A House of Her Own

PATRICIA DUSENBURY

Cover Design: Saille Graphic Design for Books / www.sailletales.com
Photography: © Michaelowski / Dreamstime.com

Ebook first published by Uncial Press
www.uncialpress.com
ISBN-13: 978-1-60174-209-4

ACKNOWLEDGMENTS

I am grateful to the many people, too numerous to name, who helped and encouraged me to keep writing, but most of all, I'm grateful to my husband George, who was beside me every step of the way. George and I spent many happy hours in New Orleans, particularly at Jazz Fest. A portion of the proceeds from the sale of this book goes to The New Orleans Jazz and Heritage Foundation, which puts on Jazz Fest and keeps the music alive through education, economic development, and cultural enrichment.

ALSO BY PATRICIA DUSENBURY

A Perfect Victim:

Secrets, Lies & Homicide

A House of Her Own is fiction, and the characters are figments of my imagination. However, the tragic 1994 Grand Prix racing season is, to the best of my knowledge, accurately described.

CHAPTER 1

Monday March 14, 1994

Those who hadn't been chosen straggled back to the jurors' room to await the next call. Some opened books, others rattled newspapers, one man studied a crossword puzzle, and a woman resumed knitting. Claire Marshall took out plans for a kitchen renovation that needed one more review before she showed them to the client.

A clerk walked in, cleared her throat, and announced, "You all can go on home. Today's juries are complete. New Orleans thanks you for your time." She added that because their service had ended before noon, they would not receive a meal voucher.

"Five minutes before noon," crossword puzzle man grumbled, but he like everyone else gathered his belongings and hurried from the room.

Claire's disappointment surprised her. She hadn't wanted to serve. Authentic Restorations was a very small company, and her absence for the days or even weeks a trial might take would cause problems. When her plea of economic hardship cut no ice, she'd resigned herself and cleared her calendar. But the judicial system had decided it didn't want her. Now what was she going to do?

If Tony were in town, she could invite him to play hooky, but he was in Italy. If it were nice out, she could go for a long walk, but the day was unseasonably cold and raining, more like January than the middle of March. She exited the elevator at loose ends.

The courthouse lobby bustled. People paused at the doors, creating bottlenecks as those coming in lowered their umbrellas and those going out raised theirs. Off to one side, several well-dressed men read official-looking documents. Some had audiences; others talked to themselves. All spoke so softly that only people standing close could hear.

Curious, Claire wandered over to one of the solitary readers. He noticed her—people always notice tall redheads—and nodded before returning to his recitation. She listened for a moment and realized that she'd stumbled upon a foreclosure auction.

The man, whose nametag identified him as affiliated with a local law firm, finished reading the legal description of a property and announced an opening bid from the lender. He looked at her, his only listener. When she said nothing, he muttered "going, going, gone," then wrote down the time and the bid amount. Barely pausing for breath, he began reading the next property description.

Someone just lost their home. It should have been more dramatic.

She left him and joined a small group surrounding a different reader. When he announced the opening bid, a woman offered a dollar more. Without skipping a beat he repeated her bid and, after a pause, announced, "going, going, gone." He wrote on the documents he held, the woman signed something, and two others in the group witnessed the transaction.

Claire had always envisioned auctions as lively contests, but no one here seemed to care what happened. She waited until the paperwork was completed then spoke to the winning bidder.

"Excuse me, but I'm curious. Just a dollar more, and he let you have it?" The woman grinned. "If it were legal, I'd bid a dollar less, and they'd still sell it to me."

"Don't people ever bid up the price?"

"Occasionally there's competition, but I've never seen unrestrained bidding." She pointed to her printout, on which half a dozen listings were highlighted in yellow. "I'm here to bid on these properties, and I have a limit for each one. If I went over it, I'd be fired."

"So this is your job. It's not even your money."

"That's right."

2

"Don't the homeowners ever come?" Claire couldn't get past the indifference to families losing their homes.

"Most have given up by the time it's gone this far." A shrug. "If I had to bid on a property with the owner watching, God forbid hoping to save their home, it would hurt my heart." Implicit was that she'd do it, pain or no. "Even with the tax sales, you don't see homeowners." She jutted her chin toward the far corner where seven or eight people surrounded one reader. "That's what's going on over there. You can get a real bargain, but you can also get burned. My investors stick to foreclosures."

Claire looked where directed. "Why are tax sales riskier?"

"Foreclosures come with appraisals; tax sales, not necessarily, and many properties have been vacant for years. You'd better have done your homework. Plus, the owner has thirty days after the sale to pay the back taxes. If he does, get in line. You're just one more person with a lien, and who knows what else is out there."

Claire held out her hand. "Claire Marshall," she said. "I'm a contractor, my company renovates old houses, but this is unfamiliar territory."

"Nicole Dennis," the woman said. "Be glad it's not familiar. I've seen plenty of properties carrying liens from contractors who haven't been paid and will be lucky to get pennies on the dollar." She looked around the crowded lobby. "Are you planning to buy a foreclosure?"

"No, no. I'm just window shopping." She and Jack had discussed buying and restoring properties rather than always working on other peoples' houses. A recent run of high-maintenance clients was making that option attractive, and they'd agreed to keep their eyes open, but that was as far as it had gone. She thanked Nicole for taking time to explain and joined the gathering in the corner.

The reader nodded a welcome and gestured toward a stack of papers on a nearby table. Claire picked up what turned out to be a list of the properties at auction and the minimum opening bid. The addresses she recognized were in neighborhoods she'd prefer to avoid. *Wait a minute.* Three-sixty-eight Chestnut Street was in the Lower Garden District, not far from Tony's house, and the minimum bid was under five thousand dollars. What's more, she knew the house. It had stood empty for years, but if she could buy that house for that price or anything near it, no matter how dilapidated it had become... Dollar signs danced in her head.

Claire wasn't poor, but she wasn't rich either, and the disparity between her finances and Tony's—he could retire tomorrow and live comfortably for the rest of his life—contributed to her sense of disadvantage in their relationship. The money she could make on this house wouldn't put her in his league, but it could give her a little breathing room.

Don't get carried away. The land alone is worth ten times what they're asking. You can afford what? Six thousand, seven at most. Someone with deeper pockets will outbid you.

Still, she decided to hang around and see what happened. She had nothing better to do, and whoever bought that house would need a contractor.

The next two properties found no bidders. Three people bid on the one after that, but two dropped out after the first round. Three sixty-eight Chestnut was up. Claire's pulse quickened as the man read the property description and announced the minimum bid, four thousand nine hundred and eighty-seven dollars.

She raised her hand. "Five thousand."

"Five thousand dollars," he repeated.

She held her breath, expecting to hear another bid and steeling herself against the inevitable disappointment, but there was silence.

"Going, going, gone for five thousand dollars." He smiled at her.

Claire signed the papers with shaking hands. This was not like her. She was a rational and cautious businesswoman who did not make snap decisions, but she'd just bought a house practically on a whim and after being warned against tax sales. She knew where the house was and what it had looked like six years ago, but nothing more. What if there was a mortgage, a fraudulent refinance for more money than the house was worth? Would creditors come crawling out of the woodwork now that the property had a new owner?

You might have just done something really stupid.

Claire spent the next hour combing through records in the Office of Deeds. Her search surfaced no easements or other encroachments, no mortgage or other liens. Three sixty-eight Chestnut last sold in 1983, eleven years ago, in an all cash sale. Phew! It's better to be lucky than smart, wasn't that one of Jack's favorite sayings? She checked her watch. If he was on schedule, he'd be working through the punch list at their Mimosa Street project.

She drove over, singing along with the radio, smiling and nodding to the other drivers, and letting in anyone who wanted to cut in front of her. Three lights in a row turned red in front of her, but she didn't care. Nothing was denting her good mood.

Jack's truck sat at the curb. Jack, himself, was inside, lying on the kitchen floor—at least those looked like his legs sticking out from under the sink.

"Hey partner," she said. "What are you doing under there?"

He inched his way out. "A leak in the supply line. What happened to jury duty?"

"I wasn't selected." Her smile broadened. "So I went downstairs and bought us a fixer-upper."

For a moment he looked puzzled, then the light came on. "You bought a foreclosure?"

"Tax sale. Five thousand dollars for a house on Chestnut Street. The Lower Garden District, do you believe it? I was the only bidder. I'm still pinching myself."

"Impossible." Jack said. "Opening bid is two-thirds the appraisal. There must be another Chestnut Street."

"There was no appraisal, minimum bid was superior claims plus cost and commission. I know the house. It needs a lot of work, but the potential is there—big time." She laughed. "I could have paid thirteen dollars less, but I wanted to scare off any other bidders."

"You know this house?"

"When Tom and I moved to New Orleans, our realtor suggested we look at it, and I walked around the outside. It was derelict then and too much for us to take on, but I remember thinking what a shame someone was letting such a nice house go to seed." She shook her head in disbelief. "I just bought that house for a fraction of what they were asking six years ago."

"If something's too good to be true..." Jack didn't have to finish the sentence. He was a man of mottos, and this was one of his favorites.

"I had to put ten percent down," she said. "Worst case, the owner reappears, they pay the taxes, and we lose the deposit. We have thirty days before the rest of the money is due."

"What about outstanding mortgages and who knows how many years of unpaid utility bills? You might have bought a cheap house and a bunch of expensive debts."

"I searched the title back thirty years. It's clean." No need to tell him that she'd done this *after* buying the property. "I found nothing that suggests any problem, but I'll make doubly sure before spending another penny. If it doesn't work out, we lose five hundred dollars and some of my time. Not good, but a learning experience. The upside potential is huge."

"There's got to be a catch, an environmental problem, something."

Claire understood Jack's pessimism. His company had teetered on the brink of bankruptcy before she invested her money and herself in saving it. The experience had left him scarred and wary. She understood, but she didn't want to spend any more time listening to him conjure up imaginary problems. Real ones would surface soon enough. She gestured toward the sink.

"Are you through here?"

"I tightened the connection. If that doesn't do it, I'll get the plumber back, but it looks to me like he didn't take time to double-check. Everyone's in a big hurry these days."

Claire, who was practically hopping up and down in her impatience to show Jack the house, waited quietly while he turned the dishwasher on and knelt in front of the open cabinet, watching.

"We're good to go." He stood up and set the machine to drain.

"Then come on, let me show you Authentic Restorations' first in-house project."

Driving over she told Jack about the auctions, and he continued looking for reasons to worry.

"Why no appraisal?" he said. "And no mortgage?"

"The previous owner paid cash."

"Why didn't anyone else bid?"

"Have you been listening to a word I've said? I saw one competitive auction, and it lasted only two rounds. Some properties, nobody bids." She pulled into the driveway. "Here we are." Strictly speaking, they should have parked at the curb, but the house was barely visible behind an overgrown hedge, and no one lived here. No one would care.

She stared at the house, trying to see it through Jack's eyes. Two-stories with a first floor gallery and side gables, the original structure was probably about twenty-five hundred square feet. It would have been built in the mid-nineteenth century, barely antebellum. A second-story bump out drooped precariously from the right side. Behind it, a big magnolia needed pruning. Weeds growing in the gutters and missing roof shingles promised water damage. Peeling paint confirmed it and gave the façade a forlorn appearance, but beneath the mess, this house was intrinsically nice, well proportioned and well sited on the lot.

"So." she said, "what do you think?"

He didn't respond.

"The siding looks solid," she said. "Given the age of the house, I bet it's cypress. We'll have to replace most of the trim, but enough of the original is there to serve as a template. This used to be a good-looking house. The neighborhood's okay and getting better. Jack, talk to me."

"I should have known when you said Chestnut Street."

"Known what?"

"The house is haunted. That's why no one else wanted it."

"Haunted?" Surprise made Claire laugh. "Don't be silly. You don't believe in ghosts do you?"

"I do, and so does the rest of New Orleans. We'll never sell this place. We couldn't give it away."

7

"I have to admit it looks haunted." Claire smiled. "If it is, we'll just remove the ghost along with the other problems." She climbed out and waited for Jack's reluctant exit. "We aren't entitled to enter the property until we've finished paying for it, but..."

"Don't walk under that bump out." He pointed at the second story extension. "How long 'til you take possession? Thirty days? It could be on the ground by then."

"It looked like that six years ago—or close to it—why would it fall down now?"

"Last I heard, the law of gravity hasn't been repealed."

"We can walk around the other side." They followed the driveway into the back yard.

Most of the houses in the Lower Garden District had long ago been expanded to the limits of the buildable lot, virtually eliminating backyards, but the only encroachment here was a glassed-in sunroom about twelve feet square. Jack pointed to mud tunnels climbing its foundation. He banged the siding with his fist, and a dozen white bugs dropped out.

"Termites." He ground them with his heel. "If they stop holding hands, this addition falls down."

"Save us the trouble of demolishing it."

"Look at your bump out from the back." He said. "See how it's pulling away from the house."

She nodded agreement. "You're right, but it's not original. Whether or not we want to keep it depends on what's inside." She climbed the back steps and tried the door. It was locked, so she wiped a clean spot on the glass and peered inside. "I can't see much; it's too dark inside. Maybe we can get in the front door."

Jack shook his head. "Curiosity killed the cat."

"Satisfaction brought her back." They went through this routine at least once a week. "Let's at least take a look in those front windows."

She led the way back around to the front of the house and climbed half a dozen steps to the front gallery. The front door was also locked. Behind her, wood snapped and Jack cursed. His foot had gone through the porch floor. He brushed aside her efforts to help him and righted himself. "I'm okay, but this floor isn't."

"The front has definitely taken a hit. A fire, a falling tree, something. I bet there used to be a second floor gallery." She shrugged. "A lot can happen in a hundred and forty years. I'm guessing that's how old the house is."

"The repairs were done on the cheap."

"We'll do it right."

He waved a piece of the splintered wood. "Untreated pine, for Pete's sake, but you're right about the original structure. It's cypress and ought to be okay."

"Except for the ghost," Claire teased.

"Except for the ghost." Jack wasn't smiling. "I've seen enough. Let's go."

She refrained from pointing out that he hadn't seen a single ghost.

Tony called that evening. He'd left her with assurances that absence made the heart grow fonder. *Maybe, maybe not.* He'd been gone two weeks, and this was only the second time he'd called.

"I was wondering how you were doing." Claire cringed at the whine in her voice. "Sorry, I didn't mean that the way it sounded."

"I'm doing fine, but I've been working long days and going to bed early. By the time you're home from work, I'm asleep." He took an audible breath. Or was that an exasperated sigh? "We're in Brazil week after next, same time zone. I'll call more often. Right now there's a lot to learn, and the curve is steep."

"Why a learning curve?" He'd been racing Ferrari's for years. "What's different?"

"Last season we heard a lot of chatter about the equipment becoming more important than the driver, so the owners decided to scale back the technology. No more anti-lock brakes, no more active suspensions, no more traction control. The cars are harder to handle, but no one is slowing down—we can't." A pause. "There will be more accidents."

Before this, Tony had brushed away her concerns about his job, insisting that a Grand Prix race was safer than a Louisiana highway. His change of attitude worried her. "Be careful, please."

"Don't worry, I'm always careful. I'm very attached to my own skin." His tone softened. "But not nearly as attached as I am to yours. I miss my beautiful redhead."

"I miss you too."

"We'll be together in June." He changed the subject to the exhibition of his father's art that would bring him back to New Orleans. "I told the gallery to call you if something came up and they couldn't reach me. The time change makes things difficult." He yawned. "Speaking of which, it's after one, sweetheart. I'm beat."

Claire wished him sweet dreams and hung up, frustrated by their five-minute conversation. Maybe Brazil would be easier, but after Brazil was Japan, the other side of the world, then back to Europe until June, when he'd be in Canada and, briefly, back in New Orleans before going somewhere else far away. The Grand Prix season ran from May through November, seven long months, and that didn't count pre-season practice.

"What did you expect?" asked the nagging little voice that questioned everything to do with Tony. "You've known him for three months. He's practically a stranger."

Claire told the voice to shut up. She thought of all the things she wished she'd said. She should have told him it was okay, more than okay, to call her at work during the day. He had the number for her mobile phone. She could have told him about jury duty, the property auction, and buying that old house; but he'd sounded tired, and she'd chattered enough. She could have told him that she loved him, but she was waiting for him to say it first, and some things are better said in person.

Tony was a client who became a friend and then a lover—too quickly. They should have spent more time getting to know each other, more time talking. She undressed for bed and studied herself in the mirror. The marks left by love had faded from her body. She slipped on her nightgown, a silky wisp Tony had given her, and climbed into bed to lie sleepless and alone on cold sheets.

CHAPTER 2

Tishanna Tenier hustled, keeping her head down and her eyes on the pavement. She didn't want to step in any of the nasty stuff that littered the alley. Overflowing dumpsters lined the walls and smelled awful, but this was a shortcut to the bus stop, and she was late. If she wasn't home by the time Gramma walked in the door, she'd get another beating.

Something screamed and Tishanna froze. *What was that?* She looked around.

Up ahead, a bunch of big kids stood around something on the ground. One of them stepped back and took a running jump. A howl echoed through the alley. That was the noise she'd heard. Another one jumped on it then another. They were taking turns, mean kids torturing some poor stray dog. They'd probably kill it. Tishanna felt bad for the dog, but if she yelled or said anything, those kids would turn on her.

The biggest kid prodded the dog with his foot, he turned it over, and Tishanna gasped. It was a man, not a dog. The man rolled onto his side and pulled his legs up, trying to curl into a ball. The next jumper flattened him back out, someone kicked him in the head, and they all laughed.

"Shit, shit, shit." Tishanna edged away, staying close to the dumpsters where she'd be harder to see and no longer caring what it smelled like or what she stepped in. She knew these guys. They hung around the park across from her school, selling drugs and taking stuff from kids. Everyone was scared of them. CeeCee said they were members of a secret gang called Players, and some of them used to go to their school. CeeCee wouldn't say how she knew, but she swore they'd killed a man last week, robbed him and beat him up, then shot him dead out of pure meanness. That man on the ground wasn't looking too good either.

"Hey! Hey you, girl."

Tishanna turned and ran. She was only thirteen, but she was tall and long-legged, fast on her feet. The crack of a gunshot and the smack of a bullet bouncing off the wall next to her made her legs move faster than she'd thought possible.

She cleared the alley and sprinted across the street just as the light turned red. Behind her, horns honked and brakes squealed, but she didn't look back. She reached the corner, cut through yards to the next block, jumped a fence, ran around a house, crossed another street, and kept going. It was all houses here, and this block was a dead end. Two houses down was a tall hedge. She pushed her way through and collapsed on the ground.

Get up, you ain't safe yet. She peeked out, praying that she'd lost them. Her prayer ended in a sob.

A block away, six of them half-ran half-walked down the middle of the street, their heads turning from side to side, looking. They reached the corner, stood there talking and then split up. Two went right, two went left and two came down the street toward her. They'd see the broken hedge. Her school uniform, a white shirt and tan skirt, would show up against the dark branches. They'd grab her and jump on her and kick her like they had the man in the alley. They'd rape her until she was dead. CeeCee said they always hurt people before they killed them.

The house behind her was dark. She should have stayed up on Magazine where there were other people around. She could have run into one of the bars, told them what she'd seen, and asked for help, but it was too late now.

No one lived here. Tall weeds filled the yard, and there was a big hole in the gallery floor. There was no one to help her, but if she could get to that hole, she could hide under the gallery. Keeping low, Tishanna raced to the house and huddled beside the steps, panting so hard her chest burned. She couldn't hear the gang chasing her, and she didn't see any movement on the street, so she started up the steps.

A deep voice yelled, "Hey, she's over here. Hurry up. We have her cornered."

Tishanna leapt onto the gallery, too late to hide under the floor, and tried the front door. The knob turned in her hand, and the door opened, practically pulling her inside. A staircase led up, and a hall went to the back of the house. She ran down the hall and found the back door. But this doorknob wouldn't turn no matter how she rattled it. The top half of the door was glass, and through it she could see two dark shadows rounding the corner of the house. The front door creaked open.

Someone cursed. "Shit, it's cold in there, and it stinks."

It did smell bad, worse than the alley. She'd been too scared to notice, but hearing him talk about it churned her stomach. She backed away from the door.

"That's the smell of the grave," a nervous voice said. "Everyone knows this house is haunted. I ain't going in."

"Don't be a pussy." It sounded like the one who'd spotted her. "Players ain't pussies."

"The haint lives upstairs. We go up those steps, she'll push us back down and break our necks just like someone broke hers," the nervous guy said.

"You believe that shit?"

"My grandma knew someone who worked here."

"We're going in," a new voice said. "You stand watch, make sure she doesn't get out a window."

The two out back had climbed up the steps and were rattling the door. Any minute now, they'd break the glass. Shaking with fear, Tishanna looked for a hiding place. Behind her a narrow staircase led up to where the haint lived—if that Player had it right. She didn't want to run into no haint, but she was more scared of the Players. Legs trembling and tears running down her face, she crept upstairs.

At the top of the stairs, a doorway stood open to a room with a fireplace too small to hide in and two more doors. The one on the outside wall was open, and through it, she saw a bathroom with a floor that ran downhill. The other door was closed. She opened it, and something long and white fluttered—the haint!

Tishanna clapped her hand across her mouth to keep from screaming. Then she realized it was nothing but an old dress hanging on the clothes rod. Someone had moved out and left a closet full of clothes. She'd have fallen to her knees in thankful prayer, except the Players had come inside, and her troubles were far from over.

It sounded like two people—no, three—downstairs and still talking about the haint, two saying there was no haint and the other one not so sure. Talking was slowing them down, but sooner or later, they'd climb those stairs. Her only chance was to go out a window.

The side window was too high off the ground to jump, and the sill was too narrow and rotten to hold on to. No matter how she stretched, she couldn't grab hold of the big old tree. She tiptoed over to the back windows and almost cried with relief when she saw a flat roof a little ways down.

She undid the latch and pushed up, but this window wouldn't open. She tried the one next to it. Same thing. She strained, pushing and pulling with a strength born of fear, but neither window budged. Too frantic to worry about making noise, she pounded the window frames with her fist, trying to knock them loose.

"Hear that? Come on. We've got her." Footsteps started up the front stairs.

"It's the haint," the nervous one said. "We gotta get out of here."

A smack and the deep voice said, "Shut up or I'll knock your scrawny ass down the stairs. You won't have to worry about no haint."

Tishanna ran to the closet and shut the door behind her. She pushed her way through to the back corner, pulled some clothes off their hangers, and covered herself. Then she crouched, knees tight to her chest, and prayed that any Player who looked in the closet would think she was a pile of rags.

Please, I don't want to die. I'm only thirteen years old.

She squeezed her eyes shut and put her hands over her ears, but she could still hear the doors opening and shutting as the Players searched the front rooms. Their footsteps came closer, came into the room. She felt the air move and knew someone had opened the closet door. Hangers scraped along the pole as he pushed the old clothes aside. A hand pulled her covers off.

"Why'd you run away, girl?" He kicked her. "You see something you shouldn't have seen?"

Warm dampness spread beneath her. "I won't tell," she whimpered. "I didn't see anything."

He grabbed her arm and dragged her out of the corner. "Look at this. She's so scared she peed her pants."

Something made a noise like fingernails on a blackboard. There was a loud bang.

"What the fuck?" He let her go.

"I told you." It was the scared one. "This house is haunted. That ain't no girl, that's a haint. She's lured us in."

"Do haints holler when you kick them?" A foot slammed into her ribs, harder this time.

Tishanna howled like the man in the alley, but the screeching and banging was even louder. The floor started to shake like the house was about to fall down. She opened her eyes.

The one who'd kicked her was standing with his hand on the closet door and his mouth hanging open. Two others stood in the middle of the room, staring at the windows. She hadn't been able to budge those windows, but now they moved by themselves, screeching up and banging down, faster and faster.

All three Players ran for the door, crashing against each other in their rush to get out. They thumped and clattered down the stairs. The front door slammed. Someone outside hollered. Inside the room, the windows slid shut and stayed there.

Several minutes passed, and everything stayed quiet. Quiet as the grave, Grandma would say. Still sniffling, Tishanna pulled herself to her feet. Her side hurt so bad she thought she might throw up, she'd peed all over herself, and she was going to get a beating when she got home. But

15

she was still alive.

"Thank you," she said to the haint. "If they'd of gotten me, I'd have been raped and tortured and killed for sure.

"I ought to get home, but I'm scared they're waiting outside." She peered out the windows. It was getting dark, and the yard with its scraggly bushes looked spooky, but she didn't see anyone or anything moving.

"They could be out front," she said. Even if the haint didn't answer, it felt like she was listening.

Tishanna stepped into the hall, and her foot sent something skittering across the floor. A gun. "I bet that belongs to them. They shot at me, back in the alley."

She knelt down and picked it up. She'd seen plenty of guns but she'd never touched one before. She held it out in front of her with both hands like the police do on TV and kept her finger on the trigger while she tiptoed to the top of the front stairs and looked down. There was no one in sight, and the front door was closed. She shifted the gun to her right hand, barrel pointed down, and went to look out the front windows.

They were at the corner, standing under the streetlight, talking and waving their arms around like they were having a big argument. Tishanna counted six. That was all of them. She was pretty sure the argument was about whether or not they were coming back in after her. She settled down to watch, the gun in her lap.

CHAPTER 3

Jack raised his eyebrows in exaggerated surprise. "It's not even eight o'clock and you're already at work. To what do we owe this honor?"

"It's April fifteenth," Claire said.

"Pay your taxes or go to jail. Is that what got you out of bed?"

"You can always get an extension, automatic until August." She gave him a thumbs up. "April fifteenth is a good day, because 368 Chestnut Street is finally ours. I paid the balance, and the deed is in the mail."

"I'm not sure that's good news," Jack said. He had argued for writing off the five hundred dollar deposit and pretending they'd never heard of 368 Chestnut.

"I want to go over there this morning—as soon as you're ready." They always did the initial once-over together. She had an eye for what had been and what might be. Jack knew about construction and structural issues; he could tell her on the spot if an idea was feasible. Plus it wasn't smart to explore a dilapidated structure alone. Accidents happen.

"Uh, not this morning. I'm meeting an inspector over in Lakeview in twenty minutes. I should have left five minutes ago." He headed for the door.

"Have it your way," she told his departing back, "but someone else can meet that inspector and you know it." She checked her messages— nothing that couldn't wait—and drove alone to Chestnut Street.

Over the last month, Claire had kept an eye on the property, driving slowly past most days and, at least once a week, taking a quick walk around the property. Three weeks ago, a new hole appeared in the gallery floor. There'd been nothing since, but she wasn't taking any chances. She'd scheduled a locksmith to come by later today and secure the house.

Her first task as the new owner/contractor was to put up an Authentic Restorations sign. Her company's results were its best advertising, and she suspected the neighbors would be especially pleased that someone was fixing up the local eyesore. She made a mental note to get a gardening service over to tidy things up, the front yard ASAP and the back after they'd completed demo.

Yesterday afternoon when she paid off the balance, the tax office gave her a key, which they said was for the padlock on the front door. If there had ever been a padlock, it was long gone, and the door wasn't locked. When she pushed it open, a blast of nasty-smelling air hit her in the face. Rodents lived here; some had died here. She added *call an exterminator* to the to-do list in her head then stepped inside.

The foyer was large and well proportioned with a classic black and white marble checkered floor and old gas sconces along the walls. The sconces were brass mermaids, thrusting forward like figureheads and holding up glass chimneys. Claire wiped the dust off one and smiled at the flowing hair and voluptuous breasts. Seashells and fronds carved into the fireplace mantel continued the nautical theme. This had probably been a sea captain's house. Back when it was built, the port would have been an easy walk.

Openings in the back wall led to a stair going up and a hall going back. Wide doorways on either side gave access to spacious front rooms. Claire's good mood, which had been dampened by Jack's desertion, returned. This house was an absolute treasure. The original detailing remained, the beautiful foyer would make a spectacular first impression, and restored, 368 Chestnut would sell itself.

Built-in floor to ceiling bookshelves marked the room on the right as the original library. The first owner—or more likely his wife—had been a reader. She would have turned to books to fill the empty hours while he was at sea. A more recent occupant had run in cable TV. Round white wires snaked along the baseboards and across the floor, a dissonant note that could easily be removed.

Tall windows dominated the front wall and opened onto the gallery. She rubbed clear spots in the glass and felt the ridges. Old blown glass, thick and wavy and lovely. Across the foyer, the living room was this room's twin, minus the bookshelves and cable wires. She danced back into the foyer for another look at the sconces.

Shivers ran up her spine. A goose walked over your grave, her mother used to call it, but there really was a cold spot at the base of the stairs. She put her hands out and felt a draft, air far colder than outside. Coming from where? A movement caught the corner of her eye, and she whipped around. Wide eyes in a pale face stared at her. She gasped then burst out laughing. From a large mirror, part of the elaborate mantel over the foyer fireplace, her reflection laughed back.

Shape up, she told herself. Don't let Jack's ghost stories spook you. The house is cold because it's been shut up all winter. Old houses are drafty. You know that.

She followed the hall to the back of the house, and the unpleasant odor intensified. Rags and yellowed newspapers littered the kitchen floor; large droppings dotted the countertops. The exterminator moved to the top of her to-do list, and she proceeded more cautiously. She didn't want to encounter whatever left those droppings, a possum or a raccoon or worse, Attila the Rat.

Off to the left, a laundry and a small bedroom with a tiny *en suite* bathroom spoke of the bygone era when even the middle class had live-in servants. On the other side of the kitchen, a butler's pantry with glass-fronted cabinets that looked original connected to a wood-paneled dining room. A sun porch off the dining room completed the first floor. Remembering the termites and Jack's trip through the gallery floor, Claire stopped in the doorway. This addition, which probably dated from the 1950s, would be the first thing to go.

She returned to the kitchen and climbed a narrow back staircase to the upstairs hall. The first bedroom she came to smelled like sweat, mold, and who knows what else. She opened a window to let in some fresh air and noticed that her footprints were one set among many.

Several people wearing large sneakers had been in this bedroom.

Someone had left a bunch of old clothes hanging in the closet and more on the floor. Claire picked up what might have been a dress, caught a waft of urine and dropped it. A cleaning crew joined the exterminator at the top of her list. Who knew what disgustingness lurked in this filth.

A door on the far wall led to the bump out, a Jack-and-Jill bathroom serving both bedrooms on this side of the house. The bump out was worth keeping—these days, people expected more than one upstairs bath—however the floor sloped away at an alarming angle. They'd have to prop it up before anyone could go inside.

A second bedroom on this side of the house was slightly larger, and its windows overlooked the street. One set of footprints crisscrossed this floor, her size but not hers. Someone had walked in and stood at the front window. A lookout?

When Claire returned to the hall, she noticed a jumble of footprints on the stairs. She hadn't seen them from down in the foyer, but they were clearly visible from above. There'd been a lot of activity in this supposedly empty house. Were neighborhood kids using it as a hangout? She hoped they had enough sense to stay out of that bump out.

A master bedroom with a large dressing room/nursery, a connecting full bath, and two good-sized closets comprised the other side of the second floor. Each bedroom had a ceiling fan and its own small fireplace, a reminder that not too long ago most houses in New Orleans had neither central heat nor air conditioning. This one still didn't. They'd have to retrofit climate control.

The ceilings were in decent shape, a pleasant surprise. The roof might not be as bad as it looked from the outside. She wouldn't know until she checked the attic, which would have to wait. Entry was through an opening in the hall ceiling, and the pull rope for the dropdown staircase had been reduced to a frayed stub that hung well out of reach.

Something banged. It sounded as if it came from the back bedroom. Had the wind blown a door shut? Claire went to investigate and saw that the window she'd opened was now closed. Luckily, the glass was still intact, but she should have checked the sash rope before leaving it open. All the sash ropes were probably rotten. Replacing them would be a simple task, but until that was done, they'd have to be careful to prop the windows open.

She followed the footsteps down the front stairs and again noticed the cold spot. Air could be coming in from under the house, which could mean rotted sub-flooring. They'd have the structural engineer take a close look while he was assessing the foundation and the bump out. Meanwhile, she was ready to go back outside and breathe fresh air.

A pregnant young woman stood at the end of the walk. "Hi," she called. "I heard that someone bought this place, and now I see the sign. Are you going to fix it up?"

"That's the plan." Claire walked down the steps. "I'm Claire Marshall. My company bought this house last month. I hope we'll have it ready to go on the market by August or September."

"That's good news." The woman held out her hand. "I'm Lindsey Tice. Bill, my husband, and I moved in three houses down from you a year ago January, and we're fixing it up as we can afford to, doing most of the work ourselves. I'm glad to see something happening here." She nodded toward the house. "Has anyone told you about the ghost?"

"I don't know about a ghost, but some good-sized rodents have moved in, and it looks as if the neighborhood kids have been using it as a hang out."

Lindsey's smile faded. "No big kids live in the neighborhood. It's empty nesters and people like Bill and me buying our first house. We don't have any kids yet, but in four more months..." She patted her belly.

"Congratulations." Claire kept her smile, but Lindsey's response worried her. Someone had been inside and recently. Those were fresh footprints.

"The woman on the other side of us, Ellen Ledet, has lived here forever. The tan house with the screened-in gallery." Lindsey pointed down the block. "When you get a chance, you should go talk to her. She can tell you all about your house and the people who lived there, including your ghost. Her name is Dorcas. She was the maid's daughter. When she was thirteen, she fell down the stairs and broke her neck. It was hushed up at the time. I'll let Mrs. Ledet give you the details. It's actually a very sad story."

Fell down the stairs? Claire remembered the icy spot at their base

21

and suppressed a shiver. "I'll be sure to talk to her."

"Well, nice meeting you. And welcome to the neighborhood." Lindsey left with a smile and a wave.

First thing Claire did when she returned to the office was cancel the locksmith. If whoever was hanging out there couldn't open the door, they might break those beautiful antique-glass windows, which she'd never be able to replace. Next, she called Bea Washington. Having a good friend on the police force could come in handy.

"I have a favor to ask," she said. "It's a long story. What if I tell you over ice cream, my treat?"

"Can't do it today, I'm sorry. We're slammed." Bea sounded harried.

"You must be busy if you're turning down free ice cream. Are you feeling all right?"

"I'm fine but our fair city is in the midst of a crime wave thanks to gangs of kids, some of them barely out of grammar school. I have a special task force meeting in half an hour. Until then, I'm at your service. What's the favor?"

"Actually this involves kids. I hope not gangs. That house I bought," Claire said. "It's supposed to be haunted, but these ghosts wear sneakers and leave footprints."

"Give me the address. I'll ask the patrol officers to keep an eye out."

"It's 368 Chestnut, two blocks off Felicity. We'll start soon, and crews will be there during the day, but it will be empty, or should be, at night. I'd really appreciate them checking. My uninvited guests are using the front door to get in and hanging out in the back right upstairs bedroom. There's a tall hedge and neither the front door nor those bedroom windows are visible from the street."

"We're investigating a string of brutal muggings near there," Bea said. "We're pretty sure it's a new gang trying to prove they're tougher and meaner than anyone else. Let's hope that's not who's hanging out in your house."

"Let's hope." *First ghosts and now gangs. Wait until Jack hears the latest.*

"We're putting extra patrols on the street this weekend, but your neighborhood isn't the only trouble spot, and we don't have as many resources as we'd like. Promise me you won't go there alone and don't go there after dark. Period."

"I'll be careful."

"Careful isn't good enough. These kids are vicious. Two of their victims have died. One was shot and the other, severely beaten. He lived for three weeks before his family gave up and let the doctors pull the plug. That was yesterday."

Claire spent a restless weekend, cleaning and running errands, and when those chores were done, shopping without buying because she didn't want or need anything. What she wanted was to take another look inside 368 Chestnut Street. Dorian sensed her irritable mood and kept his distance except at mealtimes.

Not too long ago, she would have filled empty time by calling her mother for a nice long chat, but her mother was in Florida, visiting a widower she'd been seeing for several months now. Having a man in her life had made her mother more determined than ever to see her daughter once again part of a couple. Claire still hadn't told her mother that Tony was more than a client, and the continuing omission made conversations awkward. She wasn't ready to say anything because her feelings were too ambivalent. She loved him, but she didn't trust him. What kind of future was that?

Tony had called from Brazil. She'd told him about jury duty. Twice in a row, it was a divorce case, and the wife's lawyers hadn't wanted her on the jury.

"Did you want to be on a jury?" he'd said.

"No. I tried to be excused, but the judge didn't care that Authentic Restorations needed me in the office. Civic duty trumps economic hardship."

"Then why are you unhappy about not being selected?"

"It was insulting. They seemed to think that, because I'm a widow, I resent women who have chosen to end their marriage." She sensed that she wasn't getting across. "If you'd seen this woman talking to her lawyers while I was on the stand, you'd understand. She kept peeking at me. As if I might attack at any moment."

"More likely she found you threatening because you're a beautiful young widow." Tony was trying to jolly her out of it, but he hadn't been there.

"Well," she said. "It turned out for the best. I went downstairs and bought a house, a ten minute walk from yours."

Silence greeted her news.

"Tony? Are you there?"

"You bought yourself a house?"

"Not for me. For Authentic Restorations to fix up and sell at an enormous profit. That was the plan, but Jack's not on board. He says the house is haunted and we won't be able to give it away. Can you believe that? He's always worried about something. But ghosts?"

"Since when don't you believe in ghosts?"

"Since forever." Something was bothering him. She could hear it in his voice. *What did I say?*

"The first time I saw you, you were staring, mesmerized, at my dad's studio. You jumped out of your skin when I said hello. Remember?"

"Yes." She'd never forget. They'd found a skeleton in the old studio.

"You told me the studio had demanded your attention. Like something inside was calling you."

"Kids are hanging out in this house, not ghosts."

"All I'm saying is don't dismiss the possibility."

"Okay." She didn't want to argue with him and certainly not over something so silly.

Only after they signed off and she was rerunning the conversation, did Claire realize why Tony had reacted so strangely to her news about the house. Before leaving New Orleans, he'd suggested she move into the house her company had restored for him. She had demurred. He'd barely moved in himself and now he was leaving. She'd still be alone. Why didn't they talk about it when he was back in June?

He'd been surprised by her reluctance, what he called her indecision. Tonight, when she said she'd bought a house, he'd heard her say no, she was not going to move in with him. It had been one more misunderstanding in a conversation fraught with them.

Sine then, she'd been waiting for a chance to emphasize that the purchase was purely business, but he hadn't called. The race was Sunday in Japan, and weren't they fifteen hours ahead? It had to be over, unless it was yesterday there, and she didn't think so. Tony had explained the International Date Line, it made sense at the time, but she'd forgotten how it worked.

Monday morning, Claire still hadn't heard from Tony. She called the *Times-Picayune* sports desk. "Do you have the results from the Pacific Grand Prix?"

"Are you calling about Tony Burke?"

"Did something happen to him?"

"No, baby. Tony's fine. All the girls call about him, that's all. I want to know what Tony has that the rest of us don't." He sniggered. "If he ever bottles it, I'm buying a case."

"Do you have the race results?"

"Don't get mad at me, baby."

"I'm not mad. I just want to know about the race."

"Tony came in second. He had it won, but he blew a tire on the next to last lap. I've got a phone interview with him on Wednesday. Do you want me to give him your love? Hugs and kisses?" He sniggered again. "You might have to take a number."

Claire hung up on the smart aleck sportswriter who wasn't half as clever as he thought he was. Dorian twined himself around her legs, and she told him to scoot. The cat retreated to the other side of the room, looked at her reproachfully, and began grooming himself.

"Dorian, I'm sorry." She picked him up and scratched behind his ears. "You deserve a treat for putting up with me, I was a grouch all weekend, and it's not your fault Tony hasn't called."

It wasn't as if everyone she knew hadn't warned her not to become involved with Tony Burke. International playboy, the reporters said with a wink and a grin. Womanizer was a more accurate description. Even Tony had told her not to expect him to "live like a monk" while he was away. He'd smiled when he said it and caressed her cheek. She couldn't tell if he was kidding. It was before he mentioned living together, but he never took it back. Nor did he call often.

She hung around the house until nine—midnight in Japan, whatever day it was—before giving up and going to work. Jack was in the office.

"I sent the demo crew over to Esplanade," he said.

"I thought that was next week." She knew darn well that demo on the Esplanade project wasn't scheduled until next week, and so did Jack. "They were supposed to start Chestnut Street today."

"I think we ought to cut our losses."

"What are you talking about?"

"Walk away," he said. "We've got five thousand in it. Losing that's a hit, but nothing like the hit we'll take if we restore it and then can't sell it."

"We've discussed this before. We can't walk away. It's ours, and we're liable for what happens to and on that property. Nor can we tear it down. It's a contributing structure in an historic district. The only thing we can do with that house is sell it. And, for your information, it is going to be absolutely terrific when it's finished."

"We'll never sell it," he said. "It's haunted."

"Kids are hanging out there, doing who knows what, but it is not haunted."

"The rest of the world believes that it's haunted."

Claire remembered Lindsey Tice. The neighbors even knew the ghost's name. Perception could trump reality, which meant that Jack had a point.

"Okay," she said.

"Okay what?"

"If we can't sell the restored house, I'll buy it. Our cost plus twenty percent." She raised her hand as if she were being sworn in. "You have my word. Now when can we start demolition?"

"What are you going to do with it?"

"Live there."

"Why don't you think this over?" Jack said. "I'm not going to hold you to something you said when you were ticked off."

"I mean it." *Do I really? What about Tony?* "Meanwhile, I want jacks under the bump out. Stabilize it until you can get an engineer over there to assess it."

"We'll talk again Friday. If you still want to go ahead, we'll start demo next Monday."

"Fine, but I'm not going to change my mind. Can you get the jacks in place this afternoon?"

CHAPTER 4

Claire began Monday by getting up way too early and driving over to Chestnut Street to meet the demo crew. Zach, the crew boss, Charlie, Banjo, and Pete stood in the driveway, four big burley guys shifting weight from one foot to another and looking anywhere but at each other.

Jack had warned her that they all knew the house was haunted and were not happy about working on it. Still, it appeared that no one was ready to admit he was afraid. Sometimes, the macho code among construction workers was annoying. Today it worked in her favor. She said good morning and pointed out the holes in the gallery floor.

"Jack tested the floor for you. He thinks there's a problem."

"You tell Jack we appreciate his help." Zach said. The men laughed, and the tension dissolved in jokes and stories about other times someone had stepped wrong and gone through a floor or a ceiling. Zach said they'd lay some plywood from the steps to the front door.

Claire smiled a thank you. "Do that before you leave, but there's no rush. Your work is in the back of the house. Start by taking down the sun porch, but be careful. It's full of termites. Everything inside the kitchen and maid's quarters goes. If you have time, take it down to the wall joists and subfloor. Leave the dining room and butler's pantry as is. We're going to repair what's there. Ditto the front rooms."

"Is there power?" Zach said.

"No. The exterminator found a rats' nest in the fuse box and said we should assume they'd chewed wires throughout the house. We've rented a 1000-kilowatt generator, which is being delivered this morning. If it's not enough, let me know and I'll order another."

As if conjured up by her words, a flatbed truck pulled up to the curb. Claire showed the driver where to set the generator. The crew walked around back, and she climbed the steps to the front gallery. Treading carefully, testing each board before putting her weight on it, she inspected the front windows.

The inside had been painted shut, and it appeared the outside was as well. Because the old glass was irreplaceable, she assigned herself the job of freeing them—starting with the living room. Using a thin chisel made specifically for the job, she broke the paint seal then went inside and repeated the process. That done, she coaxed the window open a couple inches, levered it up the rest of the way and propped it open with lengths of two by four. The wood would hold if the ancient sash ropes gave way.

By now, the sounds of demolition should be coming from the back of the house, but all Claire could hear was the generator. She went to investigate the hold-up and found the crew standing in the backyard. Zach was talking, and the others had their hands in their pockets. She called to them from the doorway.

"I'm opening the front windows to let in some fresh air. The house has been closed up for a long time and smells it. It's not just rats. The exterminator says we have possums in the walls. He's set traps. Look out for them." Forget playing dead—a cornered possum was a fearsome creature with razor-sharp teeth and a nasty disposition.

"You don't need an exterminator," Zach said. "Banjo will set his own traps." He gave Banjo's shoulder a punch. "This good old boy eats possum stew for breakfast."

Banjo protested and the others guffawed.

"I'll ask the exterminator to save everything he catches," Claire said. She smiled a thank you to Zach. Keeping the crew laughing would keep them working. "Now, come on in and see the kitchen, straight from the nineteen-sixties."

Zach led his crew up the ramp, still joking about who might or might not want to eat any captured possums.

Claire repeated her instructions then said, "While you're doing that,

I'm going to finish the front windows and head back to the office. Either Jack or I will stop by after lunch to see how you're coming along."

Supervising demo was Jack's job, but he'd found an excuse not to be there. He'd said he'd try to stop by, but she wasn't counting on it. Given his attitude, she wasn't sure she wanted him there, exchanging ghost stories with the crew while no work got done. She thought about it some more and called him.

"You don't need to stop by Chestnut Street. Things are going well. I'm leaving soon to prepare for my lunch meeting, but I'll stop by afterwards."

"Thanks." If he heard the rebuke, he ignored it.

Her lunch meeting was with a prospective client who, even before he'd signed the contract, was demanding a lot of handholding. She'd factor that into her cost estimate. Truth lies behind the contractor's joke that a $100 job costs $150 if the client watches and $200 if they want to help.

The meeting, like previous ones with this client, ran late, and Claire didn't return to Chestnut Street until almost three. The demo crew had been busy. Kitchen appliances lined the curb, a symphony in harvest gold and rust. She parked next to it and walked around back where the sun porch was only a memory. Windows and rotted wood filled the dumpster.

"Sorry to be late," she said. "But it looks as if you're doing fine without me."

"We got the kitchen cabinets to go, but we're running out of space." Zach gestured toward the full dumpster. "They can't get by to empty it until after five. If you want us to keep going, we can pile the stuff in the yard."

She thought a moment then shook her head. "You don't want to move everything twice. This is a good stopping place. Close up the back and call it a full day. Thank you. I appreciate your hard work."

"What about the old appliances?"

Claire made a rueful face. "I forgot all about them. Please load them into my truck. Jack or I will see you all back here tomorrow morning."

It should be Jack. He was the early bird who didn't mind being on site at seven-thirty when the crews started work. She was the slow riser who didn't come into the office until nine or, admit it, ten. It should be Jack hauling old appliances to the recycler. He should have scheduled the trash service to empty the dumpster mid-afternoon. She handled the business end, he handled the construction, and until very recently, their partnership had worked well.

She called him to say demo was moving quickly and she'd let the men off early because they'd run out of dumpster space. "I'm about to drop the appliances at the recycler. I told Zach you'd meet them here at seven-thirty tomorrow."

"I don't know if I can, Claire. I'm waiting on the electrical inspector again. He approved the new circuits but found something he didn't like with an old one. We fixed it, and he's coming back. Can't you cover the demo for another day?"

"Are you suggesting we switch jobs? Maybe you'd like to take over the check book." It was a low blow. Jack, the classic example of a skilled craftsman with no head for business, hated bookkeeping in any form.

"The electrical inspector is wet behind the ears and trying to show the world how smart he is," Jack said. "He's giving me a hard time, and I don't trust anyone else to handle him. One more inspection and we'll be through."

"Good, because I can't do this myself. I can't convince the crews to work if they see you avoiding the place. The only way this project will get finished is if you show up and work with them like you do on every other project. This is my house and my money you're wasting."

"You don't have to buy it, Claire."

Did she really want the house? The question was inextricably tangled with her uncertainty about Tony. Things had moved so quickly between them, and then he was gone. His voice on the phone, the infrequent calls, it wasn't working. Moving into his house would be a commitment on her part, but what commitment was he making? He'd still be traveling around the world, doing whatever he pleased.

"What we have in it plus twenty percent," she said. "That's the agreement, and I don't want out. Nor do I want to keep beating my head against a brick wall. Are you in or not?"

"Soon as I get this inspector off my back, I'll be at Chestnut Street from sunup to sundown if that's what you want."

"If that's what it takes."

"I wish you'd think about it some more. Act in haste, repent at leisure."

"My mother used to tell me that. Daily."

By the time Claire dropped off the old appliances, it was almost five, time to go home. She walked in the door, saw the telltale light blinking on her answering machine, and knew she'd missed a call from Tony.

He was back in Italy but still tired from traveling and the time changes. Japan had gone well. The rule changes weren't causing serious problems, and she shouldn't worry about him. He was lonely but didn't want her to call back. It was late, and he needed his beauty sleep. He'd try to call in the next couple days.

He sounded tired, but the race in Japan was a week ago. It was a lousy excuse.

There'd been an article about Tony in the newspaper. It mentioned the rule changes and wrecks in both races, but no serious injuries. It also included his picture with an overflowing bottle of champagne in his hand and a pretty young woman overflowing her dress on his arm. He hadn't looked lonely.

Claire suspected he knew about the article, assumed she'd seen the picture, and intentionally called when she probably wouldn't be home. Tony didn't like conflict. Truth was, neither did she, so they skirted around dangerous topics. Like other women. That didn't work as well on the phone as it did in person. She understood that the publicity surrounding his racing career was important advertising for the luxury car dealership that bore his name—more than bore his name, he took an active role in running it—but she had trouble accepting the contribution his playboy reputation made to car sales. His offhand explanation that sex sells had not helped.

Tony had been gone almost two months. It would be another six weeks before he was back in New Orleans, and then only for a few days. The longer he was gone, the less certain she was that they'd be able to make their relationship work—and less certain that Tony wanted to. Unless things changed drastically, she and Tony wouldn't last this racing season. Then what? She couldn't imagine not loving him.

Tony lay in bed, wide awake when he needed to get some sleep. Caring, really caring, what a woman thought was a new experience and not a totally positive one. Claire didn't make it easy. She'd listen whenever he told her about himself, but she never reciprocated. He'd never known anyone more reticent when it came to talking about their feelings and the events that had made them who they were.

In part, he understood. The background check he'd commissioned before hiring her company described a rough road. Her husband had died rescuing a stranger's children from a house fire. The mother had watched from the sidewalk, afraid to go inside.

How did you feel about this, Claire? How do you feel now?

He didn't have a clue. She never discussed her marriage. The only thing she'd ever said about her husband was that he'd been studying to be a doctor, some kind of pediatric specialist. He couldn't remember the specifics.

A year and a half after her husband died in a fire, Claire had been suspected of killing a man and burning a house down around him. That must have been a living nightmare, but she never talked about it. The investigator's report said the media had jumped all over the story. Claire had been tried and convicted in the court of public opinion although she was never arrested and was, in fact, totally innocent.

Tony knew from experience how little truth mattered when it got in the way of a good story. Racing is a team sport, and driving takes every nerve and reflex a man has, but the public thinks it's all the drivers and all play. How could they think otherwise? TV ran clips of post-race celebrations, champagne and pretty women. The newspapers followed suit. No one showed pictures of every other day when drivers drank moderately, if at all, and went to bed early because they didn't want to let the team down.

Off-season was another story, and he had played it for all it was worth. Until this year. New Orleans was a long way from the Riviera. And he was a long way from the man he'd been when he started working for Ferrari. Perhaps not the same man he'd been last year.

On the surface, which was all she let him see, Claire accepted his "take me as I am or keep walking" attitude. Women accepted it or walked—their choice. He hadn't really cared. Not even when his marriage ended in the inevitable divorce. He and Callie both partied hearty in college, but she'd thought marriage changed the deal. He, in his twenty-two-year-old wisdom, told her that people didn't change, and he hadn't. Wherever she was now, he hoped that she'd found a man who gave her the stability she wanted.

What does Claire want? He fell asleep, wondering.

CHAPTER 5

Claire wished the demo crew good morning and explained her presence. "Jack is still stuck on another job, so you're stuck with me." She made a joke of it, but she was losing patience as well as sleep. "When you finish the kitchen, we'll move on to the upstairs bathrooms. Do the master bath today. The second one is in the bump out. We've jacked it up, but I don't want anyone in there until we're sure it's safe."

"Looks about to fall off the house, jacks or no," Zach said, and the others nodded agreement.

"I hope not, but don't go in there. Meanwhile, would one of you please carry a ladder upstairs for me? I want to check out the attic, and the stair pull is broken." She walked inside and up the front stairs, ignoring the cold spot at their base.

New footprints on the stairs and in the upstairs hall showed that at least one person had been back. They were going to have to do something to keep the neighborhood teenagers—or God forbid, Bea's gang—out of the house at night.

The sound of wood screeching against wood came from the back bedroom. Claire hurried down the hall to make sure whoever was opening the window propped it open. But it wasn't one of her workers. A tall skinny girl, dark-skinned and wearing a school uniform, had a plastic garbage bag slung over her shoulder, one foot on the floor, and the other on the windowsill.

"Hey, stop. It's a long way down." Claire ran over and pulled her away from the window.

The girl squirmed. "Let go of me."

"Relax. I'm not going to hurt you, but you really don't want to climb out that window. The sun porch is gone. Look. See for yourself."

The window on the side wall squeaked open then slammed shut. It bounced open then slammed again. Startled, Claire loosened her grip. The girl twisted free and swung the garbage bag. It caught Claire on the side of her head and knocked her into the wall. The girl ran from the room and down the hall, Claire two steps behind.

The girl leapt down the stairs, taking them two or three at a time. Claire stumbled and would have fallen down the stairs if her hand hadn't, by some miracle, found the banister. She proceeded more cautiously, losing ground with every step. The girl flew out the front door and down the walk, braids bouncing and long legs pounding, just as the demolition crew came running around the side of the house.

Claire gave up. She leaned against the front door, panting.

"That's it. I ain't going back in there," Pete said.

"No need to get excited." Zach raised a calming hand, but it did no good.

"This house is haunted," Charlie or Banjo said. Both of them were talking at once. They'd felt the cold spot, sensed a ghostly presence, and now they'd seen her. They weren't going back inside.

Claire let them vent until her pulse and breathing returned to normal. "Gentlemen." She spoke loudly enough to get their attention. "I didn't see any ghost, and neither did you. There was a flesh and blood girl camping out upstairs. She tried to get away, and I chased her. You all saw her. You all have seen the footprints. Ghosts don't wear sneakers and leave footprints. People do." She held out her arm. "I grabbed her, and she scratched me. See the marks."

"I heard lots more banging and crashing than one little woman chasing another," Banjo said.

Claire drew herself up to her full five eight and looked him in the eye. "She was opening a window, planning to sneak out, when I found her. The window crashed shut when I grabbed her. The vibrations jarred the other window, and it came loose. She tried to slow me down by slamming doors." It wasn't exactly true—the girl must have rigged some ropes to manipulate that window—but it was plausible, and Claire didn't have time to figure out what had really happened.

No one contradicted her, and she continued. "She ran, I chased her, and practically fell down the stairs."

As she said, "fell down the stairs," Claire felt an icy hand on her arm. She hadn't fallen because someone, or something, helped her find the banister. Lindsey, the neighbor down the street, had said that a thirteen-year-old girl fell down those stairs and died. It was her ghost that haunted the house. The girl she'd just chased could easily be thirteen. She could be the ghost. That was what the men had been saying.

"You heard me being clumsy," she finished weakly. It was a coincidence. The girl she had just chased was a living human being.

The crew responded to her explanation with mutters and headshaking but no direct challenge.

"Look," she said. "I understand that the drama with our trespasser has thrown everyone a little off. Forget the upstairs bathrooms for now. Finish the kitchen and we'll call it a day."

No one moved toward the house, and no one would look at her, not even Zach, who had been her ally. If she didn't defuse the situation right now, these men would never go back to work. The word would spread, and no one else would take the job. The demo would not get done, and the house would never be restored. For want of a nail... It was another of Jack's sayings, and this was beginning to feel like a war.

"There's something I want to show you. I'll be right back." Claire willed herself to walk back inside as if nothing strange had occurred. *Look at me, guys. I'm not afraid. This house isn't haunted.*

She returned carrying the garbage bag. "That girl smacked me upside the head with this. It's her stuff." She pulled out a pillow, a blanket, a pair of jeans, and a tee shirt and held each item up for the men to see. "A living, breathing girl who wears clothes and sleeps under a blanket has been staying upstairs. She's your so-called ghost." She stuffed the linens and clothing back in the bag.

Either this concrete evidence or the fact that she'd gone back inside and emerged unscathed did the trick. Zach picked up his crowbar and started walking around the house. Charlie, Pete, and Banjo followed.

Claire carried the garbage bag back inside and dumped it on the living room floor, looking for a clue to her uninvited guest's identity. Two heavy objects thumped. She sorted through the clothes, inexpensive common brands that could have been purchased at the Walmart down on Jackson, and found an old book, a diary from 1961 belonging to someone named Mary Beaudry.

The other something hard was carefully wrapped in a towel. Removing the towel revealed a small gun. Dark gray metal with a crosshatched tan plastic grip, it was surprisingly heavy. Cautiously, she sniffed the barrel and smelled gunpowder. Didn't that mean it had been used recently? She wished she knew more about guns, like how to unload this one. Was there a safety catch?

She set the gun and the diary aside, stuffed the rest of the girl's belongings back into the garbage bag, and tossed the bag into a corner. She'd figure out what to do with it later. Right now, she had more pressing problems. She rewrapped the gun, then stowed it and the diary in the glove compartment of her truck, and went to see why the men weren't back to work.

They weren't even in the house. Charlie and Pete lounged against their trucks, watching Zach and Banjo argue. Claire waved to them from the kitchen door. They listened, expressionless, as she repeated her instructions about finishing up the kitchen demo.

"Let me know if you have any questions. I'll be here for a while," she said. "I want to measure all the rooms." *And I'm hoping to shame you into staying on the job.*

Her tactic worked. Several minutes later, the cracks and thuds of demolition resumed. Claire finished measuring the first floor and checked back with the demo team. All four were in the kitchen, ripping out cabinets. There was none of the usual banter, and no one looked happy, but they were getting the job done.

"I'm moving upstairs. Holler if you have any questions." She felt the crews' eyes on her back as she climbed the back stairs, pretending a nonchalance she didn't feel. Demolition continued, and she stayed upstairs, measuring and sketching, until Zach hollered.

"Hey Claire. We finished the kitchen. We'll be outside."

She kept her promise. She thanked them for giving it another chance and told them they could call it quits. She was sorry her struggle with the girl had startled them; they'd get a full day's pay for the morning's work.

"We've been talking," Zach said. "You don't have to do that. We worked four hours."

"And got a lot done. It's worth a day's pay. I appreciate the good job you guys do. Jack or I will see you back here tomorrow morning." She hoped. None of them would have gone upstairs today if she'd pulled out the gun and ordered them to. She sweetened the pot. "All that's left is gutting two upstairs bathrooms, and the second one isn't safe to enter. Tomorrow will be another half day. Demo the master bath, and I'll pay you for another full day."

"I'll be back," Banjo said.

"Still looking for that possum?" Zach clapped him on the back. "We'll talk to the others." He nodded toward Pete and Charlie who had retreated to their trucks. "If they quit, Banjo and I can finish the job."

"Thank you." Paying a full day's wages for half a day's work meant demolition would go over budget, but she'd be up the creek if they refused to return, and it was her money she was throwing around.

After the crew left, Claire finished measuring the rooms. There was nothing else she could accomplish on site, so she drove back to her office and called Bea.

"I'm still slammed," Bea said, "and I'm on my way out the door."

"I really need to talk to you or somebody you're working with. That gang you're after might be using my house."

"What about tomorrow for breakfast? Mother's at seven-thirty?"

"See you then." Claire sighed. Another early morning, and Jack would have to handle the demo tomorrow whether he felt like it or not. Plus he still hadn't hired an engineer to assess that bump out. She left a note on his desk.

That night after supper, Claire settled down on the sofa and opened the diary her uninvited guest had left behind.

The flyleaf was inscribed to *Mary B, the cutest girl in the 7th grade, Merry Christmas and Happy New Year love, Betsy.* Curling tails on the capital letters reminded Claire of the hours she'd spent in seventh grade trying to perfect her signature. Dotting her i with a little circle had seemed the height of sophistication. She smiled at the memory but wouldn't want to be a teenager again—not for all the gold in Fort Knox. Thirteen was a fraught age, girls trying to figure out what kind of woman they wanted to become, and the world sending its mixed messages.

How did you handle it, Mary Beaudry?

The diary began with a warning that it was not to be read without permission. Claire felt a small pang, but turned the page. Thirty-three years later, who still cared? She skimmed through January, February, and March. Mary Beaudry was a good student who got all As and Bs, although she hated word problems in math and thought social studies was boring. Mary loved stories and had a lively fantasy life. Sometimes, she imagined herself as a character in a book she was reading; other times, she imagined the characters as part of her life.

Although still a devout Nancy Drew fan, seventh-grade Mary had begun reading grown-up books, some of which had to be hidden from her parents. In March, she read *To Kill A Mockingbird,* a book that could not be mentioned in the Beaudry household, because Daddy said Harper Lee was a rabble-rouser. Mary identified with Scout and wished her father were more like Atticus.

Issues that worried adults in 1961 received an occasional mention, usually beginning with "Daddy says." Mary's father was a staunch anti-communist and afraid the Russians were winning the space race. Her mother's quoted opinions related to issues such as cool clothes, thirteen-year-olds wearing mascara, and staying out past ten o'clock, all of which, to Mary's despair, she opposed. Mary had no pets, and the only sibling mentioned was a much older sister named Lissie who was away at college and called home on Sunday evenings.

Mary's longest entries described the mini-dramas that Claire remembered from her own early adolescence: a growing interest in boys that led to worries about her appearance, arguments with her mom, and petty jealousies among her group of girlfriends; the tension between still liking to climb trees and her mother's insistence that she start acting like a lady now that she was a teenager; the conflict inherent in wanting to be one of the gang and wanting to be unique.

The girl who emerged from this diary was likeable and imaginative. *If we'd gone to school together, Mary, I bet we would have been friends. I used to read books up in trees, too.*

Claire read through the end of May before she put the diary aside and went to bed. Two early mornings had taken their toll, and tomorrow would be another one.

MARY: INTERLUDE # 1

June 1961

Mary leaned back against the tree trunk and admired the shifting patterns that sunlight filtered through leaves made on her tanned legs. She imagined Heathcliff and Catherine walking the moors together for all eternity. Were they finally happy? Wouldn't someone who'd been as bad as Heathcliff go to hell?

She heard the screen door slam and quickly, before her mother could round the corner, climbed down. Whistling through her teeth, she walked toward the house.

"Were you up in that old magnolia again?" her mother frowned. "You were. You've got soot all over your nice white blouse. And stop that whistling. A lady doesn't whistle."

"I was reading." She waved the book. "I have to write a book report."

"Your sister's upstairs sorting clothes. Go see what you can use before she throws everything away."

Mary climbed the stairs to Lissie's room and watched her sister rummaging through her closet. "Momma says I'm supposed to help you."

Lissie pointed to three piles of clothing on the bed. "Atlanta, you, Goodwill," she said.

"I don't know why you and Momma think I want the stuff you're throwing away." Mary stuck out her lower lip. She didn't see anything she wanted in the stack meant for her.

"I'm not throwing them away. I'm giving them to you. Those are perfectly good clothes for school but not for work." Lissie lifted her hair off her neck and raised her chin. "I need to dress like a career woman."

"I don't want your hand-me-downs."

"Don't be such a pill. The clothes I'm giving you are practically new. You'll look really cute in them."

Mary had no interest in cute. She wanted to be beautiful or fascinating. "I thought you'd move back home after graduation. I don't like being an only child."

"I used to wish I was an only child. I was until I was ten and you came along and ruined everything."

"You don't mean that."

"I hated it when Momma made me babysit." Lissie pinched Mary's cheek. "Poor little thing. You were a mid-life baby, and no one had any time for you except Dorcas, and then she died."

Mary considered asking what a mid-life baby was but decided not to give Lissie the satisfaction. "Let go of my face," she said.

Laughing, Lissie released her.

"I sort of remember Dorcas, but I don't recall her dying."

"Momma and Daddy didn't want to upset you, so they told you she'd gone to live in the country."

"I kind of remember that." Mary frowned at the effort. "How'd she die? She wasn't old."

"She fell down the stairs and broke her neck."

People were always saying be careful, you don't want to fall down and break your neck, but it had never occurred to Mary that anyone actually did. "What stairs?"

"The stairs you just climbed."

"Really? How come no one ever told me?"

"I probably shouldn't have. At least that's what Momma and Daddy will say. Don't tell them we talked about it."

"How old was I?"

"Four or five, I don't remember exactly." Lissie picked up a dress. "I swear half the girls in my sorority had one like this." She held it up so Mary could see. "Shirtwaists are always in style, but a floral print isn't sophisticated enough for work. It will look real cute on you."

Cute again. Mary pantomimed gagging. "No thanks. The material looks like pink striped wallpaper."

"Have it your way." Lissie tossed the dress in the Goodwill pile. "Some poor girl is going to be very happy to get this."

After lunch, Lissie and Momma went shopping to "fill in the blanks in Lissie's wardrobe," and Mary returned to her perch in the magnolia tree. It was funny how she remembered and she didn't. If she closed her eyes, she could almost see a body, long legs and skinny arms, all crumpled up at the bottom of the stairs, but the picture was blurry. When she tried harder to see, it went away.

That night, Mary dreamt that a Negro girl came in and sat on her bed. She knew without being told that this was Dorcas.

"I used to get Lissie's hand-me-downs, too," Dorcas said. "The raggedy ones that no one else wanted. They saved the nice ones for you to grow into."

"That's not my fault," Mary said, "and I bet I didn't want them."

"Hah," Dorcas said, and she went away.

The next morning, first chance she got, Mary asked Lissie to tell her more about what happened to Dorcas.

"Why did she fall down the stairs?"

"It was an accident. I don't know the details. I wasn't even home, and there's no point worrying about something that happened years ago."

"I want to know what happened to Dorcas."

Lissie made an exasperated noise. "Forget Dorcas. I never should have mentioned her."

"If you won't tell me, I'm going to ask Momma."

"You better not." Lissie pinched her arm until she promised never to mention Dorcas again and never ever say anything to Momma and Daddy.

Friday night, the whole family drove Lissie to the train station. They accompanied her onto the train and settled her in her own sleeping car. Tomorrow morning she'd wake up in Atlanta.

The way the bed folded out was really cool, but Mary pretended disinterest. She leaned against the door, arms folded across her chest, and watched her father fuss with Lissie's luggage, arranging and rearranging it on the shelf as if it was some kind of a big deal. Momma fussed with Lissie, pushing her hair back off her face and smoothing her dress, checking one more time that Lissie had money for a cab once she got to Atlanta.

Momma's eyes were bright with tears, and even Daddy looked a little misty. Lissie was too excited to notice how anybody else was feeling. Mary could tell she was ready for them to leave, which was fine with her, but her parents lingered until the conductor yelled "All aboard." Then Momma wanted to stay on the platform so they could wave good-bye when the train pulled away.

"Lissie can't see us," Mary said. "She's not even looking."

Her father gave her a stern look, and they stayed.

On the drive home, Momma kept turning her head to look at Mary alone in the back seat. "Lissie will be fine, and we still have you," she'd say and give Mary a big fake smile. Every time she did that, Daddy said before they knew it, Lissie would be coming home for Thanksgiving. Mary didn't say anything. When she grew up, she was going to move to New York City and go to the Stork Club for Thanksgiving. If Lissie was lucky, she might invite her to come.

She sprawled in the back seat, now all hers, and stared out the window. *Wuthering Heights* was the best book she'd ever read, even better than *To Kill A Mockingbird*, but she hadn't been able to make sense of everything. Mrs. Martin told the class that some people thought Heathcliff was really the devil come to earth. Mary didn't think so. He and Catherine were soul mates, and no one thought she was a devil— except Heathcliff. Hadn't he called her infernal?

"Momma, do you think Catherine's ghost haunted Heathcliff?" she said. "Maybe that's why he stopped eating."

Daddy asked what on earth she was talking about and Momma explained it was a book Mary had read for English class. "It's only a story, dear," she said. "Make believe. There aren't any ghosts."

Mary thought about Dorcas's visit. There was more going on than what people could see. Heathcliff thought so too. "What were the use of my creation, if I were entirely contained here?" she quoted.

"What did you say, dear?" Mama asked.

"That's what Heathcliff said."

Daddy harrumphed something about foolishness, and Momma shook her head. "You are my silly girl, Mary."

That night Mary dreamt about Dorcas again. The dream felt so real she half-expected to go downstairs and see Dorcas in the kitchen helping her mother with breakfast. But it was Annie, their regular maid, who stood in front of the sink washing up from Momma and Daddy's breakfast.

"Ten o'clock in the morning," Annie said. "Just because it's Saturday don't mean you can lie in bed all day."

"Did you ever take care of a little girl?" Mary fetched the *Cheerios* from the cupboard, opened the refrigerator, and took out a bottle of milk.

"I'm taking care of your whole family, you included."

"I'm not a little girl, and I'm getting my own breakfast, thank you very much." Mary said. "But I'm not talking about meals. I mean things like playing with her, teaching her games and stuff."

"I don't have time for games." Annie turned her back, letting Mary know that her questions were interfering with more important things.

Dorcas wouldn't have done that. Last night, Dorcas had come and sat on her bed and talked about all the fun they'd had together. She'd reminded Mary about the day she drew chalk squares on the sidewalk and showed her how to play hopscotch. Another time, she had rescued the cards Momma threw away because they were too raggedly for her bridge group and taught her how to play slap jack and go fish and fifty-two pick-up. Dorcas had been nice.

"If'n you don't put that milk back in the fridge, it's going to turn." Annie said.

Mary put the milk away and carried her barely-touched bowl of cereal over to the sink.

Annie watched, her hands on her hips. "What am I supposed to do with that soggy mess?"

Mary shrugged. "I'm not hungry." She went to sit on the front gallery, ignoring Annie's grumbles about certain people who spent half the day in bed and expected hard-working people to drop everything and clean up after them no matter what time they decided to eat.

"There you are, sweetheart." Her mother poked her head out the front door. "Go get dressed and I'll drive you to the club. It's hot enough to go swimming."

"I don't feel like going to the club."

"Don't be silly. Betsy will be there and the other girls. "

"I'm tired." Betsy was her best friend, but Mary wanted to stay home. She needed time alone to think about all the things Dorcas said last night.

"I hope you're not coming down with something." Her mother laid her hand on Mary's forehead. "You don't have a fever."

"I couldn't eat my breakfast. Ask Annie."

After Momma left, Mary climbed up the tree Dorcas had taught her to climb.

CHAPTER 6

Wednesday April 27, 1994

Claire watched amused as Bea ordered a three-egg omelet with a side of cheese grits and sausage patties. Detective Washington ate as much as a big man but was as slender as a fashion model, a build that she shared with the "ghost" who haunted the Chestnut Street house.

"Think that'll hold you until lunch?" she said. She had ordered tea and toast.

"How can you function without food? The body needs fuel."

"I'm too stressed out to eat. Remember my haunted house? Yesterday, I met the ghost. She's an adolescent girl who looks a bit like you." At least the primary ghost. She had gone over the entire back bedroom and found no ropes or anything else that would explain how the girl could have worked the windows. Nor could she find a structural explanation for that cold spot at the base of the front stairs. Dorcas remained a mystery.

"Are you accusing me of something?" Bea chuckled.

Claire described finding and chasing her uninvited guest. "She's living there, at least part time. I want her out, but I don't want to throw her onto the street if she has nowhere else to go. Can you put me in touch with a good social worker or recommend an agency that would help her?"

"If she comes back—and that's a big if—what makes you think you can not only catch her but also make her listen to you? I'll give you a referral, but I doubt you'll ever see her again."

Claire's nod conceded the point. "It's been one thing after another with this property. Termites, possums, the squatter, other kids hanging out, and a crime wave in the neighborhood. With all that going on, it's no wonder people think the house is haunted."

The waiter brought their food. Claire claimed the toast and waited while he arranged Bea's plates. When he left, she continued. "I had to bribe the demo crew to keep them on the job, and I'm not confident that they'll come back and finish. Jack says we'll never sell it. I told him, if that turned out to be true, I'd buy it and live there myself."

Bea unfolded her napkin and laid it in her lap, paying far more attention than the task required.

"What?" Claire said.

"This isn't the first time you've mentioned moving."

"Ah, moving in with Tony." She had tested the idea on Bea, who'd refused to offer an opinion. "That won't happen, if it ever does, until the racing season's over. How can you move in with someone who's not here?"

"I saw in the paper that he did well in some race."

"I saw the picture, too. That's your standard after-race photo. Models, starlets, champagne, it's a tough life."

Bea cut off a piece of sausage, mixed it with her grits, and put it in her mouth. "Mmmm, good."

"It smells good." Claire fiddled with her toast. "Tony says that every picture of him with a beautiful woman brings customers into the dealership."

"Self-sacrificing isn't he?"

Claire shrugged. "I can accept him as he is, or I can walk away, and I don't want to do that."

"I see his appeal," Bea said. "There may be a hotter man, but I haven't met him."

"I know everyone says he's good-looking." Claire shrugged. "When

I look at him, he's just Tony. I'm far from immune, but it's more about feeling than seeing." She couldn't think about him without her pulse quickening, look at his mouth without her lips parting or at his hands without remembering their touch. She always knew when his eyes, blue-gray-green like the ocean, were on her. "I miss him." *Every minute of every day.*

"You two are an odd couple, you know? You lose your husband and after a period of mourning, pull yourself together to become the majority owner of a construction company. Holding your own in a man's world, you could be a feminist icon. And what do you do? You fall for Don Juan reincarnated."

"That's not fair. Tony's a nice guy, and he respects my job."

"I'm guessing he's a terrific lover."

"You know what they say about practice." Claire tried to make it a joke, but she couldn't find a smile, and if the conversation stayed on this path, she'd end up wallowing in self-pity. She pointed at Bea. "What about the lady detective? Are you going to tell me the Homicide Department isn't a man's world?"

"Claire, you're one of the nicest people I know. I wish you well."

"But." Claire said it for her.

"It has to be tough with Tony halfway around the world. If you need a shoulder to cry one, call me. I'll understand, and I'll bring the wine."

"I'm holding on until the middle of June. He'll be here for a few days." Claire spread jam on her toast and took her first bite. Bea didn't and wouldn't ever understand. She didn't understand herself. She and Tony were oil and water. The crowds and parties he enjoyed exhausted her. Her intuitive approach to decisions appalled him. He was open, and she was reserved. Secretive, he said. She was slow to challenge authority, and he lived by his own rules. Opposites attract.

They'd both married young. His marriage lasted six months. She and Tom had been happy and, she believed, would still be married if he hadn't died. She'd loved Tom, but she'd never felt so at peace with herself and the world as she did when lying in Tony's arms.

"You stay and finish, but I have to go." Bea had cleaned her plates. "Staff meeting in thirty minutes. Should I tell my boss hello from you?"

"Of course. I like Mike." If Mike were the man in her life, she wouldn't have to see pictures of him with other women, wouldn't have to wonder who was lying beside him when she wasn't around. Mike was steady and dependable, a man who could be trusted.

"A penny for your thoughts," Bea said.

"Nothing worth a penny." She pushed her barely touched food aside. "I'm ready, too."

"My treat." Bea tossed a bill on the table. "You nibbled; I ate."

"No, my treat. My invitation, and I'm asking you a favor." Claire handed the money back to Bea. "Walk to my truck with me. I have something for you."

"A present? *Pour moi?*"

"Not exactly. I found a loaded gun amongst the ghost's belongings. It's in my glove compartment. I didn't want to bring it into the mall."

"I wish you'd mentioned the gun last night. It raises the ante. Your ghost could be involved with the gang we're tracking. They use guns. They killed a man with one." Bea threw her money back down on the table and tucked the check in her pocket. "The Department's paying. You're helping with our investigation, you and your ghost."

"The gun is why I thought the gang might be involved."

"You might be right, and that's not good news. Where are you parked?"

Happy to be rid of the gun, Claire drove to Chestnut Street to meet Jack who had better be there. They'd talked again last night, and it had been a heated discussion on her side. She'd insisted that he go through the house with her, no more excuses. They needed to draw up specs for the subcontractors, and that had to be a joint effort. They were partners, weren't they?

He'd waffled, pointed out that if there were no structural changes, she could do it without his input.

She lost her temper. "You're forgetting the bump out. And you're forgetting that I'm the client on this project. You're treating me like dirt. If I weren't your partner, I'd fire you."

"You don't want that house, Claire. It's haunted."

"The house is not haunted. Kids are using it for a hangout." She didn't mention Bea's gang or the gun. As Jack would say, why paint trouble on the wall? "There may be a squatter, but there is no ghost."

"That house was haunted before the squatter or the neighborhood kids were born."

"The demo crew will be there at seven-thirty tomorrow morning." She hoped. "I've been working with them, but it's your turn. I'll be there as soon as I can." She'd hung up without giving him a chance to say he was busy elsewhere.

Jack hadn't been happy last night, but when she turned the corner onto Chestnut Street, she saw his truck in the driveway. He met her on the front walk.

"I've already taken a look around, but I want to do it again, the two of us."

"Thank you. Where's our crew?"

"Zach and Banjo are upstairs, gutting the master bathroom. It's not a big job. Two men can handle it." He pointed at the plywood path crossing the gallery floor. "Did you tell the guys I did that?" His grin was apologetic. Beginners fell through floors and ceilings; he was an old hand.

"You and one of our uninvited visitors," she said. "There are two holes under that plywood." She resisted the impulse to say that ghosts don't make holes in rotten floors and led the way inside. Sounds of demo came from above, music to her ears.

Jack stomped the foyer floor. "No one's falling through this. The subfloor is solid as a rock, and the marble is thicker than anything sold today. Have we uncovered any more termites?"

"Nowhere but the sun room. We'll find out for sure tomorrow when the termite inspector comes."

"The interior is in better shape than I expected. Nice mantel." He patted the foyer fireplace. "What's the matter?"

"I left a black garbage bag over in the corner. It's gone."

"A garbage bag? The guys probably tossed it in the dumpster."

"I guess." Claire didn't think so. The girl had returned for her belongings. When would she notice that her gun was missing?

Jack knelt in front of the fireplace and stuck his arm up the flue. "Mortar's holding. Whoever built this house did it right."

"I think it was built for a sea captain. The mantel carvings are seashells, and check out the mermaid sconces. I giggle every time I look at them." She ran her hand along the doorframe. "The pocket doors are in here, stuck, but we'll get them out. The back rooms are another story. You saw what used to be a tiny kitchen, laundry and maid's quarters. The demo team has gutted them. I need your input before we begin putting it back."

"The kitchen is the most important room in the house."

"I knew you were going to say that." He said it on every project.

The new kitchen was a blank slate, and they spent a good forty-five discussing possible layouts before climbing the back stairs.

"The only issue upstairs is the bump out," she said. "You're right about it being ready to fall off the house, but I want to keep it. It's a Jack-n-Jill bathroom."

He slapped his forehead. "I forgot to call an engineer. I'm sorry, Claire. I'll do it this afternoon. I know a good guy for the job."

"Ask the engineer if we can save what's there or if we'll have to rebuild. Go take a look while I talk to Zach and Banjo. I want to tell them how much I appreciate their showing up."

Jack disappeared into the back bedroom and emerged carrying a black garbage bag.

"Is this what you were looking for?"

"Where was it?"

"On the closet shelf." He opened it and pulled out the pillow.

"It looks like our ghost is still living here."

Jack frowned. "We got to get rid of her. We can't have kids in here. Even propped up, that bump out is an accident waiting to happen. Some kid gets hurt, and their parents will sue us for a million bucks."

Claire shook her head in disbelief. Jack had wanted to walk away, she had preached responsibility and warned of liability, and now he was throwing this at her? "I've been talking to the police," she said. "I'll talk to them again—soon as I get back to the office."

"You going to call your buddy?"

"Not Mike—if that's your question. This is trespassing, not homicide, but Bea will help."

"She's back?" Bea said. "I'll be darned. We stepped-up patrols last weekend. Lots of activity, but no one reported seeing anyone around your house. Of course a teenaged squatter is pretty low on the priority list."

"What kind of activity?" Claire said.

"There was another mugging yesterday. This one was a block from your house. The victim is still in the hospital. Doctors say he should make it, but he may never walk again." Bea bit the words off. Claire had never heard her this angry. "The victim offered no resistance. He handed over his wallet, but they stomped him anyway, crushed three vertebrae and left him for dead."

"That's horrible. But why are you so knowledgeable about these muggings? Aren't Juvenile and Homicide separate divisions?"

"These kids kill people. Homicide is in charge. We're coordinating with Street Crimes and Juvenile."

"I was planning to hide in the house, try to ambush my guest."

"But now you're having second thoughts. As you should. It's not safe."

"I won't stay there alone after dark."

"I said it before. Don't be there alone in broad daylight and not at night. Period."

"That's what you told me, but what about the people who live in the neighborhood? If things are as bad as you say, why hasn't anyone warned them?"

"I hear you." Bea said. "We've kept this quiet for reasons you and I don't need to discuss, but that's going to change. Superintendent Vernon is holding a press conference at noon. It will be all over the news. Your ghost should hear about it and might decide to stay away."

"The way she hangs around here, you don't think she already knows? But she keeps coming back. Why is beyond me."

"I'm going to be in the neighborhood tomorrow, scouting sites for a weekend stakeout. Give me the address again. I'll take a look."

"Three-sixty-eight Chestnut, two houses down from the corner. There's an overgrown hedge on three sides. Someone standing in the front hedge could see both streets, all four directions, but no one would see them."

"Someone being a police officer," Bea said. "You will be nowhere near."

"That house is my property, and I have every right to be there. We might as well cooperate."

"Forget it, Claire. You're a civilian, and Mike would kill me. He still has a soft spot for you. By the way he says hello."

"I'm going to be in the house, not in the hedge. And please tell Mike hello from me. I hope he's doing well."

"Claire..."

"I took that girl's gun. She might have had it for protection, and now she doesn't."

"That gun is a piece of junk, inaccurate, and prone to jamming. Unfortunately junk guns kill people as dead as any other kind. I've sent it to forensics for testing. The kids we're after shot one of their victims with 22 caliber bullets, like those in the gun. If it is the murder weapon, we'll turn the neighborhood inside out looking for your ghost."

"She's a girl, not a ghost, and not much more than a child." And no matter what Jack or Bea said, until this was resolved, she couldn't lock that girl out of the house.

"Have you talked to Tony about this?"

"No." She might have told him if he'd called. "You check out the house. Neither I nor anyone who works for me will be there alone or after dark, until Saturday when I'll get there before dark and wait inside. What time will your stakeout begin?"

CHAPTER 7

Claire swore by everything holy that she'd stay inside.

"I still don't like it." Bea said.

"But there's nothing you can do. I'm determined to be here, and this is my property."

"Why?" Bea's question combined irritation and curiosity.

"Why do you spend hours of your precious free time working with The Girls' Club?"

"There's a difference, Claire. I understand your wanting to help her, but—"

"She's just a kid."

"She's not a kid the way you were a kid. Her world isn't your world, and her standards of behavior aren't yours. You don't want to get involved with her."

"Actually, that is exactly what I want, and how do you know so much about a person you've never even seen."

"Okay." Bea lifted her hands in a gesture of resignation. "If your girl returns, I'll signal you, and then come around through the back door. Give me five minutes."

"When, not if. She's still living here. Demolition leaves dust on the floor and someone is leaving footprints in the dust. They're my size but not mine, and I don't think ghosts leave footprints."

"One buzz means she's back. Three in rapid succession mean the muggers are in the area. Either signal, I'll pause and then repeat. If it's the muggers, you take refuge. Lock the doors, shut yourself in a closet, and stay put until I call your mobile phone."

"Fair enough. I'll start out right here." Claire sat on the floor in front of a window that caught enough light from a streetlamp for her to see drawings, and pulled out a folder.

"What're you doing?"

"Looking at kitchen layouts. It's what I'd be doing if I were home"

"This is how you spend your Saturday nights?"

"It beats crouching in the bushes."

"I had a date tonight." Bea's mouth turned down. "For dinner, and he's a big spender."

"And you're a big eater."

"Tomorrow, it's girl's night out. We'll go somewhere nice, eat lots of good food, drink lots of good wine, and let our hair *down*." Bea pointed at the floor with both hands.

"You have a deal," Claire said. She hadn't been out to dinner since Tony left—her fault, but still.

"Tomorrow's May Day. We'll celebrate the holiday."

"The workers or the little girls who wrap ribbons around a maypole?"

"Both." Bea grinned. "Wrapping those ribbons is work."

They exchanged high fives. Bea went back outside, and Claire settled in with the drawings. She was comparing several options for an island with a sink when the pager in her pocket vibrated once. After a long pause, it vibrated once again. She checked her watch and moved to a spot behind the hall door.

Moments later, the front door creaked open then clicked shut. Soft footsteps climbed the stairs and padded down the upstairs hall to the back bedroom. Claire glanced at her watch again. Two minutes had passed since Bea's signal. She waited for three more then tiptoed up the stairs, keeping to the outside edge where the steps were less likely to squeak.

The girl sat on the floor, reading by flashlight and too engrossed in her book to notice Claire standing in the doorway.

"Hello again." Claire stepped into the room.

The girl jumped to her feet and lifted the flashlight like a club. "Get out! Go on, get out."

"I beg your pardon. This is my house."

"This is Dorcas' house."

"Who told you about Dorcas?"

Bea, who had come in the back and up the kitchen stairs, walked in. "Who's Dorcas?"

The girl looked from one to the other, threw the flashlight between them and tried to follow it. Bea grabbed her and with no apparent effort twisted her arm up behind her back. She held her badge in front of the girl's face.

"Detective Beatrice Washington, New Orleans Police Department. You didn't know that, so I'm going to forget that you just tried to assault me, but we are going to talk." She frisked the girl. "No weapon. That's a step in the right direction."

A window slammed shut. "Let's get out of this room," Claire said. "She's rigged the windows. Can we go downstairs?"

"In the back of the house. I don't want to disrupt the stakeout." Bea pointed at the girl. "Don't even think about making a run for it. You'll run smack into another police officer and a whole bunch of trouble."

"There's a pantry off the kitchen," Claire said. "No windows."

"We're right behind you."

Claire carried the girl's flashlight and book down the back stairs. When they reached the pantry, Bea released the girl, who collapsed onto the floor and lay there, glaring at them.

"Now what?" Claire said.

"Good question. I didn't believe this young woman was going to show up, but here she is, and I have to do something about her." Bea turned to the girl. "How long have you been camping out here?"

"I don't have to tell you anything."

"At least since the middle of March," Claire answered for her. "But not every night."

"How old are you?" Sullen silence met the question, and Bea studied the girl. "I'm guessing thirteen or fourteen. You *could* be my little sister. Claire said we looked alike." She waved in Claire's direction. "Claire Marshall, she owns this house. I've already told you my name, and you are?"

"Tishanna."

"Just one name? Like Cher or Madonna?"

"Tishanna Tenier."

"What are you doing here Tishanna Tenier?"

"None of your business."

"I could take you down to police headquarters and talk to you there."

The threat produced a worried frown but no response.

"Don't you have a home?" Bea said.

More silence.

"No? Then I'll have to find you one." Bea called for a squad car to come by the house. "We have a stakeout in progress. Ignore them and they'll ignore you. Park out front and walk in the front door. We'll walk out with you and leave in your car. The stakeout is for that gang. They've been active in this neighborhood, and if they see us, it might spook them, but there's not much we can do about it. I've apprehended a juvenile runaway. I can't leave her here."

When Bea mentioned the gang, Tishanna's eyes widened. Her demeanor had ranged from surly to insolent and back again, but now she was biting her lower lip.

"You know who she's talking about, don't you Tishanna?" Claire said.

"If she's been around for the last six weeks, she's seen them." Bea frowned. "And they've seen her. I'm surprised they're leaving you alone, Tishanna. Are they friends of yours? An older brother? A boyfriend? Is someone protecting you?"

"She's not protecting me from you." Tishanna sniffled, her rebellion crushed. She looked to be on the verge on tears.

"She? Who are we talking about?"

"Dorcas."

"Dorcas again?" Bea raised an eyebrow.

"Dorcas is the ghost," Claire said. "I told you. People think this house is haunted." Not only did everyone in New Orleans believe her house was haunted, they were all on a first name basis with the ghost. When she had some free time, she'd talk to Mrs. Ledet and bring herself up to speed.

"Are you going to arrest me?"

"Only if Claire wants to press charges."

Claire shook her head.

"Then you got to let me go."

"You're too healthy to be living on the streets. I think you have a home. Give me your address and I'll take you there. Otherwise, we're going downtown and Juvenile will find you a bed for the night." Bea looked her up and down. "If I were you, I wouldn't want to spend the night in a juvenile facility."

"I live with my grandmother."

"Okay." Bea said. "Where does your grandmother live?"

"Desire."

Claire winced. This child lived in New Orleans' most notorious public housing project. No wonder she was looking for another place to stay.

"I'll get one of the patrols to drive us there," Bea said. "As soon as Claire leaves."

"I'm on my way." Claire gave Bea the flashlight and the book Tishanna had been reading, *To Kill A Mockingbird,* one of Mary's favorite books. "This belongs to her."

"That's Mary's book," Tishanna said.

"Mary Beaudry," Claire nodded. "You had her diary. Did you read it?"

"You the one who took it? You better put it back. If you take Mary's books and don't put them back, Dorcas will get mad."

Bea and Claire exchanged looks.

"The ghost, right?" Bea said. "We have a ghost with a temper?"

"You laugh, you're going to be sorry," Tishanna folded her arms across her chest, once again the picture of defiance. "Dorcas can do stuff."

CHAPTER 8

Bea was already seated, at a table overlooking the garden, when Claire arrived.

"I hope I'm not late," Claire said. "It was so nice out I walked."

"No, I'm early, but you should think twice about walking around by yourself at night. Even in the Garden District."

"Bea, you're off duty."

"Right, but I'm driving you home."

Claire waited until the waiter had taken their order before asking about Tishanna. "What kind of reception did you get when you took her home?"

"Grandma started yelling the minute we walked in. She also believes in Dorcas, but she's not a fan. According to Grandma, Dorcas is an angry spirit who will cause real trouble for anyone who has anything to do with her. Warning delivered, she moved on to more earthly concerns. She accused Tishanna of turning into a tramp like her mother, taking off and staying out overnight. I told her that Tishanna had been staying in an empty house by herself and, as far as I knew, hadn't been doing anything else wrong. I suggested she lighten up a little, but I'm afraid our girl is in trouble with her grandmother."

"What's the address? I could stop by, talk to her grandmother, and see if there's anything I can do." Claire lifted her hands in a gesture of helplessness. "I don't know what, but I feel responsible."

"Don't go there." Bea was emphatic. "Cops don't go in alone. I'll follow up."

"You have a tough job."

"Look who's talking," Bea said. "Last time I saw you at work, you were crawling around under a house." She shuddered. "Snakes, spiders, ugh. I wouldn't do that on a bet."

"You would if you were chasing a criminal."

"Maybe, but not just to check the plumbing or whatever you were doing under there."

"Confirming the structural walls." Claire raised her glass. "To interesting work."

They clicked rims and Bea said, "I read somewhere that seventy percent of people hate their jobs. I'm grateful to be in the other thirty percent."

"Me, too." Claire took another sip of wine. "So, what else is going on in your life? How many men do you have on the string?" She marveled at how gracefully Bea juggled a demanding job, an active social life, and work with the Big Sisters program that she rarely discussed.

"Competition adds spice to romance." Bea grinned. "Unlike you, I'm not ready to settle down."

"I'm not sure I am either. Would a woman wanting to settle down become involved with Tony Burke?"

"You'd have to hope not."

"Tony lives in the moment, and at this moment, we're thousands of miles apart. He calls and then he doesn't. Out of sight, out of mind—isn't there a song about that?" There were days when she thought her feelings for Tony represented temporary insanity, a stand-in for all the mad crushes she didn't have growing up. She'd become Tom's steady girlfriend in ninth grade, his fiancée in college, and was his wife until he died. There'd never been anyone else.

"Why don't you call him?" Bea said. "You must know how to contact him."

"Of course I do, but women are always calling him."

"So?"

"He finds it annoying. He has two phones, one he never answers, just checks the messages to see if he wants to talk to the person or not, and one with a number very few people know. If that number gets out, he changes it."

"Which number do you have?"

"Both."

"Which takes us back to why don't you call him? You're obviously not on his nuisance list."

Claire shrugged. "I don't know. The time difference makes it hard. I'm afraid I'll be interrupting something important." *I'm afraid he'll be with another woman.*

"I hesitate to defend Tony Burke," Bea said. "But those may be the reasons he's not calling you."

The arrival of their food ended the conversation.

They left the restaurant a little before ten, tired but feeling the rosy glow produced by good food, good wine, and good company. Bea dropped her off, and rather than go inside, Claire sat out on the porch, rocking in the swing and thinking—about Tony, about 368 Chestnut, about Tishanna who believed the ghost that scared everyone else protected her.

Tonight was a night for believing in ghosts. Moonlight turned the magnolia trees into dark sentries. A cool breeze sent their leaves rustling and their shadows in motion. Even fluffy orange and white Dorian looked sinister as he stalked a bug crawling along the porch.

"Do you believe in ghosts, Dorian? Were you a witch's familiar in one of your previous lives?" She leaned down to scratch behind his ears, and he purred loudly. Whether he was saying yes or a no wasn't clear. *Feed me* was the most likely message. She picked him up and settled him in her lap. "Do you miss Tony?" she said. "Or are you another out-of-sight-out-of-mind guy?"

Bea had stuck up for Tony tonight, but they both knew she had serious reservations about him. When Claire first confessed that she could be falling in love with him, Bea had suggested caution. "You're walking on shaky ground, Claire. You know his history. If his mother ever loved him, she hid it well. A child who grows up feeling unloved might not know how to love."

"His father loved him."

Bea had said no more. They both knew the truth was complicated. The man Tony called his father had been a heavy-drinking womanizer prone to leaving home for weeks at a time. Tony had never admitted that he remembered his father's absences, but he must. Jack, who also viewed Tony with suspicion, would say that the acorn hadn't fallen far from the tree.

Still, Claire had shrugged off her friends' warnings and convinced herself that, in time, Tony would come to love her as wholeheartedly as she loved him. Her perspective changed after he went back to Europe. Without him around to fog her mind, her optimism had faded, and a nagging little voice took residence inside her ear. Tony had strayed before and would again, the voice said. Sooner or later, she would add her name to the list of women with hearts broken by Tony Burke. It wasn't a short list.

Tony told her the other women were no more than diversions, temporary pleasures soon forgotten—neither he nor they had any delusions about their time together—but he'd never expressed regret. Now, with thousands of miles separating them, she asked herself, What if one time was different? Wasn't it inevitable that, eventually, he'd become bored with her? She was a reasonably attractive thirty-four-year-old woman. He was a glamorous celebrity, living in a world full of younger, prettier, all too willing women. For perhaps the hundredth time, the nagging little voice told Claire that she was playing way out of her league.

Dorian jumped down and skulked into the shadowy garden, abandoning her comfortable but boring lap for the pursuit of some night creature. Claire watched him disappear into the shadowy garden then went inside. As soon as she saw the blinking message light, she knew it was from Tony. Why hadn't she checked when she got home? She pressed the button.

"I'm in Imola. Call me, no matter what time you get in." He left a number, a new one.

Claire had never heard of Imola, but she recognized the country code for Italy. Ten-thirty in New Orleans was five-thirty tomorrow morning in Italy. Tony had sounded tired—exhausted. Did he really want her to call? She dithered a moment, then dialed.

"Pronto," Tony answered, his voice rough with sleep.

"I'm sorry, Tony. I shouldn't have called, but you said no matter what time."

"Give me a minute. Where've you been?"

"Out to dinner with Bea Washington. Are you okay?"

"I am but other people aren't. San Marino—" His voice broke.

"What happened?"

"It started during practice. Barichello hit a tire wall, swallowed his tongue. He could have died, but he was lucky. The medics got to him in time. He's okay."

Claire waited to hear who wasn't okay.

"Ratzenberger lost a wing flap early in the qualifying run, but he kept going. Next lap, he hit the wall at Villeneuve. He never regained consciousness."

"He died?" There were accidents and drivers got hurt, but they didn't die. They wore helmets and other protective gear. Medics and fire trucks stood at the ready.

"First lap of the race, another accident. No drivers were hurt, but flying debris injured several spectators—serious but not fatal. Then, on the seventh lap, Senna, one of the best drivers and nicest guys on the circuit—" He took a ragged breath. "Senna went off the track on the Tamburello curve. Hit the wall head-on. A piece of the suspension went through his helmet. He died at the hospital."

"How awful. I'm so sorry." The dead men were strangers, she'd never heard the foreign names that rolled off Tony's tongue, but she was horrified by the carnage. Two men dead, other people badly injured, and for what? A car race?

"It didn't end there. Alboreto threw a wheel leaving the pit. It hit one of our crew. The doctors don't know if he'll make it."

Tears rolled down Claire's cheeks. "I wish I were there. It wouldn't change what happened, but I could be with you." She wanted desperately to hold him, comfort him, feel his warmth and know he was safe.

"The owners changed the rules, but drivers died, and we get the blame. A reporter said we drove too fast, like Icarus flew too close to the sun."

"Are you going to keep on racing? Please say no. Tell me you're coming home. Now. Tomorrow."

"I'm part of a team, Claire. I can't quit three races into the season. We're going back to Fiorano to regroup then on to Monte Carlo."

I hate your job, she thought but did not say. She didn't trust herself to speak. Continuing as if nothing had happened was stupid, not honorable.

"After Ratzenberger died, we decided to organize. The owners would have to listen if all of us spoke with a single voice and demanded safety improvements. Senna was going to head it." Tony's voice caught. He was crying, too. "Senna was Brazilian, but they found an Austrian flag in his car. He intended to win the goddamned race and dedicate his win to Ratzenberger."

"I'm so sorry." She'd said it before, but she had no better words.

"They're talking about improved pit safety. We're going to demand more."

"You can't just go on as before." *Please, no.*

Before they hung up, Tony gave her a number where she could reach him in Fiorano. "I'll be there through the twelfth."

Too strung out to sleep, Claire returned to the porch and watched purple clouds slide across the moon. More than responsibility to the team kept Tony racing. She'd felt his passion when he described powering through a curve, fighting his way through the pack, and overtaking another car. The accidents were forcing him to look at racing's dark side, but he'd never quit. He'd told her once that racing had saved his life. She prayed it wouldn't take it.

The next race was in two weeks. Practice runs would begin before then. And qualifying runs. A driver died in a qualifying run. Another driver died in the race. Someone else might or might not survive his injuries. She rocked back and forth, hugging herself but finding no comfort. Thousands of miles away, Tony was alone and hurting, and she wasn't there to comfort him.

The little voice whispered in her ear, "You're not there, but other women are. Tony won't be alone long. You're going to lose him, you know."

Men had died, and she was worried about Tony cheating on her. Claire buried her face in her hands. Loving a man she didn't trust was turning her into a person she didn't want to be.

CHAPTER 9

Jack had promised to put 368 Chestnut on a fast track, and he was true to his word. On Monday, a team of carpenters framed the back where the sun porch had been attached, and on Tuesday, they re-sided it with old cypress that Jack had tracked down in an architectural artifacts warehouse.

Today, two finish carpenters were framing up the opening for French doors that would lead from the dining room to a future terrace. A steady rhythm from above punctuated the sounds of their power saws as the roofers nailed down the tarpaper underlay.

Tomorrow, they'd put on the shingles, and the gutter man would take measurements. Friday the carpenters would begin repairs on the soffit and fascia. When they finished, the gutters would go on. By the end of next week the exterior would be watertight, the house would be secure, and they could begin work on the inside.

Claire had down days when she imagined owning this house forever, unable to sell or rent it, a slave to the mortgage she'd have to take out in order to buy it from the company. But as days passed with no strange occurrences, her normal optimism returned. If there was a ghost named Dorcas, she was biding her time, and Tishanna did not reappear. Their crew and all the subs had heard that this house was haunted, but no one had refused to work on it. Of course, the real test would be when they began restoring the interior.

Between working on the kitchen layout, negotiating a construction loan with the bank, and talking to potential new clients—not to mention hours spent thinking about Tony—Claire had little time to worry about her ghost. It was Wednesday afternoon before she found time to visit Mrs. Ledet.

The house was similar to hers, two stories with tall windows flanking the front door but in much better shape. For starters, it boasted an intact second floor gallery. Mature but not overgrown shrubs eased the transition from house to yard, and a mix of ferns and brightly blooming impatiens invited visitors up the front walkway. The first floor gallery was screened, not pretty. If it were hers, she'd take the screens off, but they did keep the mosquitoes at bay.

An elderly woman answered the doorbell.

"Mrs. Ledet, I'm Claire Marshall, the new owner of the haunted house."

"I know who you are, dear. I keep up with all the neighborhood gossip." She smiled. "You might even say I am the neighborhood gossip. May I offer you a glass of tea? You're welcome to come inside, but it's such a nice day, we could sit out." She directed Claire to a rocking chair, one of four lined up on the front gallery, and bustled away, calling over her shoulder that she'd be just a minute.

The rocking chairs, like their owner, were old but comfortable. Worn spots along their armrests showed dark red beneath the more recent forest green, and the seats bore the imprints of previous sitters. Claire rocked back and forth, admiring the yard. She was reconsidering impatiens, a flower she'd not always favored, when Ellen Ledet returned with two glasses of iced tea and a plate of cookies.

"Please help yourself," she said. "I'm full of questions, but I'll give you a moment's peace before I start."

"Ask away, Mrs. Ledet." Claire helped herself to a cookie. "I have questions for you, too."

"The whole neighborhood wonders how you came to buy that house and what your plans are for it. And please, call me Ellen."

"We're going to restore it to its former glory," Claire said with a smile. "And then we're going to sell it." She hoped.

"Your name's familiar," Ellen said, "but I can't quite place it."

A year and a half ago, when Claire was a murder suspect, her name and picture were all over the news. That was probably what Ellen half remembered, but it wasn't what she'd come here to discuss. "Maybe Lindsey Tice mentioned me. We chatted briefly a couple weeks ago. She told me that a ghost named Dorcas haunted my house and suggested I ask you to tell me the whole story."

"Poor Lindsey. You've heard what happened, haven't you?"

"No. What?"

"Last week. Bill was coming home from a business dinner about ten-thirty at night. He'd been drinking so he decided to take the streetcar rather than drive. A gang of young thugs attacked him. Just a block from here."

"Was he hurt?"

"That's the worst of it. They beat him, knocked him down and kicked him as he lay there."

"I'd heard there was a mugging near here, but..." She shook her head. Bea hadn't mentioned the victim's name, and it had never occurred to her that she knew anyone connected to the crime.

"They broke his back. He might never walk again." Indignation brought red blotches to Ellen's face. "He would have died if someone hadn't come along and seen him lying in the gutter."

"That's just awful." Claire remembered Lindsey's wide smile, her warmth and friendliness, the baby on the way. "I only met Lindsey that once, but I really liked her."

"I'm sure she'd appreciate a note. There's a lot of heartache in this world, and kind words do make a difference."

"I'll do it tonight. And if you don't feel like talking about my house, I understand."

Ellen rocked back and forth, looking out over the street. "I'd much rather talk than sit here alone thinking about all the bad things that are happening, I've seen a lot of changes in this neighborhood. Good and bad. It's been good for a while, but lately things have turned bad—young hoodlums with no respect for anything."

"Lindsey said you'd lived here a long time."

"I came here as a bride in the year of our Lord 1946. That was 48 years ago. As you may know, there was a housing shortage after the war. Alan and I felt so lucky to have found this place." Nostalgia softened her expression. "We raised four children here. Three of them still live in Louisiana, and now their children come to visit. This old house is practically a member of the family."

Claire settled in to listen.

"Alan went home to Jesus six years ago. The children worry about me living in this big house all alone, and my son keeps pestering me about moving in with his family, but I intend to spend the rest of my days right here. I'd rather be stabbed in my bed than live in a home like— Oh dear, I'm getting ahead of myself. You asked about Dorcas."

"I like to learn as much as I can about the history of the houses we work on. A ghost is something new."

"And something tragic. When we moved here, your house belonged to the Beaudrys. Charles owned the pharmacy that used to be around the corner. He and Lucinda had two daughters. No one discussed such things back then, but I believe they had difficulty conceiving a child. They'd been married eight years before Lissie was born, and poor Mary didn't come along until ten years later. Charles was perhaps past wanting a baby in the house, but Lucinda was delighted."

Claire nodded. She knew something about the Beaudry household from reading Mary's diary.

"Dorcas was their maid's daughter and not much more than a girl herself. She'd be there after school and on weekends, helping out around the house some, but mostly looking after little Mary—playing with her really. Mary became very fond of Dorcas.

"When Dorcas died, the family tried to shield Mary by saying that Dorcas and her mother had gone to live with relatives in the country. They gave Dorcas's mother a generous severance, and she did move back home. It wasn't a cover-up as some people think. Charles and Lucinda were protecting Mary, who was a highly excitable and imaginative child."

Ellen Ledet sounded defensive, and Claire wondered on whose

behalf. "How old was Dorcas when she died?" she said.

"Dorcas was probably thirteen, Mary would have been five. Naturally, she was unhappy about Dorcas leaving, but she got over it soon enough and for years was a normal happy child. Then, when Mary was thirteen, Lissie told her the truth." Ellen shook her head. "She told me later that she'd never forgive herself, but she had no way of knowing what an impact her words would have. Would you like some more iced tea, dear?"

"No thank you." Claire had asked about Dorcas, but Ellen was telling Mary's story. Did she see them as one and the same?

Ellen sighed. "Mary became obsessed with Dorcas's death. I don't know all the details. Lucinda Beaudry and I were good friends, but Alan and Charles never really hit it off. Charles was a standoffish and stern man. I could count on one hand the times I saw him smile. I don't believe I ever heard him laugh.

"When Mary's troubles began, Charles and Lucinda circled the wagons. I could tell that Lucinda was dying to confide in someone, but Charles forbade it. Once I tried to bring it up, and he told me that family problems belonged within the family."

"What happened to Mary?" Claire said. The girl whose diary she'd read had been happy and normal.

"The poor child suffered a nervous breakdown. Walking past the house, you'd hear her screaming and the crashes from her throwing things. I can't imagine how terrible it must have been inside. The school sent her home and told her parents to take her to a psychiatrist. Have you ever read Freud?" Ellen waved her hand as if shooing a pesky fly. "I think it's a bunch of nonsense myself, and it didn't help Mary one whit."

She stopped talking and pointed a long finger at a teenager sauntering up the street. "I don't know him. It used to be I knew everyone in the neighborhood, but times have changed and not for the better."

"Lindsey said there weren't many children in the neighborhood."

"I don't think he lives here."

Claire watched him pass, his gold necklaces flashing and baggy pants flapping over untied sneakers. Perhaps his footprints were among those she'd found. Her suspicion hardened when he paused to stare at her house before continuing on toward Jackson.

"You don't go out by yourself at night, do you?" she said.

"No, dear, I'm not a fool. I see these young men who don't belong here, and I stay inside."

"If you see anyone around my house, please call the police. People are hanging out there, and I want it to stop."

"We all do, dear, and you're right in suspecting that they've been in your house. I don't sleep as well as I used to. Sometimes I'm up half the night, reading or watching television. Just last week, I saw several young men on your property. I called 911, but by the time the police arrived, they were long gone. We'll all be glad when someone is living there again."

Ellen took a sip of tea and resumed her narrative. "It's easy to know better after the fact, and people are quick to judge what someone else has done, but we have to remember that Mary's breakdown was more than thirty years ago. We've learned a lot about mental illness since then. Mrs. Carter made a big difference. I always liked her, although I wasn't so sure about her husband."

"Learned a lot and have a lot more to learn." Claire said. She'd suffered panic attacks after Tom died and knew firsthand not only the devastation of emotional problems but also the dangers of the drugs used to control them. "Did Mary recover?"

Ellen shook her head. "No. Lucinda and Charles tried everything under the sun, but Mary only got worse. Eventually, they had to put her in a home. She'd been hospitalized before, but this was permanent. Lucinda passed two years later. From cancer, the doctors said. Of a broken heart, if you ask me. Charles passed the next year. A stroke."

"What happened to Lissie?"

"Lissie had moved to Atlanta after college. She married a man she met there. They live in one of the suburbs and have one child, a son who's in college up north somewhere. College," Ellen said. "Only yesterday, he was a toddler. You know, it's children growing up who show us the passage of time."

Claire nodded, although she didn't know. She wondered if she'd ever have a child. Tony once told her, out of the blue, that he thought she'd be a good mother. She'd been startled and asked where that came from. He hadn't elaborated. She pushed thoughts of Tony away and returned her attention to Ellen, who had resumed talking.

"Lissie inherited the house. She tried to rent it out, but long-distance landlording proved troublesome. No tenants stayed for long, and some left owing several months' rent. One family moved out in the middle of the night. Lissie sold the house to someone who sold it to someone. The most recent owner was a man who has rental property all over the state. He bought the house ten or fifteen years ago. His tenants moved out, too. Word got around about strange things happening, people said the house was haunted, and eventually no one wanted to live there. It's stood empty for years."

Finally, they'd gotten to the ghost. "Have you ever seen or heard anything to make you think the house really is haunted?" Claire said.

"Mary was haunted. I don't know about the house. She turns forty-six later this month. I'm working with the staff to have a little party for her. Maybe you'd like to come."

"Mary is still in New Orleans?" Ellen's story had seemed like ancient history, but this brought it squarely into the present. "You see her?"

"I try to visit once a month, depending upon when my son can drive me. I promised Lucinda. That poor woman had a cross to bear. And you know how people can talk."

Claire suppressed a smile. People certainly did talk, her hostess among them. "How is Mary now?"

"She's peaceful, but she'll never be right." Ellen put her hand on Claire's arm. "That's enough about sorrowful things. Tell me a little about you." She asked Claire where she was living now, how long she'd lived in New Orleans, did she have family here, all the standard questions people asked.

Claire admitted that she was from up north, Michigan in fact. "But I'm very fond of New Orleans. I've lived here going on six years and intend to stay." She thanked Ellen for the neighborhood history and the iced tea.

"Please visit again. And do think about coming with me to see

Mary. Her birthday is May 26th. I believe that's a Thursday, a workday for you, but if you could take off an hour or so early..." Ellen's eyes misted. "Mary doesn't have much in her life."

"I'll try," Claire promised. She left without learning much about Dorcas. Ellen had made her a bit player in the larger tragedy of Mary's problems, but it was Dorcas who had died, and at thirteen. Wasn't that a tragedy too?

That night, Claire went back to Mary's diary, looking for the disturbed young woman that Ellen had described. Early June brought the first mention of Dorcas. Lissie had indeed told Mary that Dorcas died after falling down their stairs.

Until then, Mary had been a lackadaisical diarist, sometimes writing only a sentence or two and other times skipping several days in a row, but now, a recurring dream of Dorcas inspired daily entries. The obsession Ellen had described emerged, and as the summer progressed, Mary's emotional health deteriorated.

MARY: INTERLUDE #2

August 1961

Momma sat down on the sofa. "School starts in three weeks," she said. "Your daddy and I have been talking about taking a long week-end and renting a house over at Pass Christian."

"I don't want to go," Mary said.

"Mary, you love the beach."

"Sounds to me as if she'd just as soon stay home," Daddy said.

"We discussed this, Charles, and you said yes."

"You presented the trip as something Mary wanted. I was going along with the majority."

Mary made a face. Her father talked about majority rule, but his one vote outweighed everyone else whenever he wanted it to.

"Mary will be happy when we get there," Momma said. "You can invite a friend, dear. I bet Betsy would love to come with us."

"I will not and I don't want to."

"I've recently hired a new clerk," Daddy said.

"What does that have to do with anything, Charles?" Momma sounded exasperated.

"I'm not sure I can trust him not to close early if I'm not around. We'll go to the beach another time." Daddy picked up a magazine and started reading. Momma went upstairs.

That night when Dorcas came to visit, Mary told her about the beach trip argument. "I don't want to go because I don't want to leave you behind," she said, "but I feel bad about making Momma unhappy."

"I don't know why," Dorcas said. "I'm the one who stayed home and played with you when you were little. Your momma was always off to her clubs and card games."

The next day Momma made her go to the club, which turned out to be kind of fun. Betsy and the other girls were there, and they played cards and Marco Polo and talked about school starting up again. The letters giving them their schedules and homeroom assignments had come out. Mary and Betsy were in different homerooms, but they had the same lunch period and the same English class. When Momma came to pick her up, Mary was sorry to leave.

That night at dinner, they talked about what clothes she'd need for school. Daddy said they needed to remember that he wasn't made of money, and Momma said that they'd start by going through the clothes Lissie had left.

"Why don't we do that tomorrow?" Mary said, "I want to go to bed."

"Are you all right, dear?" Her mother had that puzzled line between her eyes. "What happened to my little girl who never wanted to go to bed?"

"I'm reading a good book, and I like to read in bed." That wasn't the real reason, but if she told Momma and Daddy that she went to bed early and lingered under the covers in the morning because she wanted to be with Dorcas, they'd put her in a lunatic asylum.

"It's early yet," Momma said. "Why don't you go put on that nice pleated skirt Lissie gave you and let me mark it for Annie to hem."

"I want to read."

"You can read when we're finished." Momma used her no nonsense voice, and Mary knew not to argue. "Annie should be through cleaning up. Go put on the skirt and meet me in the kitchen."

Mary did as she was told, and five minutes later was standing on the kitchen table, while her mother adjusted the hem marker so it hit just below her knees.

"Don't stick out a hip or it won't be even." Momma closed the marker over a piece of skirt, put in a pin, slid several inches of fabric through, and did it again. "Okay, turn just a tiny bit. This skirt looks nice on you. The flare gives you a little shape. My baby is growing up."

"How much longer is this going to take?"

"Mary Amelia Beaudry. You've been mopey ever since your sister left. I understand that you miss her, but I will not have whining. Now stand up straight."

"I'm sorry, Momma." Mary squared her shoulders. Did she really miss Lissie? She didn't think so.

"Of course you don't miss her. Why should you?" Dorcas appeared out of nowhere and sat at the table. "She always took the biggest piece of cake and left you the crumbs. Just like this skirt. You get what she doesn't want."

Mary froze. Dorcas had never come out of her bedroom before. Could Momma see her? Could she hear her?

"I used to hide things for you, remember?" Dorcas said. "One day my momma made two dozen red velvet cupcakes with butter cream frosting, and Lissie said she needed all of them for a party at her friend's house. While she was talking your momma into it, I hid four of them in the back of the cupboard, two for you and two for me."

"I remember," Mary said.

"What do you remember, dear?"

"Nothing, I was just thinking." Mary pressed her lips together. She hadn't meant to speak aloud.

"I bet you remember the day I taught you the fifty-two pickup trick and you played it on Lissie," Dorcas said.

Mary nodded.

"Don't move your head," Momma said. "If you can't stand still, we'll never get this done."

"I'm trying." Mary didn't see how one little head bob could make any difference way down by her knees.

"Lissie was mad as a wet hen," Dorcas said.

Mary smiled at the memory. She'd been sitting on the gallery floor playing the real fifty-two pickup with herself, which was good practice but not a real game, when Lissie's friends dropped her off.

Lissie had waved good-bye and hurried up the steps. "What are you doing pumpkin?" she said.

"Playing fifty-two pickup. Do you want to play?"

"Not now."

"Please, please, pretty please."

"Okay, but just one game." Lissie knelt down beside her.

Mary threw the cards high in the air. "Pick them up, Lissie. Pick them up. Fifty-two pickup." She had laughed so hard. It wasn't often that she got the best of her big sister.

A pinprick on her leg startled Mary back to the present. "Ouch!"

"I'm talking to you, Miss. I said turn." Her mother stuck her again, not hard enough to draw blood but hard enough to hurt.

"Ouch! I hate this skirt. Betsy's getting new clothes for school, and all I get is hand-me-downs that Lissie doesn't want anymore." She stomped her foot.

The box of pins rose off the table, turned over, and dumped all the pins on the floor.

"Hah," Dorcas said. "Five hundred pickup."

"Now look what you've done." Her mother slapped her leg.

"But I didn't." Mary started to cry. Dorcas and Momma were driving her crazy, both of them yelling. She jumped off the table, ran upstairs to her bedroom, and slammed the door.

Later, Dorcas came in and sat on her bed. Mary told her to go away. "I'm mad at you for causing trouble. You're mean, and I don't want to be friends anymore."

"You're not getting rid of me that easily," Dorcas said, but she went away.

CHAPTER 10

Friday May 6, 1994

Ignoring Bea's warnings, Claire returned to Chestnut Street Friday evening after the workers left. Tishanna's belongings had reappeared. This morning, Vinnie, their HVAC sub, found them crammed into the far corner of the linen closet's top shelf. How long they'd been there, no one knew. Claire had told him to leave them where they were.

It was too late to do anything for Mary, except perhaps attend her birthday party, but Tishanna was still around and, beneath her rough exterior, both young and vulnerable. Claire climbed the stairs to the back bedroom.

A little after seven, Tishanna came in and went straight to the mantel. She fiddled with something, and the mirror slid aside to reveal a hidden bookshelf. She selected one of the books.

"What are you reading?" Claire said.

Tishanna dropped the book. "Who are you, sneaking up on me like that?"

"I was here when you walked in. This is my house. Remember?" She bent down and picked up the book. "Another of Mary Beaudry's diaries. That's how you know about Dorcas. Her mother was the Beaudrys' maid back when this was the Beaudrys' house."

"This is Dorcas's house." Tishanna grabbed the book back. "And this book ain't none of your business."

"Are you planning to spend the night? Your grandmother will be worried."

"No she won't." Tishanna bit her lip. "She's working nights this week."

"Why do you keep coming back?" Claire walked over to the window. Dusk was moving toward darkness, and the streetlights had come on. A movement in the yard caught her eye. "Someone's outside. Are you meeting them here?"

Tishanna peeked out the window then ducked down, pulling Claire with her. "They're looking for me. They think I got something of theirs, but I lost it. Don't let them see you. If they catch us, they'll kill us and rape us and torture us."

Claire took out her mobile phone. "Who are they? And if they're looking for you, what makes you think they're not going to come inside?"

"They don't want to mess with Dorcas. We're safe as long as we stay here."

"We'll be safer when the police come."

Bea picked up on the fourth ring. "Thank God you're still there." Claire kept her voice calmer than she felt. "I was about to hang up and call 911. I'm at the house with Tishanna."

"The house? On Chestnut?"

"Yell at me later. We need help now. There are two young men in the yard, maybe more. Tishanna says they're after her. She's terrified."

"Hold on." When Bea came back, she said there was a patrol car on the way. "Where are they, how many are there, and can you see any weapons?"

"Two were in the side yard, headed around back." Claire moved to a back window. "They're now standing in the back yard, talking. Let me check the front." She crept down the hall into the front bedroom. "There are four more out front. They're young men. Teenagers? I can't tell. One of them looks familiar. I think I saw him walking up the street a couple days ago."

The young men stood on the front walk halfway between the hedge and the gallery steps. Angry gestures said they were arguing. The one she'd recognized left the group and approached the house. He reached the steps, turned back, and said something. After a brief argument, he started up the steps. The other three followed.

"It looks like they're coming inside," Claire whispered into her phone. "I can't see any weapons, but that doesn't mean much. It's getting dark."

"Hide if you can or barricade yourselves in a room. We don't want a hostage situation. A squad car is on the way. I reported an emergency."

Claire returned to the back bedroom where Tishanna huddled beneath the window. "The police will be here soon. Our job is to stay out of sight until they get here. We're going to shut all the upstairs doors. If those guys come inside, they'll have to open everything to look for us. We'll hide in the attic." *If we can reach the rope pull that I keep forgetting to fix.* "Hurry. We don't have time to waste."

Tishanna shook her head, scared but not about to follow orders. "I'm staying right here."

"They'll find us here. It was the first place I looked."

"Dorcas will scare them away."

"Dorcas is dead." Claire grabbed Tishanna's arm. "Come on. We'll be safer in the attic."

"I ain't going nowhere, and you better stay here, too. This gang is mean."

The sound of the front door opening ended the argument. Footsteps crossed the marble foyer and started up the stairs.

Claire pulled Tishanna over to the bathroom. She tiptoed inside and felt the floor shift. The structural engineer had said the bump out was unsafe but not likely to fall any time soon. She hoped he was right.

"Dorcas will scare them away." Tishanna's tone wasn't as confident as her words, and her lower lip wobbled. "Help us, Dorcas," she murmured. "Please, help us."

"Get in the bathtub and lie down. Careful, parts of the floor are rotten."

Claire locked the doors. A locked interior door wouldn't stop anyone, but it would slow them down. The intruders were in the upstairs hall now. Where were the police?

Something slammed.

"What was that?" a male voice said. He sounded young and scared.

"Nothing, you pussy. The wind must have blown the front door shut. I've been watching this house all day. People go in and out and nothing happens. It ain't haunted."

"I saw her go in," a third voice said. "She's here. And she's not a haint."

"So what? You and Waylon already searched the house," the scared one said. "It's not here."

"She must have hid it. We'll make her tell us where."

Claire recognized the metal on metal squeak of the pull-down staircase. The attic would have been a poor hiding place.

"Hey man look out!" A loud thump. "Those fucking stairs 'bout hit me. Why'd you open them?"

"I didn't open nothing. The haint did it. She's up in the attic."

A slap. "Stop talking shit. There's no haint."

A cacophony of slamming drowned out any response. It sounded as if every door, except the ones she'd locked, was in motion. More yelling, footsteps thudded down the stairs, and the front door banged shut. Weak with relief, Claire leaned against the wall, scarcely believing what she'd just heard.

"I told you." Tishanna climbed out of the tub. "Dorcas looks out for me."

A siren whooped, and moments later blue light flickered on the wall opposite the window. The crackle of a police radio replaced the siren. Someone yelled, "Stop. Put your hands over your head."

Claire dialed Bea's number. "Tishanna and I are safe inside the house. Up the front stairs and on the right, there's a bathroom between the two bedrooms. We're in it, and we're on our way out." She didn't want to press their luck with the bump out.

"Is anyone else inside the house?"

"I don't think so. I saw six young men. Three or four came into the house, and it sounded as if they all ran back out."

"Dorcas scared them away," Tishanna said. "You tell her Dorcas scared them."

"Sit tight until someone knocks on the door and calls you by name," Bea said.

"Knock gently."

It was Bea who tapped on the door. She said the police had apprehended two young men who were running down the street as they pulled up. Two others got away.

"Four got away," Claire said. "There were six."

"The two we caught are outside in patrol cars, but I'm afraid we're going to have to let them go."

"Let them go? Bea!"

"The front door wasn't locked. They didn't damage anything. We can't charge them with anything but trespassing, and they know it. This is Jazz Fest. The jail is already full of drunk and disorderlies. A couple kids entering a house under construction don't make the cut."

"Their being here wasn't random. They're after Tishanna. I didn't really get a good look at all of them, but I'm pretty sure I can identify the one I'd seen before, maybe others. They were inside talking. I might be able to identify their voices."

"It's not worth the risk of letting them see you. And those 'pretty sure' and 'maybe' identifications wouldn't stand up to any scrutiny." Bea turned to Tishanna who was sitting in a corner, chewing on her lower lip. "Why are they after you?"

Tishanna shook her head.

"Let me guess," Bea said. "You saw them rob someone, maybe kill someone. And they saw you. Right?"

Another head shake.

"They think she has something of theirs," As she spoke, Claire realized it probably was the gun.

"I don't blame you for being scared, Tishanna," Bea said. "But you're safe now. If you cooperate with us, tell us what you know, we will protect you."

"Ain't nothing you can do to protect me, and I don't need you. I got Dorcas. She's the one scared them away. You didn't do nothing."

Bea looked at Claire, a question in her eyes.

"The ghost, remember?" Claire said. This time she wasn't laughing. "I think we have a poltergeist." Ellen Ledet had said that disturbing things happened in the house only when Mary was home. And now they happened when Tishanna was there. She started to explain, and Bea interrupted.

"I know what a poltergeist is." She nodded toward Tishanna. "And this is the adolescent female who sets it off? Do you really believe that?"

"You would, too, if you'd been here. Every door in the house was slamming, it sounded like a war zone. That's what scared the gang away." Bea raised a skeptical eyebrow, and Claire said, "The ones who were running down the street, what did they say? I bet they were scared."

"They claim they were running away from the two who got away. Of course they have no idea who was chasing them or why. But you're right about them being scared. I think they were almost glad to see us." A frown replaced the smile that had flickered for a moment. "I don't want them to see you. We'll take them downtown, keep them out of circulation while you make your exit."

"What about the others?" Claire said. "There were six."

"Before you leave, we'll make sure no one's around who shouldn't be around."

"You can't make me leave," Tishanna said.

"Claire asks you to go, you have to go," Bea said. "It's her house. I'll take you back to your grandmother's apartment."

"You take me home now, and I'll get a whipping." She pulled up her pants leg and pointed to bruises striping her calf. "This is what happened last time you brought me home. My other leg too. I ain't going back there."

Claire looked at the welts on Tishanna's legs and felt queasy. "You can spend the night at my house," she said. "Tonight, tomorrow night, long as you want, but you can't stay here." She turned to Bea. "She'll be safe with me. What if you call Grandma and tell her Tishanna is visiting a friend?"

Bea looked at the bruises. "It's your house or wherever Juvenile can find to put her. The system stinks. But are you sure?" Claire nodded and Bea walked them out the back door. She stood watch while they climbed into Claire's truck. "If they saw your truck, they'll be looking for it."

"I'll stop by my office—my car's there—and switch vehicles. That's what I'd be doing if nothing had happened."

"A squad car will follow you and make sure no one else is. That doesn't mean you can stop being careful. Watch your back, Claire. This is serious."

Claire nodded.

"Coming here tonight was a bonehead stunt."

"I know."

"We'll talk tomorrow."

CHAPTER 11

Claire parked her truck behind the office and pointed to her bright blue Miata. "Over there," she said.

A grin brightened Tishanna's face. "That's your car?" she said. "Way cool."

"I think so, too." Claire put the top up on the slim chance that they'd drive past any of the gang. "Her name is Felicia, because driving her makes me happy. Felicia Miata." Tony called Felicia her little toy car, but even he admitted that she handled nicely "for a car with no power."

"Shotgun seat." Tishanna settled herself in, still beaming.

Claire marveled at this girl's resilience. "Are you hungry? We can get some take-out."

"Fried chicken's my favorite, and I could eat a whole bucket, but I don't have any money."

"No problem." Claire detoured by a fried chicken franchise and, following Tishanna's advice, bought what looked like dinner for a family of six. She started to toss the bag behind the seat but Tishanna wanted to hold it on her lap "to make sure nothing spills," said.

The smell of fried chicken set Claire's mouth watering. She glanced over and caught Tishanna swallowing. "We'll be there in five or ten minutes, but if you're starving, help yourself. Just don't get grease on the leather upholstery."

Tishanna's hand dove into the bag. "I'll be careful."

They rode in a silence disturbed only by the rustle of the bag as Tishanna reached in for another piece of chicken. Claire pulled up to the driveway and gestured toward the Clarke's big house. "I don't live in the mansion. I rent a little house at the far end of their garden. It used to be a carriage house, back when people rode around New Orleans in horse-drawn carriages."

"You live where the horses used to live?"

"Uh-uh, where the man who drove the carriages used to live. The horses lived in a stable, where they keep the lawn tractor and garden tools now."

The gate swung open, and they followed the winding driveway through the Clarke's gardens. Tishanna's head swiveled from side to side. Claire couldn't imagine what this opulence looked like to a girl who lived in Desire.

"Do animals live in these woods?" Tishanna said. Her wide eyes had been apprehension not awe.

"Nothing bigger than the possums living in the other house. You might see them or you might not. They're more afraid of you than you are of them."

"What about snakes?"

"I've never seen any, but they're here. You leave them alone, they leave you alone." She parked beside the porch. "You'll be safe here. The Clarkes employ a security service, there's an alarm system, and that gang doesn't know you're here."

"You live by yourself?"

"Nope," Claire shook her head. "Come on in and meet my cat. His name is Dorian, and he likes to be scratched in that little space right behind his ears."

Curled up in his favorite chair, Dorian looked like a large orange and white fur ball. He opened one eye when they walked in, saw a stranger, and twitched his tail.

"Wow, he's big. Does he bite?"

"No, but be gentle or he might scratch."

"When are we going to eat?" The two pieces of chicken Tishanna had devoured on the way apparently weren't enough to ward off starvation.

"Soon as I check my messages." Claire nodded toward the red light blinking atop her answering machine. "You talk to Dorian while I see who's called."

Let it be Tony. She pressed the button and heard his voice. There had been more rule changes, good ones. She shouldn't worry. The only thing bothering him was spending his nights in a cold lonely bed. He missed his beautiful redhead. He left a number, another new one.

Tishanna giggled. "Is your boyfriend coming over?"

"Not tonight." Claire felt heat rising in her cheeks. A thirteen-year-old didn't need to hear that bit about the bed. "He's in Europe. I'm not going to call him back right now, but I should tell my business partner what happened tonight."

"I'd call my boyfriend first."

"It's seven hours later where he is. Three thirty in the morning, he's probably asleep."

"What? That's the craziest thing I ever heard of."

They spent dinner discussing the concept of time zones, which led to the revolution of the earth around the sun and the fact that summer is cold and winter hot in the southern hemisphere. All of this came as news to Tishanna, who guessed maybe they'd talked about some of this stuff in school, but she hadn't been paying attention.

"Me and Mary don't like science," she said. "But this solar system stuff is pretty cool."

Between questions about the planets and stars, Tishanna finished off the fried chicken. She fed Dorian bits of skin under the table, trying to be sneaky, but the cat purred so loudly that there was no missing his presence or what was going on. By the time they finished eating and cleaning up, it was nine o'clock.

"Time for the X Files. It's my favorite show," Tishanna said. "Where's the TV?"

Claire pointed her toward the living room, and they settled on the sofa.

Mulder and Scully saving a skeptical world from a paranormal threat provided a natural lead-in to a discussion of what had happened at the house. Tishanna worried that Bea would tell the FBI about Dorcas, and Claire assured her that was unlikely.

"In the real world, the FBI has no X-files."

"Dorcas is real."

"She was. Her mother worked for the people who lived there." Claire repeated what Ellen Ledet had said about Dorcas's fatal accident. "Mary is real, too. She still lives in New Orleans."

Tishanna sat up, her eyes wide. "You're fooling with me. You know Mary?"

"Mary lives in a home for people who can't take care of themselves."

"I wondered what happened after Dorcas got through with her."

"Tell me about Dorcas."

Tishanna shrugged. "Dorcas won't let anyone hurt me. Plus she showed me Mary's books so I could read them. Me and Mary like the same books."

"I've been reading Mary's 1961 diary," Claire said, "the one you had in your bag. If there are others, I'd like to see them."

"I don't know if Dorcas wants you to read them." Tishanna chewed on her lip. "You don't want to get her mad. She can go inside your head and make people think you're crazy."

"Go inside my head?"

"That's what she did to Mary."

"Why? What does Dorcas want?"

Tishanna looked away, an adolescent fielding adult questions about something she'd rather not discuss. Claire tried another tack. "What about those hoodlums? What do they want? It sounded as if they think you have something of theirs."

Another shrug and this time Claire hazarded a guess.

"The gun?"

"What gun you talking about?"

"The gun I took out of your stuff."

"You've got it? You? I should have guessed." Tishanna glared at her. "You better give it back. They're mean, and they don't care nothing about hurting people."

"If I don't know who they are, how can I give it to them?"

Tishanna was back to chewing on her lip, saying nothing.

"I know they hurt people," Claire said. "They mugged one of the neighbors, took his wallet and beat him so badly that he's paralyzed, maybe forever."

"That guy's gonna live? Man, I thought they'd killed him." Tishanna put her hand over her mouth. "I didn't say nothing."

Claire attempted to continue the conversation, but Tishanna retreated into an adamant silence, so she backed off. "I'll bet you're tired. We've had a big night. You can sleep out here. The sofa opens into a bed."

"I ain't sleeping where there's no curtains. Anyone outside can see in and shoot me or break-in and rob me."

Tishanna's anxiety provided a depressing insight into life in Desire. Claire had driven past the huge project, buildings like dirty dominos lying on their sides amid trash-strewn courtyards, and thought how living in such an ugly place would damage the soul. She hadn't factored in the fear.

"There's no one around," Claire said. "But if it will make you feel better, I'll hang sheets over the window while you wash up."

The next morning, when Claire went in to check, the sofa bed was empty. Tishanna lay wrapped in bedclothes on the floor behind it. Dorian curled at her side. Claire let them sleep and went into the kitchen to call Tony.

"Pronto," a man, not Tony, answered. She could hear engines in the background. Saturday on a non-race weekend, but Tony was at a track somewhere.

"Please, do you speak English?"

"How may I help you, signora?" he said in heavily accented

English.

"This is Claire Marshall. May I speak to Tony Burke?"

"Signor Burke isn't available right now."

"I'd like to leave a message."

"Certainly, and I will deliver it, but I cannot promise he will return your call. Signor Burke is a busy man who receives many messages."

"Please ask him to call Claire Marshall." She spelled her name. "Tony has my number."

"He sure does," the little voice said. "You think you're special, but this man works with Tony, and he's never heard of you."

"Who you talking to?" Tishanna stood in the doorway, a sleepy-eyed child wrapped in a blanket.

"Trying to talk to my boyfriend, but he's not there. Are you hungry? How about pancakes?"

Tishanna shoveled down a stack of syrup soaked pancakes and asked if there were more. This girl not only looked like Bea, she ate like her. After her second stack, Tishanna slowed down, and Claire mentioned the sleeping arrangements.

"I saw that you and Dorian slept behind the sofa. You're really nervous. I would be too, if that gang was after me."

"Then you better be nervous, because they want their gun back. They figure out you took it, they'll come after you."

"How do you know?"

"None of your business how I know." Tishanna's insolence had returned.

Claire started to say she'd already given the gun to the police but stopped herself. "I could give it back if I knew who they were and where to find them."

"I'm not telling you nothing. You'll tell your friend the lady detective."

"You need to help Bea," Claire said. "Tell her what you know."

"I talk to any police, I'm dead." Tishanna pushed her plate away.

"Those guys won't be satisfied with the gun. You saw them hurt someone, maybe kill him. If they know that, you're not going to be safe until they are in jail."

"I didn't see nothing."

"Last night a little bit slipped out. It's going to slip out again." Claire watched Tishanna struggle with herself and softened her tone. "Were they in my house? Is that where you got their gun? How did that happen? I want to help, but I can't if I don't know what's going on."

"I don't need your help." Tishanna folded her arms across her chest and stared at the wall. Conversation over.

"Well, if you're through eating, I need yours. How about clearing the table?" She and her mother used to do the dishes together. It had been a good time to talk, and maybe she could re-establish some of last night's rapport. The phone rang before she could try.

"I'm on my way to get Tishanna," Bea said. "I've had a frank conversation with her grandmother, and I'm comfortable bringing her home."

Claire left Tishanna rinsing dishes and carried the phone into the living room. "How can you? You saw those bruises. Her grandmother beat her with a cane."

"Her grandmother loves her. Plus, she's providing a stable home, which is a big deal. Tishanna's mother is a drug addict who was convicted of armed robbery right before Christmas. When Mom goes to prison, Tishanna goes to Grandma's. As a repeat offender, Mom won't be eligible for parole. She is out of the picture until 2002."

"Tishanna will be 21 in 2002."

"Her grandmother is doing her best, but she works twelve-hour days as a housekeeper in a downtown hotel."

"Tishanna has bruises up and down both legs."

"Grandma errs on the side of strictness, but we've had a good talk, and she's going to lighten up. I'll be there in fifteen minutes. Please have Tishanna ready."

"What's the rush?"

"I'm working today."

"It's Saturday."

"Don't rub it in."

Claire lowered her voice. "Tishanna saw that gang beat a man so badly she thought he was dead. I'm not sure when, but it was near Chestnut Street. She also says the gun belongs to them and they want it back."

"I bet they do," Bea said. "And I want Tishanna to tell me what she saw."

"She won't talk to me, but maybe you can earn her trust."

"Or maybe not." Bea sighed. "The law of the jungle governs Desire. Neither Tishanna nor her grandmother is fond of the police."

"Desire is across town." Claire hadn't thought about this before. "Why is Tishanna hanging out in the Lower Garden District?"

"Before her mother became a guest of the state, they lived in Saint Thomas Homes. When Mom went to prison, Tishanna wanted to stay at her old school. She has friends there. The school administration might make her transfer if someone told them she'd moved, but no-one's going to. Fifteen minutes max." Bea hung up.

Ten minutes later, she knocked on the door. "Where's our girl?"

"In the kitchen playing with Dorian. Come on in. Do you have time for a cup of coffee?"

"No thanks. I had two cups with Grandma." Bea slipped her shoes off and left them beside the door. "Desire was a sea of mud. My beautiful shoes will never be the same."

"I don't know how you can work in those high heels."

"There is a woman behind this detective's badge." She pointed at Claire's bare feet. "Look at your fire engine red toenails. No one sees them under those clodhopper boots you wear to work, but you know."

"You're right." Claire smiled. "Except the color is called Scarlet Woman." Bea couldn't see the silky underwear she'd started wearing since becoming involved with Tony. Although why she still did was a mystery. Tony couldn't see it either.

"Is Tishanna ready?" Bea said.

"As ready as she'll ever be. She's in the kitchen, eating again."

When Bea wished her a good morning, Tishanna frowned. Her

frown deepened as Bea described her negotiations with Grandma, but she didn't argue when told it was time to go. Claire gave her a good-bye hug, which wasn't returned, then stood on the porch and waved until Bea's car disappeared up the driveway.

Back inside, she tossed Tishanna's sheets in the washing machine and pulled out the vacuum cleaner. Dorian, who considered the vacuum his mortal enemy, exited through the cat door. "If you didn't shed so much, I wouldn't have to use this so often," she called after him.

She turned on the vacuum cleaner and attacked the rug like a woman possessed. The phone rang, and she ran to pick it up. Tony.

They chatted about things that didn't matter, the incredible meal he'd eaten at some famous restaurant and how much cooler the weather was in Fiorano than in New Orleans. Then, he asked about "the house that isn't haunted."

"Actually, I think it might be." His teasing question was the perfect opening for a sanitized version of last night's events, and she took it. She made the story as entertaining as possible, emphasizing the ghost and glossing over the danger.

"What were they after?" Tony said.

"I don't know." She lied, wishing that he hadn't asked that particular question. "But I doubt they'll be back. All the doors banging, they were frightened."

"And you weren't?"

"It had happened before, although it was windows and not quite as dramatic." She told him about the first time she encountered Tishanna. "I seem to have a poltergeist. As long as there're no young women around, things are relatively calm."

"Sounds like life on the circuit." He chuckled.

She matched his tone. "I don't want to hear any lurid stories."

"You're the star of my lurid fantasies."

"I miss you, too." There wasn't much else to say, except good-bye and stay safe.

Claire put the phone down, frustrated with Tony and with herself. After the tragedy of San Marino they'd been candid with each other, but the openness hadn't lasted. Today's conversation could have been banter between casual friends who joked and flirted but didn't share their feelings.

No, that would have been easier.

When they were together, she felt as if she'd known Tony all her life. Now they were apart, and there were times, like today, when he seemed to be a total stranger. They'd not squabbled, but their conversation had been fraught with the underlying tension of things unsaid. Tony must have been to funerals or memorial services for the two drivers, his friends who had been killed. But neither of them mentioned the accidents. He didn't say anything about the impact of the new rules, and she didn't ask.

Nor did she ask who ate that wonderful dinner with him or what they did next. If she'd asked, he would have told her, and she didn't want to know. She'd rather live with doubts that he'd been alone than know that he hadn't.

She'd never told him about finding a gun among Tishanna's belongings, or about the muggings, or about Bea's warnings. She didn't trust him to understand why she felt responsible for Tishanna or not to be angry about her recklessness, so she'd left things out and purposely misled him.

The encounter with the gang hadn't been a freak occurrence. They wanted their gun, and they'd try again. Tonight's lies compounded the ones she'd told before. A lie of omission is still a lie.

CHAPTER 12

Claire had slept badly, tossing and turning as a kaleidoscope of disturbing images whirled in her head: one young girl tumbled down a flight of stairs while another sat up in a tree crying; a racecar spun out of control and crashed into a brick wall; young hoodlums kicked a prone man; Tony raised one arm in victory, while his other hugged a beautiful woman.

She took two aspirin for the headache that was gathering strength behind her eyes and splashed cold water on her face, twisted her hair up and clipped it in place. No time for breakfast—she was meeting Jack and Vinnie at eight-thirty, and it was twenty after already. Dorian, who never missed a meal if he could help it, twined around her legs, purring loudly. She dumped a can of food into his dish, grabbed her purse, and headed out. She might not be late after all—barring a traffic jam, the house was only a five-minute drive.

The house. She and Jack usually referred to their projects by the street address, Prytania, Esplanade, Mimosa, but 368 Chestnut had become *the house*. The house she never should have bought and was never going to be able to sell, not unless she could figure out how to get rid of their ghost—no, their poltergeist. Poltergeist was German for noisy ghost, and Dorcas was nothing if not noisy.

Saturday afternoon, after talking to Tony, Claire had distracted herself with a trip to the mall. She'd bought a book about astronomy for Tishanna and one about poltergeists for herself. Five shelves of books about the paranormal, each one filled with descriptions of strange incidents, had reassured her that many apparently rational people had encountered the irrational. Maybe she wasn't losing her mind after all.

The book she selected had confirmed her recollection that an active poltergeist was associated with the presence of an adolescent girl. Some so-called authorities blamed the events upon the hysterical energy such girls possessed. That didn't seem fair, but Claire had to admit that thirteen-year-old girls dominated the history of her haunted house. Dorcas had been thirteen when she died. Did she haunt the house, or did the wild energy of other thirteen-year-olds, Mary Beaudry and now Tishanna Tenier, set the old house vibrating?

If she wanted to sell the house, she'd have to find a buyer who would never have a teenage daughter—a confirmed bachelor or an older gay couple perhaps. Claire imagined a realtor's reaction to that suggestion. Forget a realtor, her smile faded, she still hadn't told Jack about Friday night. She turned onto Chestnut Street and saw two trucks parked in front of the house. She might not be late, but she was last to arrive.

Jack and Vinnie were in the upstairs hall, deep in conversation. They looked up as she approached. "Hey, Claire," Vinnie said. "Jack says you want me to run my ducts inside the closets."

"That's the plan," she said. "Let's see how we can make it work."

This meeting went the way all meetings with Vinnie went. They quickly agreed how many vents were needed in each room, and then Vinnie, apparently unable to remember the discussion about putting ducts in closets, suggested a more expedient option. Claire vetoed it because she was not about to lower a ceiling or destroy the symmetry of a room with a cased duct. Jack mediated, gently reminding Vinnie that he was working for them. When the dust settled, Vinnie agreed to do what they asked and for a reasonable price. Claire didn't know why they couldn't go there directly. She suspected that Vinnie enjoyed the sparring sessions.

"Barring unforeseen disaster, we'll be ready for you to start next week," Jack said. "What's your schedule like?"

"If Claire can get me the contract and first payment by Wednesday,

I'll be good to go."

"Is four o'clock Wednesday afternoon good enough?" Claire asked. When Vinnie nodded, she said, "Stop by the office. Your contract and check will be waiting."

Vinnie left, and Jack said, "You look like something the cat dragged in. Eight-thirty isn't that early. Are you okay?"

"I haven't been sleeping well." She told him what had happened Friday night. "I think we have a poltergeist."

"You can call the ghost any fancy name you want, but like I've been saying all along, this house is haunted."

"It looks like you've been right." While she'd keep searching for proof that the doors and windows were rigged, Claire no longer expected to find it. Nor had she been able to find a source for the cold air that collected at the base of the front stairs.

Jack shook his head. "I don't get it," he said. "You see for yourself that the house is haunted, but we just hired Vinnie to put in HVAC, and you're about to write him a check for a couple thousand. That's throwing good money after bad. Face the facts. The house is haunted, the neighborhood isn't safe, and we'll never find a buyer."

"I think the safety issue is a short-term problem. At least I hope so."

"And the ghost?"

"I wish I knew."

"Wishing and hoping, even I know that's no way to run a business."

"You're right." Claire ate more crow. "But I think it's going to work out. The key is keeping the workers on the job, and you're doing that."

"Until something else happens to scare them off." He shrugged. "Are you headed back to the office?"

"There's something I want to check first, Go ahead. I'll be right behind you." She waited until he left, then called Bea.

"Perfect timing," Bea said. "I was about to call you. Forensics reported back. The gun you gave me is a murder weapon. We need a statement about how and where you found it. When can you come in?"

"I told you, it was with Tishanna's belongings."

"I'll need formal statements from both of you." A pause. "What would really help is a little more cooperation from Tishanna."

"Maybe if we talk to her together, she'll tell you the whole story. That is, if she can forgive you for sending her back to her grandmother."

"You're too hard on Grandma, but I agree that Tishanna needs another place to stay—at least until we have that gang off the street. I've lined up a detective to keep her for the short-term. She'd be there now, but I'm still negotiating with Grandma. The chicken bones advise against getting too close to the police. On the bright side, they also warn against fraternizing with Dorcas."

"Bea, I already have a headache."

"Grandma practices voodoo. Or she relies upon a voodoo princess for advice. I haven't been able to sort it out, and it doesn't really matter. We just have to deal with it."

"Voodoo? Really? This is 1994."

"This is New Orleans, Claire, the most haunted city in America. How many of your crew believe in ghosts?"

"Funny you should ask. I was mulling that over when you called."

"I'm amazed you've been able to keep them working."

"Knock on wood when you say that," Claire joked. "Why doesn't Tishanna come stay with me? I like her, and I'm neither the police nor a ghost."

"That's a kind offer, and if Grandma continues to balk, I may take you up on it, but for now, I think our detective is the best solution. His name is Crawford, but everyone calls him Crawdad because he's such a proud father. His office is wall-to-wall family pictures, and you'd better have time to listen when you ask how the kids are doing.

"Crawdad has twin daughters, a year older than Tishanna. Grace and Joy go to the same school and actually know her. They're not best buddies, but they're not enemies either. His wife works but part-time, when the kids are in school. You have no kids, work long hours, and don't live three short blocks from her school."

"The offer stands." If Tishanna's grandmother and Bea couldn't come to a resolution, Claire suspected Tishanna would return to the house. "Better with me than with Dorcas."

Bea sighed. "Chestnut Street was quiet over the weekend."

"Does that mean you're through using my front yard for a stakeout?"

"For the time being."

"Well, that offer stands, too."

"When can you come in? You gave me the gun, and I need a signed statement."

"This afternoon but not until late. Five-thirty at the earliest."

"Stop by when you finish. I'll be here."

"We could grab a bite afterwards," Claire said.

"I'd love to, and I could use a change of scenery, but I have another gang task force meeting tonight. We're trying to get the community on board. It's slow going."

Bea was waiting when Claire arrived at Police Headquarters. She had neither news about Tishanna nor any progress to report on tracking down the gang. "The only good news is they haven't killed anyone else. I think they're keeping a low profile after last weekend. I wish I believed it would last."

"I'm worried about Tishanna," Claire said.

"Worry about Claire Marshall."

"Have you talked to her grandmother again?"

"I will, tomorrow. Now, let's get your statement."

The process went quickly. Bea hurried off to her meeting, and Claire walked slowly back to her car, thinking about Tishanna and Dorcas and Mary Beaudry. When she got home, she stuck a Lean Cuisine in the microwave and ate it while reading the rest of Mary's 1961 diary.

Mary started eighth grade that fall. Dorcas went with her, a querulous voice that only Mary could hear. The distraction brought trouble. Mary was chastised, and then given detention for speaking out in class. She'd been talking to Dorcas. Her grades plummeted, and her parents were called in for teacher conferences. As time passed and the incidents piled up, Mary's friends wanted less and less to so with her. They whispered about her being a weirdo and a troublemaker. Even once-faithful Betsy wavered.

Claire put the diary aside. Tishanna had read this. She'd talked about Mary as if they were friends. Me and Mary this, me and Mary that. No wonder she found the diaries scary.

MARY: INTERLUDE #3

January 1962

Lissie had come home with special Christmas presents for everyone: a silk tie for Daddy, a pair of real gold earrings for Momma, a Villager blouse and a copy of *Marjorie Morningstar* for Mary. Lissie said it was her favorite book when she was in eighth grade, and she knew Mary would just love it.

At first she did. Marjorie's thoughts felt like her thoughts. They both wanted to be actresses; they both had long dark hair and dark eyes and parents who didn't understand. Although she was Baptist and Marjorie was Jewish, it didn't matter. Neither cared much about religion.

Mary thought *Marjorie Morningstar* was going to be her most favorite book of all time, but the second half wasn't as good as the first, and she hated the ending. How could Marjorie abandon her dreams and become a Shirley? Maybe Lissie thought that was fine, but Mary considered it a betrayal.

She flipped back through the pages and found Wally's denunciation. "You couldn't even *write* about her." No one would ever say anything like that about Mary Beaudry. She would never become a boring housewife like her mother. She began working on a new ending.

In Mary's revision, Marjorie didn't abandon her dreams. She became a famous movie star and met a European prince who fell head over heels in love with her—sort of like what had happened to Grace Kelly except this prince would never ask his new wife to give up acting. She was trying to decide if they would have any children when her mother called her for dinner.

"Coming." She scrambled down the stairs and took her place at the table.

Momma smiled at her. "Why don't you ask Betsy to spend the night tomorrow? It's not a school night." She asked the same question every Thursday.

"I don't want to," Mary said, like always. That usually ended the conversation, but this time, Momma wasn't letting it go. She frowned.

"Is there trouble between you and Betsy?"

Mary heard what her mother really meant. Was there trouble between her and Betsy like there was trouble between her and everyone else at school? Dorcas hadn't been around for a while, but the trouble she'd created lingered.

"Why do you keep asking me questions? I hate questions."

"Apologize to your mother," Daddy said. "And don't let me ever hear you talk to her in that tone of voice again."

"I'm sorry, Momma."

"I just want you to be happy dear." Her mother patted her hand. "I worry about you."

"May I please be excused?" Without waiting for permission, Mary pushed away from the table and hurried up to her room.

That night she drifted off to sleep thinking about *her* Marjorie Morningstar, a daring young woman who never surrendered to conformity. Mary Marjorie lived in New York City and was starring in a play that was the toast of Broadway. People stood in line for hours outside the theater, hoping to be able to buy a ticket or at least get a glimpse of the glamorous star.

The sun had set and the lights of Broadway come on when a limousine pulled up in front of the theater. Mary Marjorie stepped out, looking elegant in clothes the prince had bought for her in Paris. The people cheered, and Mary Marjorie smiled and waved. Despite her wealth and fame, she wasn't the least bit stuck-up.

What would have been a perfect dream was disrupted by the appearance of Dorcas, standing in the front of the crowd that lined the sidewalk. While the other people smiled and waved, Dorcas stared straight ahead, stone-faced, like she was mad about something.

Mary Marjorie walked past Dorcas without noticing her. She and the Prince went backstage to a dressing room filled with orchids and other exotic flowers that admirers had sent. The Prince didn't mind all the flowers. He knew that he and Mary Marjorie shared a true love and no one could ever come between.

A bell rang the five-minute warning. The Prince and Mary Marjorie embraced carefully so he didn't muss her make-up, and he went to his seat. She took her place in the wings.

Dorcas was there again. She sat in the front row with her arms folded across her chest and a sour expression on her face. When the curtain rose and Mary Marjorie walked on stage and everyone else jumped to their feet to give her a standing ovation, Dorcas kept her seat.

"Go away," Mary muttered. "You're being mean."

Her slumber became restive as she tried to get her dream back on track. Suspended between sleep and consciousness, she abandoned the theater and inserted Mary Marjorie and the Prince into pictures of New York City that she'd seen in Life Magazine.

She fell back asleep, dreaming that they were riding down Fifth Avenue in a horse-drawn carriage driven by a man wearing a tall black hat. Big fat snowflakes drifted down, but Mary Marjorie and the Prince stayed warm, wrapped in ermine blankets.

Their carriage drew up in front of a hotel that looked like a castle. A uniformed doorman with gold braid on his jacket helped them out of the carriage and ushered them inside. He bowed and waved his arm toward a long curving staircase that led up to their honeymoon suite.

The Prince smiled into Mary Marjorie's eyes. He took her hand and led her up the stairs. When they reached the top step, they turned to wave goodnight to the doorman, but he wasn't there anymore. The fancy hotel had turned into Mary's house, and Dorcas was lying in a crumpled heap at the base of the stairs.

Dorcas raised her head. "Do you remember now?" she said.

"No, no, no," Mary screamed. "Go away."

The light came on, and Momma ran into the room. She sat on the bed and rubbed Mary's back. "It's all right, baby. It's only a bad dream. You're going to be fine."

Mary gasped and gulped great sobs. The dream had been so real and so horrible.

Daddy stood in the doorway. "What's going on here?"

Before either Momma or Mary could answer, the glass of water that had been sitting on the bedside table flew through the air and smashed against the doorframe right next to Daddy.

Shock silenced Mary's sobs. She stared, aghast, at her father, dripping wet, his feet surrounded by shards of broken glass. He strode into the room and reached for her. She cowered behind her mother.

"No, no, please, Momma, don't let him get me. It wasn't me. Dorcas did it."

CHAPTER 13

Wednesday, May 12, 1994

Claire spent Wednesday afternoon at the office, paying bills and sending out invoices. Vinnie stopped by for his check, and they chatted briefly. When he left, she called Jack, who was working on the house.

"Is there any reason for me to stop by?"

"Go home. I'm leaving early too. We've both been working long hours, and it's not going to stop, not with the two new projects you just signed." For once, Jack didn't sound worried.

"I'm halfway out the door." Two minutes later, she was. She set the lock, turned around, and froze.

Across the street, a tall young man leaned against the bus stop sign. He was wearing a shiny jacket over the baggy pants and tee shirt. Heavy gold necklaces shone where the jacket hung open. The first time she'd seen him was walking up Chestnut Street the afternoon she visited Ellen Ledet. She'd seen him again—she was certain now that it had been him—on the front walk, leading the way into the house where she and Tishanna huddled. And now he was here, watching her office.

Not her office. Her. He was staring right at her.

Claire kept her eyes cast downward. *Don't react. Pretend you don't see him. Don't let on that you recognize him.*

His glare burned her skin as she walked down the steps. She reached the sidewalk and stopped, opened her pocketbook and rummaged through as if she was looking for something. Then she shook her head and hurried back into the office. Once inside, she locked the door and called Bea.

"A member of the gang, I think he's the leader, is at the bus stop across the street, watching my office."

"Are you sure?"

"I've seen him twice before. I didn't see him today until I was leaving. I acted as if I'd forgotten something and hurried back inside, but I'm going to have to go back out eventually."

"Can you see what he's doing now?"

Claire dragged the phone over to the window. "Standing there, watching my door. He's not pretending to be doing anything else."

"Are there any other people at the bus stop?"

"No. Wait, I take that back. Here come two women."

"I can send a patrol car but who knows how long it will take one to get there. Can you see your car?"

"It's parked around back. Another person is coming down the block, a middle-aged man. It looks like he's going to the bus stop, too."

"How long would it take you to walk out your door to the bus stop."

"If the light's green, a minute."

"Can you see the light from your office?"

"Yes."

"Okay, leave again. Time it with the light so that you can cross the street without waiting. When you get to the bus stop, keep your distance from the gang member and start a conversation with one of the women. Say you lost your car keys, but lucky for you, the bus stop is right here. Make up a story to keep her interest. When the bus comes, get on it. Do you know where it goes?"

"Downtown and then—"

"Get off downtown, at a stop where there are a lot of people around, and look for a police officer."

"I could get off in front of police headquarters."

"Even better."

When Claire got off the bus, Bea was waiting. "Is he on the bus?"

"He never got on. When the bus came, he nodded to me, then walked away." She rubbed her arms, remembering his cold eyes and the shiver they'd sent up her spine. "If he was trying to intimidate me, it worked."

"Let's go inside. Mike wants to see you. I told him what was going on, and he says he has questions, but I think he mostly wants to reassure himself that you're safe."

Mike's position as head of the NOPD Homicide Division warranted a good-sized office with a window that, although it looked out on a brick wall, let in plenty of light. The first time Claire had been here, she'd marveled at the lack of personal touches. There were no pictures or diplomas, no plants, and the only papers on his desk were tidy stacks in the in and out boxes. Nothing had changed, but now she saw their absence as defining the man.

He stood up when they entered. "Please have a seat. How are you Claire?"

"I'm happy to be here." She held her hands out. "They're steady now, but I was shaking back at the bus stop."

"You may have just had a narrow escape. When the patrol car arrived at your office, they found a young man, a suspected gang member, standing by your car. He said he was admiring it."

"They want their gun back," Claire said. "Tishanna warned me that they'd come after me if they thought I might have it. It seems they do."

"We're preparing a press release saying that a gun was found at the scene of a gang-related incident last Friday night. Forensic tests have identified the gun as that used to kill at least one of the victims of recent gang muggings. The press release will go out in time to make the late news tonight and the morning paper tomorrow."

"What if the gang doesn't read the newspaper or watch the news?"

"They'll still think you have it." His mouth tightened. "We're making as big a splash as possible."

Claire remembered the young man's stare, insolent and threatening, Tishanna's terror when she saw the gang in the yard, and Ellen Ledet's concern. She thought about Lindsey Tice's husband, possibly paralyzed for the rest of his life. She took a deep breath.

"I appreciate the concern you've shown for my safety and the effort involved in issuing a press release so soon after the gang showed an interest in me, but what about Tishanna?" Her indignation grew as she spoke. "You have the gun because I gave it to Bea. Two weeks ago. I'm sure she told you that I'd found it among Tishanna's belongings. If you knew what was going on, you knew they'd come after her. Why didn't you put out a press release then? Why didn't you publicize that gun as soon as you knew it was a murder weapon?"

His blue eyes turned ice cold. "I realize, Claire, that your experience with the police department has not always been positive. But do you really think we'd use a thirteen-year-old as bait?"

"No, of course not. I didn't say that."

"That's what you implied."

"That's not what I said and not what I meant, but I am worried about Tishanna. She's barely more than a child."

Mike's expression shifted into neutral. "We're all under stress."

Claire held out her hand. "Friends? Please."

Bea took her hand and held it. "The gang would be after Tishanna if there were no gun. She saw them kill a man, and they saw her. You know that, Claire. You're the one who told me. Right?"

Claire nodded.

"Unfortunately, she still refuses to cooperate with our investigation. We've asked her point blank, and she denies seeing any mugging or ever mentioning it to you."

Mike pushed a stray lock of dark hair off his forehead, a gesture Claire recognized as frustration. "We're doing all we can to protect her," he said. "Unfortunately, Tishanna is not the only person at risk. The question today is whether or not you should return home."

"Why not?"

"They tracked you to your office; they may have followed you home. We don't know. We're issuing the press release within the hour. How long it will take the information to filter down to the gang members is another unknown."

"I don't think they followed me anywhere. Every house we work on, we put up a big sign with the company name, address, and phone number. It's advertising. I doubt they have any idea where I live, and if they did, they couldn't get onto the property without setting off alarms. My landlord has become very security conscious."

"You could stay at a friend's house," Bea said.

Claire shook her head. She knew Bea meant Tony's house, and she had a key, but she wasn't going to stay there. She'd have to tell Tony and explain why. He'd ask questions, and she would have to admit that there'd been significantly more to the encounter with the gang than she'd told him.

"I don't think that's necessary," she said.

"It's your decision." Mike used his official voice. He was washing his hands of her if she wouldn't take his advice.

She set her jaw. "It is."

"I'll drive you home," Bea said.

"My car's at the office."

"Which is a good place to leave it. You lost your car keys, remember? Tomorrow, call a cab to take you to work, and don't stay at your office alone."

"Okay, but can we stop and grab a bite on the way? It's past dinner time." And she wanted to talk to Bea without Mike listening. "There's an Italian place on the way, homemade pasta and fast service."

Bea looked at Mike.

"Enjoy your meal." He lifted a file folder out of his inbox, opened it, and began reading.

Claire studied the top of his head. What was he thinking? She had believed their friendship, although tested by her relationship with Tony, could survive. Bea said he still cared for her, but he'd displayed no warmth today.

"Let's go," Bea walked to the door. "I'm starving."

Claire waited until they were in the restaurant. "I didn't mean to offend Mike. I have a knack for saying the wrong thing when I'm talking to him."

"It's not what you said. It's what you're doing, putting yourself in danger and refusing to take good advice. He's worried, not angry."

"Do you really think I'm in danger?"

"Until the gang learns you don't have their gun, you are." Bea dipped a piece of bread in the seasoned olive oil. "This isn't your typical gang. They don't wear colors, tag buildings, or do anything else to broadcast their presence, which is one reason we're having a hard time getting a handle on them. Another reason is their age. These kids are young and don't have records, at least not records we can access readily."

"The ones I've seen look to be sixteen, seventeen at the oldest. One of them looked about fourteen."

"You're out of your element here. Finishing last doesn't make nice guys."

"That's a saying worthy of Jack." Claire made a face. "But I never thought that gang was nice guys."

The arrival of the waiter, bearing their food, interrupted their conversation. When he left, Bea said, "I'm talking about Tishanna. It's possible she sicced them on you. And she knows where you live."

Claire's jaw dropped.

"Why else would they think you had their gun?" Bea said.

"They've seen me at the house, maybe even the night they came after her."

"Maybe. The good news is that she's moving in with Crawdad and his family. Grandma finally agreed. It's a temporary solution, but better than any other option. We can keep an eye on her, and the change in environment might help her straighten up." She looked down at her plate for a moment before continuing. "I know you like her, but you have to understand who she is and where she is from."

"She's a child." *We've had this discussion before.*

"She's thirteen. Kids grow up fast in Desire." Bea picked up her fork. "Let's eat. We can talk later. I'm hungry."

Claire pushed her food around her plate while Bea wolfed hers down. "Give me Crawdad's home number," she said. "I want to call Tishanna. I have a book I bought her. I'm going to see if she wants to come over again."

"Don't have her over. If you want to get together, take her somewhere, the mall, the movies, any place where there are lots of other people. Play it safe. Please."

"Tishanna isn't part of that gang. She's afraid of them."

"I know that, but when people are afraid they can behave badly. Tishanna has learned to look out for herself—she had to." Bea signaled the waiter for their check. "I don't want to rush you, but I have to get back to the office."

Claire pushed her plate aside. "I've had enough."

As they were leaving the restaurant, Claire heard a familiar voice coming from the television behind the bar. It was the smart-aleck sportswriter she'd talked to when she called the newspaper about racing results. He was discussing the rash of serious accidents on the Grand Prix circuit. The screen showed a tangled mess that had once been a racecar, probably footage from San Marino.

"Wait a minute." She put her hand on Bea's arm. "I want to see this." She really didn't, but she couldn't look away either.

"Last night, we caught up with Scuderia Ferrari's Tony Burke on his way to a party," the sportswriter said.

The picture switched to footage of Tony walking along a dock. Claire's heart jumped at the sight on him, tanned and relaxed in white slacks and an open-neck shirt. He smiled, and desire weakened her knees. A slender brunette waved to him, he stopped, and she caught up with him. She stood so close their bodies were almost touching. She was gorgeous. Whatever she said made him laugh.

The sportswriter kept talking, but Claire couldn't hear over the roar in her ears. *Let this be an old picture. Please, let this be an old picture.*

"Don't torture yourself," Bea said. "He just ran into an old friend."

"Right. Let's get out of here."

Tony had called late yesterday morning, evening his time, just hours before that footage had been shot. "I'm planning to stop by the casino tonight," he'd said. "Wish me luck."

"I wish I were there to blow on your dice." She'd flirted, willing herself not to think about the other women who would actually be at that casino.

"We could start there."

She'd heard the wink in his voice, but she hadn't heard word one about any party. And that was no chance meeting. That woman had been waiting for him.

CHAPTER 14

Tony called her at work Friday morning.

"I was just thinking about you." She kept her tone light. "How's Monte Carlo?"

"You haven't heard?"

"What happened?" She knew it was bad.

"Another accident. Wednesday, our first free practice, Wedinger hit the Nouvelle Chicane Wall. He's in a coma. The doctors still don't know if he's going to make it or not—or if he makes it, what shape he'll be in."

Claire didn't know what the Chicane Wall was or who Wedinger was. She didn't know anything about Tony's life when he wasn't with her. She pressed the phone against her cheek to keep her hand from trembling. "I didn't know."

"It was all over the news."

"I didn't see it." But as she spoke, she realized that wasn't true. Wednesday night, leaving the restaurant, she'd assumed the sportscaster was talking about San Marino. She'd turned away when the footage showed Tony with another woman. What if she'd stayed and watched the whole story? She would have known; she could have called him.

"The wall is right after the tunnel," he said. "You come out into bright sunlight and it's in front of you. You have to adjust fast. It's a tough part of a tough course."

"I thought the drivers were organizing to demand safer conditions."

"We did and we are. Pit rules changed after San Marino. There's a pit speed limit, and the crews can't be outside unless they're working on the car. The cars will be modified after this race. They'll be more stable."

"Why wait until after this race? Tomorrow you'll drive another race under the same old rules, and everybody will just have to hope nobody else is killed or maimed?"

"Qualifying tomorrow, the race is on Sunday."

"Tomorrow, Sunday, what difference does it make? How much longer, Tony?"

"One month, sweetheart. We have Barcelona on the 29th, and then Montreal June 12th. We'll be together before you know it."

"I could fly up to Montreal before the race."

"Not a good idea. I'll be busy."

"But..."

"I don't want any distractions until the race is over, and, believe me, you're a distraction. What have you been up to? How's your poltergeist?"

She could have turned his question around, demanded to know what he'd been up and who that woman was, but she didn't want to argue, not now, and all he'd done was talk to the woman. She told him about Tishanna. "She's bright and curious, but it's as if she's never been to school. I told her about time zones, and she was incredulous. I bought her a book on astronomy, but what I really want is a model that shows how the earth revolves around the sun and the moon around the earth. We're going to the mall tomorrow to look for one."

"It sounds as if this girl has awakened your mother instinct."

"Certainly my teacher instinct." Tishanna was rough around the edges, immediately sullen when she didn't get her way, defiant one minute and giggling the next. Claire didn't remember being quite that mercurial, but she'd had a stable upbringing. "I like her. I bet you'd like her too."

"I look forward to meeting her."

Before they hung up, Tony told her not to worry. Everything was fine, and they'd be together again in no time. He'd try to call after the race. If she wanted to reach him before then, call him at the Hotel de Paris. He gave her the number.

Claire sat at her desk and reran the whole conversation. This time, they really talked to each other. She'd been right not to mention the brunette. Tony sounded pleased about the safety modifications, but they wouldn't affect Sunday's race, and there'd already been one serious accident. She rested her face in her hands and took slow deep breaths. Another month.

Jack walked in. "Are you okay?"

"I'm praying," Claire said, "and I'm finished. Are you heading over to the house?"

"After lunch. First, I'm checking on Prytania."

"I'll come with you. I want to take a good look at the glazing in that front room before I pay the painters."

Like *the house*, their Prytania project was in the lower Garden District and as they drove along St. Charles, Claire recited the street names. "Clio, Erato, Thalia, Melpomene, Terpsichore, Euterpe, Polymnia." She laughed. "Streets named after Greek Muses. I love that."

"You're in an awfully good mood for someone who was praying ten minutes ago. Have your prayers been answered already?"

"I'm going to have faith." She'd concentrate on the fact that Tony would be home in a month.

"But not in the painters?"

"Glazing is tricky," she said. But when they got there, she saw that it looked even better than promised.

A light application of brown stain had turned yellow walls into warm amber and transformed an uneven plaster surface from a problem into a positive. Jack was less pleased with the installation of the wall oven. Claire left him measuring the clearances and walked over to Chestnut Street.

Ellen Ledet was sitting on her porch. She welcomed Claire and said she'd been watching all the activity at the house with great interest.

"We had a slow start, but things are coming along nicely now,"

Claire said.

"Do you have time for a glass of iced tea?"

"I was hoping you'd offer."

They settled on the porch with their drinks, and Claire asked how Bill Tice was doing.

"Lindsey says, better than expected. I'm not sure how much better, but no one is giving up hope."

"I wrote her a note but wish I could do something more substantive."

"Fixing up that house is substantive," Ellen said. "Have you given any more thought to visiting Mary?"

"That's why I wanted to talk to you." Without explaining how it happened, Claire told Ellen that she'd come across one of Mary's diaries and had read some of it. A small frown puckered Ellen's brows.

"From what I read," Claire said. "Mary was in pretty bad shape."

"And if you're going to visit her, you'd like to know what to expect."

"Yes," Claire said, "but that's not all. The diary, along with several other books I found, belonged to Mary. I don't know if she'd like them back or if it would be better not to mention them. Reading her diaries could prove traumatic. I certainly found it harrowing." And she'd only read 1961. Mary's mental state had been deteriorating; the others would be worse.

"If I were you, I'd talk to her doctor before I did anything," Ellen said. "But let me reassure you, the Mary of today is a gentle and peaceful woman. If her diaries reflect the girl she was then, you're probably expecting a frothing-at-the mouth crazy person. The truth is just the opposite."

"Why does she live in an institution?"

"It's more of a half-way house." Ellen ran a finger through the condensation covering her glass. "The best of intentions can go awry."

Claire murmured her agreement and waited to hear what had gone wrong.

"Mary had always been a bit of a tomboy," Ellen said. "The doctors told Lucinda that she had difficulty coming to terms with growing up and becoming a woman. That conflict was expressed in her relationship with her father because he was the dominant male in her life. She would make wild accusations. To the extent she remembers and understands, Mary feels quite guilty about all she put that poor man through."

This was a strange explanation from a woman who scoffed at Freud. Claire studied Ellen's expression. Did she believe what she was saying or was it an excuse? And if so, an excuse for what? Ellen might define herself as the neighborhood gossip, but she held certain cards close to her chest.

"The medicines sedated Mary," Ellen said, "but they cured nothing, and she continued to behave outrageously. Her doctor recommended a residential facility for disturbed young people. She would go there and seem to be better, but each time she came home, it was only a matter of time until she was back to screaming and throwing things around. Everything came to a head in 1963. Were you even born then?"

"I was three-years-old."

"It was a terrible year and not just the Kennedy assassination. You can't imagine how stirred up things were with the civil rights demonstrations, especially after those little girls were killed over in Birmingham."

"We studied the civil rights movement in US History."

"Studying it and experiencing it are two very different things."

Claire nodded. She'd read about the church bombing along with the Freedom Riders and the March from Selma to Montgomery. Across the South, local law enforcement officials had been complicit in attacks on civil rights workers. People in Michigan had not forgotten that a woman from Detroit was among those murdered. She and her classmates had found it hard to believe that these events occurred in the United States and not that long ago.

Living through it must have been awful, but what did this dark page of history have to do with Mary Beaudry's mental illness? Or with Dorcas? Or with her house being haunted, the real reason for her questions.

"Those protesters put little children right out front," Ellen said. "And that Bull Connor set the dogs on them. And the fire hoses. You'd see it every night on the news. It was horrible. Feelings ran high on both sides." She rubbed her forehead as if the memory caused her physical pain and changed the subject. "Mary's birthday is a week from next Thursday. I'm making her a cake. I always bring a treat. She has a sweet tooth."

"I'd like to meet her. If not on her birthday, another time soon." Next time she saw Tishanna, she'd ask for the other diaries. And she would ask again if Tishanna knew why Dorcas stayed in the house.

What did Dorcas want? If Ellen knew, she didn't want to talk about it. Maybe Mary could tell her.

CHAPTER 15

Monday, Claire woke before dawn and lay in bed brooding. The race was yesterday, and once again, Tony hadn't called. She couldn't help worrying, although common sense told her someone would have notified her if he'd been hurt.

"Really?" The nagging voice had become a full-fledged green-eyed monster. "What makes you think anyone over there even knows you exist?"

Worries about Tony's wellbeing morphed into jealousy and an argument with herself that covered familiar territory. She and Tony had spent a lot of time together in the weeks before he returned to Italy, but they rarely went anywhere people might see them. They'd order take out and eat at his place or hers. The few times they did go out, they went to restaurants where the proprietor whisked them in the side door and seated them in a dark corner. They went to one movie. They arrived after the lights had gone down, sat in the back, and hurried out when the credits started rolling. Tony wouldn't go to music clubs.

He didn't want the tabloids to know about their relationship, and he promised, neither did she. The paparazzi would drive her nuts, lurking in doorways and trying to get embarrassing photos. It would happen soon enough. She should enjoy her anonymity while it lasted and not worry about what she read in the papers. His so-called dates were set up by public relations people and designed to promote his image and that of his companion.

The nagging voice said that Tony found her invisibility to be very convenient. Her sense of fair play reminded her that she didn't go around talking about their relationship either. The part of her that had faith in Tony pointed out that he'd given her the number of the hotel where he was staying. Would he have done that if he weren't sleeping alone?

It's time for me to have a little faith. She crawled out of bed and called the hotel. Reception said Mr. Burke had checked out.

"Is he okay?" The question slipped out unbidden.

"I beg your pardon, madam?"

"Mr. Burke isn't ill or anything is he?"

"Not that I'm aware of, madam," he said, long-suffering but still polite.

"Thank you." She hung up, feeling like a fool.

Dorian stationed himself beside his dish and watched her pace back and forth in the kitchen. "If you were a dog, I could take you for a walk," she said. "The exercise would do me good."

He yawned.

"If I were a cat, I could sleep 20 hours a day and not worry about Tony."

Dorian looked at her, at his food dish, and back at her. He meowed.

"Okay, okay." She opened a can of tuna.

By now, she was too awake to go back to bed. Might as well get a head start on Monday. She pulled on her work clothes and drove to the office. Jack was already there.

"What're you doing here?" He folded the newspaper he'd been reading and put it aside. "It's not even eight."

She shrugged. "I woke up early. We have a full week ahead of us."

They reviewed work for the upcoming week, progress on the three on-going projects for paying clients plus the house on Chestnut Street. Two new projects were under contract and ready to begin. Authentic Restorations was firmly in the black and booked solid through July. Claire was grateful. Jack, who had children approaching college age and a mortgage, was even more grateful. He'd hired another carpenter and another laborer. Perhaps, Claire thought, he'll be able to stop worrying for a day or two. She was wrong.

"Did you see the article in the paper?" he said. "Some gang of kids is mugging people, beating them to death for the hell of it? They're working the area around Magazine and Jackson. That's too close to Chestnut. It sounds like the same gang that was in the papers end of last week. They shot somebody, and the cops have the gun."

"Let me see," she said.

Jack put a protective hand over the newspaper. "This is today's paper. It was in yesterday's." A pause. "You told me one of the neighbors was mugged, but this is worse than I thought, one thing after another. We'll never sell that house."

"By the time we've finished the house, the police will have caught the muggers, and everybody will be talking about something else."

"We need to secure the house."

"Soon," she promised. She didn't want to lock Tishanna out, not until she was settled in at Crawdad's—or somewhere.

"Can't be too soon." He headed for the door.

Claire watched him walk away with the office newspaper tucked under his arm. Jack did not have the gift of subtlety.

What now, Tony?

A shiny black Ferrari, one of the new 456 GTs, pulled up in front of the hotel. Tony opened the passenger side door, tossed his suitcase into the back, and climbed in. Rico, the newest member of the team, was at the wheel.

"Nice place you have here," Rico cast an envious glance at the lavish entrance. "The pit crew doesn't stay at the Hotel de Paris."

"I know," Tony said. "I used to be a mechanic." He'd been about Rico's age when he started. He'd worked his way up: mechanic, test driver, driver. Ten years. He felt like an old man.

Rico put the car in gear. "Someday, I'll be a driver." He accelerated sharply, downshifted, and took the corner without using the brakes.

The car swung too wide and skidded into the oncoming lane. A Fiat coming in the other direction had to swerve onto the sidewalk to avoid them. The driver shook his fist and shouted insults that were, in Tony's opinion, richly deserved by Rico if not by his mother. He fastened his seat belt and reminded Rico that the race was over.

Five minutes later they crossed into France. Rico glanced in the rearview. "Say good-bye to Monaco."

"I already did."

He'd gone to bed about three and wakened two hours later with a cottonmouth and a headache. He never should have had that last drink— or those last three drinks. He'd taken a glass of water onto the balcony to watch the day break. The sun rose behind him, illuminating the clouds and sea with rose and a deep gold that lightened into pink and pale yellow. It was stunning, but the beauty couldn't wash away his regrets about last night, the race, and every minute he'd spent in Monaco—face it, the whole season. For a man who didn't believe in regret, he was carrying a full load.

He'd gone back inside, intending to call Claire, but calculated the time in New Orleans and decided against it. Even if she was still up, God knows what she'd seen or read, and he was in no mood to be conciliatory. He went back to bed and slept fitfully until his wake-up call. If they weren't driving back to Italy today, he'd still be in bed.

Rico zigzagged through the crowded streets and accelerated onto the highway "Ten more minutes and you can say good-bye to France."

Tony grunted.

"You going to sit there like a black cloud for the next four hours?"

"Sorry, Rico. I'm hung over."

"It's not like you to drink too much." Rico glanced over, his expression worried.

Tony turned away and stared, unseeing, out the window. Getting drunk was something he'd left behind—until last night—and nothing he wanted to talk about. But he and Rico were on the same team, and he owed him reassurance.

"It was a mistake, one I'm not planning to repeat."

"I can't believe what you left on the table."

"Neither can I. Either drink or play baccarat. Don't do both."

"That's not what I'm talking about." Rico took his hands off the wheel and traced an hourglass shape. "La Contessa. Louisa DeLucca was yours for the taking, and you left the party without her."

Tony exhaled a long, exasperated breath. Louisa was a lovely woman, and in her arms, he'd been able to forget San Marino. But he had no intention of reviving their so-called romance, which, even at its height, had existed mostly in her mind. He'd tiptoed from her room before dawn and hadn't seen her again until she wangled an invitation to the team's post-race party. She'd shown up, trailing an army of paparazzi, and nabbed him before he could clear the door.

"I felt like gambling," he said.

"And la Contessa was a sure thing." Rico chuckled at his own wit.

Tony grimaced. The sure thing was Claire seeing at least one picture of him with Louisa.

"How much did you lose?"

"It was a bad night all around."

They merged onto the A8 and entered the tunnel. Rico shut up, forced by the change in lighting to concentrate on his driving, and Tony closed his eyes, thankful for the silence and the darkness.

Tony woke up when the car stopped. They were parked in front of an unfamiliar roadside café, and the sun was low in the sky. "Where are we?" he said.

"Piancenza, only an hour more, but I have to pee."

"Not a bad idea." He unfolded himself from the front seat. "Thanks for letting me sleep."

"The 456 rides smooth as a baby's bottom." Rico patted the fender. "You selling lots of these in New Orleans?"

"Americans buying a Ferrari want a sports car. We're selling the 512TR, and we'll start offering the F355 this summer."

"What if they want a gran turismo?"

"They ask for a sedan, and we sell them a BMW."

"BMWs." Rico spit on the ground. "They're nothing compared to a

Ferrari. Or even a Fiat."

"If I could stay in business selling nothing but Ferraris, I would." His salesmen were delighted to sell one to any customer willing to pay six figures for a car, and they'd been selling about one a month. The dealership made its money selling BMWs, which were fine cars despite Rico's Italian chauvinism.

They used the facilities then bought coffee and sandwiches, which they carried out to the terrace. Tony's mood improved. He'd be home and unpacked by seven, one in New Orleans. Claire would be in her office. He'd call her there. He leaned back, closed his eyes, and let the sun's warmth banish the remnants of his headache.

"You're having a good season," Rico said. "That should help you sell more Ferraris."

Tony rocked forward in his chair. Rico with a thought was like a terrier with a bone, but how could anyone call this season good? "Four races in," he said, "two drivers are dead and two more seriously injured—if Wedinger makes it—and we almost lost one of our pit crew."

"I know. I was there, in the pit." Rico put his right hand on his heart. "It's affected us all."

That, thought Tony, qualifies as a major understatement. You couldn't change history. He knew that. "Travel light and keep moving" had seen him through a lot. Becoming a driver might have saved his life. Without question, it had given him one worth living, but...

"I could have won," he said. "I had a chance to move up, and I backed off. If I'd taken the lead, I could have held it." Another second place. He hated coming in second.

"The 67th lap?"

"Yeah. You saw?"

"From the pit, I saw. I thanked God when you didn't go for it. Everyone on the crew thanked God." Rico crossed himself.

"There was an opening. I had time, but I hesitated. I didn't trust the car." *The car or myself? Maybe neither.* Monaco was the toughest track on the circuit, 78 tight laps on narrow city streets. Senna had owned Monaco, won the last five years straight. When you thought about

Monaco you thought about how to beat Senna. His ghost had haunted the race, his and Ratzenberger's. The first two positions had been painted with the Brazilian and Austrian flags and left empty. It was a sign of respect but also a reminder for every driver that he, too, could die. Was that why he'd hesitated?

"The cars will be better for Barcelona," Rico said. "You can make your move then."

"Speaking of moving, let's go." Tony stood up and stretched. "You want me to take a turn at the wheel?"

"You rest; I'll drive."

"*Grazie.*" He knew the favor really went in the other direction. Rico didn't get many chances to drive a car that cost more than his annual salary.

They were almost back to the highway when a movement caught the corner of Tony's eye. Something big was approaching from the right. He turned and saw the white van barrel through the stop sign. His foot hit the floor, an instinctive attempt to accelerate out of trouble. But he wasn't driving. He opened his mouth to tell Rico to speed up, get the hell out of the way, but Rico had already seen the van. He hit the brakes.

"No," Tony said. "No!" The impact knocked the words from his mouth.

CHAPTER 16

Claire walked to the corner grocery, an old-fashioned store that could have existed in the last century. Bins of fruits and vegetables along one wall, a butcher counter in the back, dairy on the other wall, and stuff that came in boxes and cans in between. If she were an artist, she'd paint this store.

A shelf by the cash register held sandwiches and pastries, all made fresh daily by Ralph and Marie, the owner and his wife. Claire hoped she'd find Marie tending the register. Ralph liked to chat, and she was not in the mood.

The head that popped up when she approached belonged to Ralph. "You're either late for breakfast or early for lunch. Which is it, baby?" His smile showed off two gold-capped teeth.

"I'm just looking for today's paper. Jack walked off with the office copy. And I'm wondering if you have one left over from yesterday."

He pulled two papers from piles behind the counter. "Yesterday's news is staler than yesterday's croissants. You can have it for nothing. Today's will cost you fifty cents, and for another dollar, I'll throw in a carrot muffin—extra raisins today. You don't want to read all this bad news without something to sweeten your morning."

Carrot muffins were their standing joke. Ralph knew she didn't like them, especially with raisins. He'd admitted that he agreed with her, but he was a businessman. If people wanted carrot muffins, he'd sell them carrot muffins.

"I'll take a dozen," she said. "And one of those almond croissants for dessert." If she didn't buy something to eat, Ralph would start inquiring about her health, which would lead to his lumbago and a ten-minute conversation. She handed him the money. "Please say hello to Marie for me."

"Marie's not feeling too good today." He shook his head. "There's a nasty cold going around. It happens every spring."

Claire conveyed her wishes for Marie's improved health and left, feeling guilty about not lingering, but the newspapers burned her hand. She hurried back to the office where she could read in private.

The article about the muggings was front page and essentially what she'd expected. She set it aside and thumbed through today's paper, looking for something she didn't want to see. It was in the Sports Section, a picture of Tony with a stunning brunette holding onto his arm. Claire recognized the woman from the yacht. The article, really just a paragraph, said Tony had celebrated his second place finish in the Monaco Grand Prix with Countess Louisa DeLucca. Their romance, which had been the talk of the circuit last season, was rekindled when they met again in Monte Carlo.

That's why he didn't call.

Anger competed with heartbreak, and one of them put a lump in her throat. Tony had said he didn't want her to come to Montreal before the race because she was a distraction. Well, if the woman hanging on his arm wasn't a distraction, no one was. An old flame, the paper said. Tears prickled her eyes, and she blinked them away. She wasn't going to cry or feel sorry for herself this time. She'd hang onto her dignity and her self-respect, and there'd be no taking Tony back on his terms or any others.

The nagging voice, always ready to make things worse, pointed out that Tony hadn't asked her to take him back. He hadn't even bothered telling her about his countess.

Claire told the voice to shut up. She didn't care what Tony said or what Tony wanted. He was no longer part of her life, and she did have a life, a life and a job and other people whose livelihoods depended upon her. She threw both papers in the trash, along with the almond croissant, and drove to the house. With Jack at Versailles Street all morning, it fell on her to check in with Vinnie. His truck was in the driveway. She pulled in behind it and walked around back. Vinnie stuck his head out an upstairs window.

"Hey, Claire," he said. "I'm glad you're here. We got a problem."

"I'll be right there." She climbed the back stairs, prepared to shoot down a suggestion for a cheaper, perhaps more efficient, but definitely ugly duct placement.

"There's somebody been in here. Me and Bill—" Vinnie gestured to his helper who'd just emerged from the linen closet. "We arrived early, about seven fifteen, and walk in the front door, which wasn't locked by the way, and we hear people running down the back stairs. By the time we get to the back door, they're jumping the neighbor's fence."

"What did they look like?"

Vinnie shrugged. "I didn't get much of a look. There were two guys, dressed in those baggy jeans the kids wear. We checked upstairs. Didn't see anything out of the way, no more garbage bags. It doesn't look like they took anything, but you might want to secure the place before the pipes go in."

"You're right." Jack had said the same thing, and he was right, too. When Vinnie finished, the plumber would begin laying copper pipe, which was a popular target for thieves. Now that Tishanna was living with the Crawfords, there was no reason not to secure the house. "I'll call the locksmith," she said. "Meanwhile, be careful. A gang has been mugging people over on Magazine and here in the neighborhood. They're young, but they're dangerous. The guys you saw could be part of it."

"Don't worry about us." Vinnie patted his toolbox. "We have Smith and Wesson on our side."

"I sincerely hope it doesn't come to that," she said. "I came over to see how things are going. With all the excitement, have you had a chance to start work?"

"Me and Bill have been looking around. You know how you said you wanted us to run one duct down through the master bedroom closet, another in the space at the end of the hall, and another in the front bedroom closet?"

"Uh huh."

"Well if you just dropped the ceiling in the foyer, you could run one big duct and go off it to serve all the front rooms. It'd save you a chunk of money."

Claire started laughing. "Thank you, Vinnie, I knew I could count on you."

"For what?" He looked mystified.

"To be who you are, but I don't want to drop the ceiling. It looks like I'm going to be living here, and I like high ceilings."

She left Vinnie with firm instructions to put the ducts in the closets, and went to find Jack, who was supervising the demo crew on their newest project, converting a cottage from duplex back to the original single family.

"Hey, Claire," Zach greeted her with a big grin. "How's your ghost?"

"Haven't seen her since you guys left. I do believe she's sulking."

Zach and Banjo laughed, and Pete half-smiled, but Charlie wasn't amused. "Ain't nothing funny," he said. "There's evil afoot in that house."

Claire became serious. "You're right, Charlie, but it's not a ghost. Remember those big sneaker prints we saw upstairs? There's a gang of kids that's really bad news, and I'm afraid that's who they belong to."

"It's past time to secure that house," Jack said.

"Let's go somewhere quiet and talk about it." She waved goodbye to the demo crew then walked with Jack over to her truck. "Vinnie surprised two intruders this morning. From his description, they could have been gang members."

"He should have shot them," Jack said. "Good riddance to bad rubbish."

Claire considered the implication that Jack knew and approved of Vinnie bringing a gun into her house. She decided to let it pass. "I don't want to secure the doors without covering the windows. Can you free up a couple carpenters this afternoon?"

"We're stretched pretty thin. Tomorrow would be better."

"Okay. I'll have the locksmith come by tomorrow. One more day won't make much difference, and it would break my heart if anyone broke that glass."

"Have you told the cops about this morning?"

"Not yet, but I will, soon as I get back to the office."

"I was going to call you," Bea said. "I heard you took Tishanna to the mall."

"Saturday. We had a good time. We talked about her staying with Detective Crawford and his family. She likes them. I think you're gaining her trust."

"She also likes you. I stopped by Sunday night, and she told me you were her second best friend. Someone named CeeCee is number one."

"Foxhole friendship," Claire said. "We bonded that night in the house. Did she tell you about the mugging?"

"She's relaxing, but she's still not talking, and we can't make her. Anything you can do to speed things along would be appreciated."

"You know, Bea, the more I think about that, the more ambivalent I am. I don't want to talk her into doing something that could get her killed."

"No one wants you to."

"Can't you match the fingerprints?"

"Yes and no. The gun you found is a murder weapon. Among the many fingerprints on it are some belonging to one of the punks we picked up the other night. When we confronted him with that information, he said that he'd found the gun in your house, picked it up, looked at it, and left it there."

Claire thought a minute. "I found the gun several days before they came into the house after us. You know that."

"He says they were in and out of the house on a regular basis before you bought it. It was their clubhouse. You saw large sneaker prints in the first time you went inside. According to my notes, that was ten days before you found the gun. He's lying, but we can't prove it."

Claire sighed. "They've been back. That's why I called. Two young men were in the house this morning at seven fifteen when my HVAC contractor arrived. He and his helper ran them off. Maybe they haven't heard that the police have their gun."

"Did anyone get a good look at them?"

"Only their backs as they ran away."

"We'll get the gun on the news again—somehow. And I'll send a team over to search the house. There could be something else they're after. Meanwhile, be careful."

"Why do I feel you know much more than you're telling me?"

"I can tell you that Tishanna holds the key. It's more than the gun. It's how and when she came into possession of it. It's the man in the alley."

"Do you know who he is?"

"*Was* is the applicable verb. Someone stomped a man to death in an alley off Magazine back in March. Witnesses saw a group of young men chase a tall skinny black girl out of that alley about twenty minutes before a busboy carrying out garbage discovered the victim. We believe the girl was Tishanna."

"She mentioned the man in the alley. I'll testify under oath."

"You'll say that, but she'll deny it. That doesn't work. We need her to tell us."

"If Tishanna testifies, she'll say Dorcas protects her. You know, the ghost. The defense lawyers will jump all over it. They'll discredit her testimony and make her look foolish."

"In this town? Not necessarily, but don't worry about it. She'll never have to step foot in a courtroom. She's a minor. If a defense attorney questions her, it will be under tightly controlled conditions."

"If she helps you, she puts herself at risk. How are you going to protect her?"

"She's already at risk, Claire, trust me. And we're doing what we can to keep her safe, short of protective custody."

"I'll talk to her again." Claire had run out of reasons not to. "And I'll come by this afternoon and give you my fingerprints so you can eliminate them from those on the gun."

"We don't have them on file?"

"No."

"Don't get testy." Bea chuckled. "Why don't you pick Tishanna up after school today. She's expecting Mrs. Crawford, but I'm sure she'd be happy to see you. Bring her down here, and we'll do your fingerprints together."

"Bea, you're relentless."

"If you want Tishanna to be safe, and if you'd like to be a bit more secure yourself, convince her to help us get that gang off the street. I'll be in my office and hoping to see you both."

CHAPTER 17

"Both of us, right?" Tishanna squirmed in her seat.

"Right. There were lots of fingerprints on that gun. If we give the police ours, they can eliminate them. Then, maybe they can use the others to prove one of the gang killed that man." *Maybe, but according to Bea, probably not.*

"I didn't see them shoot anyone. I just saw them stomp a guy. They shot at me, but they missed."

Surprised, Claire looked over at her passenger. "You never mentioned that."

"I don't like remembering."

"I wouldn't either, but you can't just pretend it never happened. If they shot at you once, they'll do it again. The fingerprints will help convict whoever shot the gun, but first, the police have to figure out who he is, and who else is in the gang. Tell Bea what you saw. When the police arrest the gang, you'll be safe."

Neither spoke for several minutes. Claire concentrated on her driving, and Tishanna frowned out the window.

"How about some music?" Claire turned on the radio. "Find a station you like."

Tishanna fiddled with the tuner and settled on a bluesy song with lyrics that would have been banned from radio back when Claire was thirteen, but take out the explicit references to sex and it was the same old story. Somebody did somebody wrong. Hers wasn't the only broken heart.

When they arrived at police headquarters, the officer on duty directed them to the lab where a technician was waiting. The tech demonstrated what he'd be doing and explained how people left fingerprints on almost everything they touched. Claire went first. After she finished, the tech pointed out the unique characteristics that would identify her prints.

Tishanna's curiosity overcame her apprehension, and she watched, fascinated, as hers were taken. "Can I have a copy?" she said. "I want to show CeeCee."

"Sure," the tech said.

"I don't think it's a good idea to draw that kind of attention to yourself," Claire said. "Why don't you wait until this is all over?"

Tishanna put her hands on her hips. "They're my fingerprints."

"You could go ahead and get a copy while we're here. I'll keep it for you until the gang has been arrested. Then you can show CeeCee."

"I want to show someone now."

"You can show Bea. And you could tell her what you saw in that alley. Are you ready to do that?"

"I guess."

"Let's go see her right now." *Before you change your mind.* Claire asked the tech to tell Detective Washington that she and Tishanna were on their way.

Three people were waiting in Bea's office: Bea, Crawdad, and a woman from social services who told Tishanna she was there to make sure everyone treated her properly. Tishanna started chewing on her lower lip, and Crawdad put a fatherly hand on her shoulder.

"You'll be fine," he said. "All you have to do is tell the truth."

Bea placed a tape recorder on her desk. "I have a mind like a sieve, and Crawdad is worse. So I'm going to tape what you say to be sure we get it right." She recorded the time and date and the people present then looked at Tishanna. "Please tell me your full name, your age, and how you came into possession of a gun."

Tishanna abandoned her lip and began gnawing on her thumbnail.

"Everybody here is your friend." Crawdad said. "Now get your hand out of your mouth and speak up so we can understand what you're saying."

Tishanna sat up straight. "I was late on account of going to CeeCee's after school. We did homework and watched MTV, and I forgot about the time. I didn't want to be late, so I cut through the alley."

"Can you tell us which alley?" Crawdad said.

Tishanna rolled her eyes, but she answered. Then she described seeing the man on the ground and the gang, which she called the Players, chasing her. "They shot at me but they missed. Claire says if they did it once, they'll do it again." She sounded aggrieved, and Claire realized, with regret, that her comment had turned the triumph of escape into a threat of future attacks.

"Not if we arrest them and put them in jail, they won't," Bea said. "What happened next?"

Crawdad interrupted with an occasional request for clarification as Tishanna told of running away and hiding in an empty house, but he listened without comment when Dorcas came on the scene. When Tishanna finished, Bea asked her exactly where she'd been when someone shot at her.

"I told you. In the alley."

"Did you hear the bullets hit the building?"

"I felt them zoom right past my head. About scared me to death."

"You're a brave young lady. I'm proud of you." Crawdad hugged Tishanna.

"Can me and Claire go now? I'm hungry."

"How about a bucket of fried chicken?" Claire said.

"Only one bucket, Claire?" Bea smiled. "What are you going to eat?"

"She gets one skinny leg." Tishanna skipped out the door, happy now her ordeal was over.

"Can we stop by Dorcas's house for a minute? Tishanna said. "I want to get another of Mary's books. Me and Mary like the same kind of books."

"Okay. We'll go there first." Claire said. It was daylight; there'd be people around.

She turned the corner onto Chestnut Street and parked at the curb. The house looked empty. The crew and subs had been on the job earlier this afternoon, but they must have left early. No one worked late or alone at this house.

"I'll go in with you," Claire said. "Let's make it quick."

Tishanna ran inside and up the stairs, apparently oblivious to the cold spot at their base. Claire followed more slowly. By the time she reached the back bedroom, Tishanna was sorting through the books.

"I want one of the Nancy Drews. Nancy's a detective, like Bea."

"Take anything you might want, because you won't be able to come back here for a while." Tishanna cut her a sharp look and Claire said, "Living with the Crawfords has to be way better than staying here."

"It's cool."

"I was talking to the neighbor again," Claire said. "She wants me to go see Mary with her. I said okay, but first, I want to read the other diaries."

"I don't know if Dorcas wants you to read them."

"Why not?"

"She did bad stuff to Mary."

"Well then, don't tell her."

"You can't keep secrets from Dorcas." Tishanna scoffed at this display of ignorance. "She sees everything that goes on."

Claire felt a tingling on the back of her neck. "She's watching us now?"

"Uh huh, but you don't have to be scared. She thinks you're okay."

"That's good to know, but why is she still here? What does she want?"

It was a question she'd asked before without getting an answer. This

139

time, Tishanna was looking thoughtful, perhaps ready to confide something, but the moment passed, and she just shrugged.

"Well," Claire said. "She's not slamming any doors. It must be okay." She picked up two diaries, 1962 and 1963. "Is this it?"

"That's all I've seen. You can take one and bring it back when you've finished reading. We'll see if Dorcas wants you to read the last one."

"Really?" Claire was amused by Tishanna the librarian, but she went along.

"They get worse." Tishanna showed her a toggle beneath the mantle that opened and closed the mirror. "Don't forget. Otherwise you won't be able to put it back."

"I won't. Now let's go get us some fried chicken."

At dinner, Tishanna once again snuck pieces of skin to Dorian, who'd attached himself to her as soon as she walked in.

"Your poltergeist likes me, and my cat likes you," Claire said.

A discussion of the fine points defining a poltergeist and a haint lead to the topic of Mary's diaries.

"That stuff had me waking up scared in the middle of the night," Tishanna said. "You're gonna see."

"Mrs. Ledet down the street told me Mary had a nervous breakdown."

"What's that mean?"

"Like going a little crazy."

"Mary wasn't crazy. Dorcas got inside her head and tried to make her tell the truth. That's how come I decided to tell Bea what I saw. I don't want that man in the alley doing me like Dorcas did Mary."

"Dorcas is real, and Mary wasn't crazy? Is that what the other diaries say?"

"Dorcas is real and you know it. You saw her scare those Players when they came after us."

"I heard her, that's for sure." Claire stood up and started clearing the table. "Why don't you feed Dorian while I put our dishes in the dishwasher."

"What about dessert? We forgot to get dessert."

"Don't panic. There are ice cream sandwiches in the freezer."

They carried the ice cream out onto the porch and sat in the rockers. "Like two old ladies," Tishanna said with a giggle.

The sun had gone down, and Claire pointed to Venus rising on the horizon. "See how the light is steady. That's how you recognize planets. Venus is the planet closest to the earth."

"I know. I been reading that book you bought me. And that's the little dipper over there with the North Star at the end of the handle. If I'm ever lost, all I have to do is find the North Star."

"When you finish that book, I'll buy you another one. But right now, it's time for you to go back to Crawdad's. You have school tomorrow, and I have work."

"Am I coming over again?"

"What about Saturday? We can go shopping for another book on astronomy, get dinner and catch a movie."

"Saturday night and you're not going out with your boyfriend? Is he still in Italy?"

"He's not my boyfriend anymore."

"You'll get another one. I bet you've got lots of boyfriends."

"Bea's the one with lots of boyfriends."

"I'm going to have lots of boyfriends. I don't have my figure yet, but when I'm grown up, I'm going to be hot." Tishanna pranced down the steps, switching her skinny hips, a big grin on her face.

"You'll have to ask Bea for tips," Claire said. "Maybe we both should."

When they got to Crawdad's house, Claire walked Tishanna to the door. "I want to make sure you get safely inside."

"I'm safe. Crawdaddy gave me a phone. If anything scares me, I can call for help." She pulled a cell phone out of her pocket and displayed it proudly. "I'm not supposed to tell anyone I have it, but I can tell you."

Before they reached the door, Crawdad opened it. Tishanna gave Claire a hug and scampered inside.

"Don't look so worried," Crawdad said. "We'll take good care of her."

"You'd better."

Driving home, Claire marveled at how Tishanna's hug had touched her heart. Tony could be right about this gangly adolescent arousing maternal instincts that she didn't even know she had. Tony. It was time to stop filtering her every thought through him.

Claire turned on the television when she got home. Despite her resolution to forget Tony, she wanted to watch the news. The story about his rekindled flame was in the paper; would it be on TV? Was he engaged? Married? Her imagination knew no limits. The news had already started, and the screen showed a car wreck.

"One of New Orleans' favorite sons has been seriously injured." The newscaster looked straight into her eyes. "Formula One driver Tony Burke was a passenger in a car broadsided by an out-of-control delivery van."

"No."

"The accident occurred this afternoon, European time, near Piancenza, a city in northern Italy. Tony was taken to a local hospital where he is reported to be in critical but stable condition. I know all of New Orleans joins me in wishing him a speedy recovery."

Critical but stable, what did that mean? Please, not a head injury. Afternoon in Europe would have been morning here, hours ago. They should know more about his condition by now. What was the name of the hospital? Would the doctors talk to her? What about that Louisa woman? Had she been driving? Was she with him?

Claire rocked back and forth on the sofa. *Calm down and think. Stop crying. Think!*

Her phone rang. She ignored it until Bea's voice on the answering machine ordered her to pick up.

"Have you seen the news?" Bea didn't bother with hello.

"Yes."

"I'll be there in fifteen minutes. Open the driveway gate."

CHAPTER 18

"I haven't tried to call the hospital. I haven't done anything," Claire said. "There was an article in today's paper. Tony is back with an old girlfriend, some countess. I recognized her from that clip on the news the other night. She's probably at the hospital with him. She might have been with him in the car, even driving it. The news said he was a passenger."

"The news I saw said the driver was a mechanic, employed by Ferrari, who suffered minor injuries. No one else was in the car." Bea walked into the kitchen. "Where's your coffee? It's going to be a long night."

"You don't have to do this."

"I want to." Bea glanced at her watch. "Ten-thirty in New Orleans, five-thirty tomorrow morning in Italy. American doctors start making their rounds about six; we'll see how early the Italians start. I wrote down the name of the hospital."

"Did you see the article about Tony in today's paper?"

"I did, and I recognized her too. Let's start with the picture. As you know, I'm not a Tony Burke fan. But I am a detective whose job involves reading expressions and body language, and I promise you, Tony was not happy to have that woman clinging to him."

"You can tell from one newspaper picture?" Claire wanted to believe.

"It wasn't subtle. To begin with, he wasn't smiling, and Tony always smiles for the camera. He looked annoyed, he was leaning away from her, and his other arm was coming across his body. The next picture, if there were one, would show Tony removing her hand."

"You really think so?"

"I'd bet a month's salary."

"The article said—"

"Do you believe everything you read in the paper?"

"Of course not." She hadn't, long before Tony asked her not to. "I remember what they said about me, back when I was a murder suspect."

"Exactly. Now, would you rather make the coffee or track down the hospital's phone number?"

"You make the coffee. It's in there." Claire pointed to the cupboard. "What's the name of the hospital? I was too stunned to catch it." She paused. "And thank you, Bea, thank you very much."

The international operator spoke English, which made getting the hospital's main number relatively simple. The woman who answered at the hospital did not, but she understood "Tony Burke" and responded with a tidal wave of Italian that sounded both negative and exasperated.

"*Por favor. Soy una amiga.*" Claire's rudimentary Spanish got the same response, followed by a dial tone. She dialed the number again, and the same woman answered. She hung up, temporarily defeated.

"I can't believe it." She pressed her hands to her head. "So close, but I can't get through. Do you know anyone who speaks Italian?"

"Jimmy Vignati." Bea said. "I used to walk a beat with him. Let's wake him up."

Fifteen minutes later, Bea called the hospital back. In brand new Italian, she identified herself as a detective with the New Orleans Police Department and said that she was calling for information about Tony Burke. "*Si, la polizia. Parli inglese?*" She gave Claire a thumbs up sign. "I'm on hold while they get someone who speaks English."

Unable to stand the waiting, Claire went out onto the porch. *Please be okay, Tony, please be okay.*

She knew he wasn't. Critical but stable condition was far from okay, but it did mean they thought he would survive. *Just don't die.* Shivering cold, she stared at the star-spangled night sky and prayed that Tony would be okay. If he loved her or twenty other women, please just let him be okay. Bea knocked on the window and beckoned her inside.

"They're putting me through to his doctor." She listened for a moment then said, "No, sir, this is not official business. I'm calling on behalf of a friend who is very close to Tony. She's too distraught to speak on the phone."

Too distraught to learn any Italian was the real problem. Claire's brain wouldn't stop spinning from one *what if* to another. Jimmy had given up on her and taught Bea what to say. But now they were speaking English. She held out her hand and Bea shook her head.

Whoever was on the other end spoke loudly enough for Claire to catch the angry tone.

"This is not a trick," Bea said. "I have not asked for medical information. I'm calling on behalf of Claire Marshall. Please tell Tony that Claire is worried about him." She glanced at Claire. "She sends her love."

"Is he conscious?" Claire whispered.

"Don't know," Bea mouthed. "That's right, Claire," she said into the phone.

Claire strained to hear what the person on the other end was saying, but he'd stopped yelling.

Bea looked puzzled. "Red. Why?" She listened again then held out the phone. "He wants to talk to you."

"Signora Claire, I am Dr. Chinetti, one of Signor Burke's physicians."

"How is Tony? Is he conscious? What were his injuries? Are they..." She trailed off, unable to make her mouth form the words, life threatening. "How serious is it?"

"He suffered several traumatic fractures, his right radius, four ribs on his right side, and most critically a fracture of his right femur. We've stabilized the leg and will operate on it this morning. Any operation is a serious matter, infection is a great concern with this type of fracture, but our patient is strong. We can hope for a full recovery."

"No head injuries?"

"I am happy to say, no."

"Is there significant displacement of his femur? You mentioned infection, is the skin broken?"

"Yes and yes, as may be expected with high impact trauma. The other fractures are no cause for concern. We'll put the arm in a sling. It's what you Americans call a greenstick fracture and requires no further medical intervention. The ribs require only time." He paused. "Strictly speaking, I shouldn't be giving you this information. You could be another intrusive reporter, one who knows more about Signor Burke's personal life than the others, but I suspect that you're the woman we should have been looking for. We thought you were a car."

"I beg your pardon?"

"When he first arrived, Signor Burke kept asking for Claire, his bella Testarossa. The medical team assumed he was talking about his car." She could hear the shrug in his voice. "Injured people, especially when they are in great pain, say strange things. He drives for Ferrari. A Testarossa is an iconic Ferrari racecar."

"I know."

"And you must know that, translated literally, testarossa means redhead, a female of course."

"Yes."

"He never had an opportunity to correct our misunderstanding. Once we determined there were no head injuries, we began administering painkillers. Since then, he has been drifting in and out of consciousness. When he is wakeful, he asks for Claire, his bella Testarossa. I'm glad that you called."

"So am I." Her face wet with tears, Claire choked out a thank you. She handed the phone to Bea and walked back outside.

Several minutes later, Bea joined her on the porch. "I gave the doctor your number. Someone will call when Tony is out of surgery, which should be about 4:00 AM our time. Do you want to catch a nap while you're waiting?"

"I can't sleep," Claire said. "Too much coffee and too many emotions." She shook her head, unable to continue.

"From what I overheard, the news is good?" Bea said.

"Tony has half a dozen broken bones, all on his right side, but no other injuries they are aware of. The only one the doctor is concerned about is his femur, which is broken in more than one place and protruding through the skin. But there are no head injuries, and they expect a full recovery.

"I'm so ashamed of myself, Bea. If it weren't for you, I wouldn't have called the hospital. Tony is hurt and asking for me, while I'm damning him because of a stupid picture in the newspaper. I'm so quick to believe the worst of him. What's wrong with me?"

"Suspecting that Tony Burke fools around is nothing to feel guilty about," Bea said. "He has a history. Now come back inside where it's warm and tell me why red is the magic hair color."

Claire repeated what Dr. Chinetti had told her.

"It sounds as if Tony has realized how lucky he is," Bea said. "Did you know about this name game?"

"Not at first. We met when he was looking for a contractor to restore his house. He seemed amused that his would-be contractor was, in his words, a beautiful redhead. I thought he was flirting. He was, but it was also his private joke."

"When did he let you in on it?"

"When he had little choice." Despite her distress, the memory brought a smile. "Tony was talking about a racecar—she this and she that. I teased him about it, and he insisted that all racecars were female and the bella Testarossa, the one he'd been describing, the most womanly of all. I asked what Testarossa meant."

Tony had also said that driving a Ferrari was like making love, and driving a Testarossa second only to loving his own beautiful redhead, but she'd keep that tidbit to herself. She glanced at her watch.

"They'll start operating any time now. You don't have to stay Bea. It's late. I'll be fine."

"You don't look fine, you don't sound fine, and you're pacing like a caged animal."

"I'll be okay once they call and tell me the operation was a success." She'd been married to a doctor and had picked up enough medical knowledge to be frightened for Tony.

"That's when I'll leave," Bea said.

"It could take hours, easily, and it's already tomorrow morning. What time do you have to be at work? I remember you saying that you were swamped."

Bea hesitated. "Are you sure you're okay?"

"Yes, and thank you." Claire hugged her. "You're a true friend."

Bea left, albeit reluctantly.

Claire picked up Mary Beaudry's 1962 diary. Reading would help pass the time and remind her that hers weren't the only troubles in the world.

MARY: INTERLUDE #4

May 1962

"Fourteen years old," Momma said. "My little girl is growing up."

"I ain't telling you no happy birthday." Dorcas had moved into Mary's head. She looked out through Mary's eyes and listened through Mary's ears. Sometimes she talked through Mary's mouth, and that was always trouble, because Dorcas said mean things about people.

"Annie made all your favorite foods for dinner," Momma said.

"Thank you, Momma." Mary looked at the floor. She dreaded dinner. Dorcas was angry today; there'd be trouble.

Sure enough, as soon as Daddy sat down, Dorcas glared at him. He thought Mary was giving him the evil eye and asked why she was in such a bad mood on her birthday.

"I'm not in a bad mood. Honest." She closed her eyes, hoping that would be the end of it but knowing it wouldn't.

Dorcas had made a hole in Mary's forehead so she could see and hear even if Mary shut her eyes and covered her ears. The hole was disgusting, all infected looking and oozing pus. No one else had noticed it or seen the little Dorcas head sticking out—not yet. Mary had only seen it when she was asleep. When she was awake, she stayed away from mirrors. The tiniest glimpse of her reflection tied her stomach in knots.

Momma passed the platter, and Mary took the littlest crab cake and one fried shrimp. She kept her head down, her hair falling over her face to hide Dorcas, and took a tiny bite of the shrimp. She chewed and chewed, but she couldn't bring herself to swallow—not with Dorcas's head sticking out of hers. She held the napkin to her face and spit into it.

"May I please be excused?"

"You need to eat more," Momma said. "You're getting too skinny."

"I'm not hungry." Mary kept her eyes on her plate.

"Are you sick?"

She shook her head, and her bangs swung back and forth. She could feel Dorcas up there.

"Try a bite of that crab cake. You know how you love Annie's crab cakes."

Momma was watching this time, so she couldn't spit her food in her napkin. When she tried to swallow, the crab cake stuck in her throat. Gagging, she jumped up from the table and ran to the bathroom.

"Let me in, Mary." Momma rattled the doorknob. "I'm taking you to see the doctor first thing tomorrow morning."

"I have a stomach bug. That's all."

Mary rested her forehead against the cool porcelain. Her stomach was empty, she couldn't throw up anymore, but she stayed there, kneeling at the toilet until she was sure Momma had gone back to the dining room. Then she crept upstairs and lay on her bed, staring at the ceiling.

I wish I were dead.

Dorcas jumped out of her head. She stood at the foot of the bed, grown to full size and spitting mad. "You wish you were dead. I am dead. I didn't get no fourteenth birthday." She leaned forward her hands on her hips. "I died when I was thirteen."

"I know. Lissie told me. She said you had an accident."

"It wasn't an accident. Lissie is a liar."

"You're the liar."

"No. You're the liar. Liar, liar pants on fire." Dorcas jumped up and down on the bed. "Liar, liar, pants on fire."

"You're not real," Mary said. "Dead people don't live inside alive people's heads."

"If I weren't real, could I do this?" Dorcas pointed at the bookshelf, and one by one, the books fell onto the floor.

"Stop, please stop."

"I'm gonna tear this place apart." The lamp flew off the bedside table and crashed into the wall.

Mary scrambled over and started picking up the big pieces. She was putting them up against each other to see if maybe she could glue them back together when Momma opened the door.

"Mary Amelia Beaudry, what on earth are you doing?"

"It wasn't me. Dorcas did it."

Her mother looked at the books all over the floor and at Mary holding pieces of broken glass that used to be a lamp. She put her hands over her eyes.

"I'm sorry, Momma." Mary realized that Momma was crying, too. She walked over and hugged her, sliding her hands up and down her mother's back as she tried to give and receive comfort. "I told her to stop, but she wouldn't listen." Mary's words tumbled out between gasping sobs. "Dorcas is mad cause she died and never had a fourteenth birthday. I told her it was an accident, but she says that's not true."

Her mother pushed her away. "Last I heard Dorcas was living with her grandmother in Mississippi. The only person who could've made this mess is you. Now you get busy cleaning it up."

Mary trembled so hard that her teeth chattered. She stumbled to her bed and lay down, her whole body shaking. No matter how tight she held the pillow against her ears it couldn't mute the sound of Momma's voice, hard and angry, telling lies.

CHAPTER 19

Tuesday May 17, 1994

Dr. Chinetti called a little after five New Orleans time. "Tony is in surgical recovery. I hope you don't mind if I refer to Signor Burke as Tony. No disrespect is intended. He is well-known, and we all feel as if he is our friend."

"Not at all, and please call me Claire."

"The operation went as well as it could have, given that Tony had fractured that femur before. Did you know this?"

"He fell off a horse when he was a child."

"Due to the extent of the recent trauma, we didn't see the old fracture until we were operating." He paused. "We changed our strategy midstream." Another pause. "We have inserted a metal plate. Screwed to the bone, it will serve as an internal splint."

"Do you still expect a full recovery?"

"It is still reasonable to hope for one; however, the healing will take longer. Of course, there are always questions and uncertainties." He paused as if searching for the right words. "When Tony is ready, I will discuss the operation and his prognosis with him. When he is out of the anesthesia, I will tell him that we have spoken and you're awaiting his call."

Claire's heart ached for Tony who would talk to his doctor alone. He had an agent, publicist, lawyers, the racing team, and fans galore, including beautiful contessas. But at the end of the day he went home alone, and now he faced serious injury alone.

"I'd like to talk to him," she said. "When will he be ready for a phone call?"

"Maybe later today; more likely Wednesday. The time difference causes difficulties."

"It doesn't have to. Please tell him to call me any time. Middle of my night, I don't care. All day, everywhere I go, I'll have my phone with me and turned on. I just want to talk to him."

Worry formed a cold lump in Claire's stomach. Both her father and her husband had been doctors. She was familiar with the combination of tired and triumphant a medical team felt after a complicated procedure went well. Dr. Chinetti sounded tired, but the note of triumph was absent.

Claire's alarm went off at nine, and she called Jack. "I won't be in this morning, maybe not all day. I was up half the night."

"I heard on the news about Tony. How's he doing?"

"The doctors expect a full recovery."

"I'm glad to hear it. When you talk to him, give him my best."

"Will do. And thank you."

"For what?"

"For being a nice man." Jack's natural sympathy had overcome his disapproval of Tony, and she appreciated it.

She went back to bed and slept until afternoon. Then she puttered around the house, waiting for Tony's call. Her phone finally rang a little before five. *Almost midnight in Italy. Will Tony be awake?* She raced to answer it, but the call was only Bea, checking in.

Claire went to bed wondering why Tony hadn't called. Was he still too groggy? Had something gone wrong?

Wednesday morning, he still hadn't called, so she called the hospital. The switchboard connected her to a public relations person who told her that Tony's condition had been upgraded from critical to serious and that he remained in the intensive care unit. Further information would become available when the doctors scheduled a press conference, probably tomorrow.

"May I speak to him?"

"I'm sorry, madam. That isn't possible."

"What about Dr. Chinetti? He and I spoke yesterday after Tony got out of surgery."

"Dr. Chinetti has finished his rounds and left the hospital. You are not the only caller, madam. I have to answer the other lines."

"Please tell them both that Claire called. And ask them to call me." She figured the odds of having her message delivered at something less than fifty percent, but for now, it was the best she could do. And, she reassured herself, Dr. Chinetti had at least implied that he would call if anything changed.

She stopped by the office long enough to pick up the active files and set up a temporary workspace on her kitchen table. Neither Tony nor his doctor called back.

Thursday morning, mobile phone fully charged and in her pocket, Claire dropped the files at the office and drove over to the house. She was surprised to see no boards over the downstairs windows. Emile, one of their carpenters, and two helpers were reframing the kitchen. She asked them to put that on hold.

"I'd like you to cover the downstairs windows with half-inch plywood top to bottom, no gaps," she said. "If you could do it right away, I'd appreciate it."

"Jack and I already talked. You cover up those windows, it's going to be dark in there, and we don't have a lot of lights. We'll do it after the house is rewired."

"Not good enough." Claire shook her head. "That old glass is irreplaceable. I want the first floor windows covered before we run new wires."

Emile, who was usually as friendly and eager to please as a large puppy dog, set his jaw.

"What?" Claire said. Then she saw the problem or, more accurately, realized what she had never seen. No worker was using the front door, walking up the front stairs, or spending any more time than was absolutely necessary in the front of the house. They'd all heard the ghost stories and felt the cold spot at the base of the front stairs. If the front rooms were dark, they didn't want to be in the house. She'd suspected there'd be problems when work moved inside, and here was the first.

"Okay," she said. "I'd like to secure the whole first floor, but if that's not going to work, just board up the front windows."

Emile shook his head.

"Hear me out. All I'm asking you to do is stand on the front gallery and nail boards across the tall windows. Forget the side windows, it would take a ladder to reach them, and the shrubbery is in the way. Forget the back windows, they're small and if one gets broken, that's life."

"We can get on the front windows right now, but someone's going to have to go pick up the wood, and it will put us behind on the kitchen."

"No problem. Long as those windows are safe, I'm happy."

Emile's nod signaled agreement, but instead of going back to work, he remained standing in the doorway.

"Is there something else?" Claire said.

"Me and the guys want to say we're sorry about Tony. We hope he's going to be okay."

"Thank you." *How do you know? Did Jack tell you? You and how many others?*

Emile must have seen the questions written on her face. "We worked on his house, remember? At first he wasn't around much, then he was there 'bout every day. We watched him watching you. I was thinking about having a little talk with him, doing the big brother bit, but you started looking back, and I decided to mind my own business."

"Thanks for the good wishes." Claire found a smile. "I'll pass them on."

"Some things you can't keep secret."

"I guess not."

"The glass in the kitchen door is old. We can board it up. Won't make any difference to the light, because we leave the door open when we're working. The other back windows—if you want, we can throw up a couple boards when we leave and take them off in the morning."

"That would be great. Thank you."

Claire went home and called the hospital. It was dinnertime in Italy; Tony should be awake. The nurse who answered the phone spoke English, but it didn't matter.

"Mr. Burke isn't accepting phone calls."

"Please tell him that Claire wants to talk to him." In truth, she was frantic with worry and desperate to talk to him. Why hadn't he called? "Ask him if he wants me to come see him."

"Mr. Burke isn't seeing any visitors."

"Please, just give him the message. I want very much to talk to him. He can call me any time."

Two hours later, Tony returned her call. She was on the way to the Prytania project and pulled over to talk to him.

"It's so good to hear your voice. How are you doing? Stupid question." Claire's words tripped over one another. "I know this is hard—more than hard. I wish I were there with you. I've been checking flights."

"No. I don't want you to see me like this."

"Like what? In a hospital bed?"

"Claire, I'm as weak and helpless as a baby."

"How could you be otherwise? You've been in a bad accident, you've had major surgery, you've been through a lot, but Dr. Chinetti said he expected a full recovery."

"I intend to recover, and when I'm further down that road, I'll fly back to New Orleans. If I'm lucky, you'll meet me at the airport. Until then, I'm handling this myself."

"The nurse said you weren't accepting phone calls or seeing visitors." *It's not just me, is it?*

"That's right," he said.

"Why, Tony?"

"I'll call you again tomorrow or the day after. Don't worry. Everything's going to be okay." A click and he was gone.

He doesn't trust me.

The insight floored Claire. She didn't trust him, but it had never occurred to her that he didn't trust her either. Not only did distrust run both ways, his ran deeper. She didn't trust him to resist the temptation of other women. He didn't believe her feelings for him would survive seeing him at less than his best. *I'm not that shallow,* she wanted to shout so loud he could hear her in Italy.

"Tony knows you're not shallow, but he doesn't know what's underneath." The nagging voice was back. "Why should he trust you when you hide yourself from him?"

"Shut up," Claire said, "just shut up."

She drove the truck back to the office and headed out in her Miata. As soon as she left the city and its traffic behind, she pulled over and put Felicia's top down. She drove fast, not caring when her wind-tangled hair slapped her cheeks. She was past Houma when she heard the siren.

The officer ambled up to her car, ticket book in hand. "I've been following you for the last five miles, young lady. Do you know how fast you were going?"

"No sir." Fast enough to blow away tears. She didn't want to guess how many miles per hour.

"I clocked you at eighty-seven miles per hour."

"I'm sorry. I was upset about something and not paying attention to my speed."

"Not paying attention for sure. Driving like that, you could get hurt." He frowned. "Look at what happened to Tony Burke, and he's a professional racecar driver."

"Tony wasn't driving. It wasn't his fault."

"No, darlin', it wasn't. But you were driving this little car seventeen miles an hour over the speed limit, and if you'd hit something, it would have been your fault."

"Yes, sir."

He let her off with a warning.

CHAPTER 20

Tishanna checked her pockets. She checked them again, slowly, trying not to panic. Crawdaddy had given her the phone and told her not to leave the house without it. His number was programmed in, and all she had to do was hit star one. Monday, she'd checked her pocket every five minutes, worried about losing the phone or, if anyone saw what she had, having it stolen. She hadn't even shown it to CeeCee who wasn't always good at keeping secrets.

Monday night, she told Crawdaddy that taking a phone to school made her too nervous, but he wouldn't take it back. He said he'd be way too nervous if she didn't have a way to contact him and told her to be sure to plug it in overnight so the battery didn't go dead.

The rest of the week, she'd carried it around, gradually getting used to weight in her pocket, checking less often and, in between almost forgetting it was there. This morning, she had forgotten, and now it was gone. She told CeeCee to go to class without her and hurried back to the cafeteria.

There was nothing but dirty napkins and spilled food under the table where she'd eaten. She tried to remember if she'd felt the phone in her pocket during lunch. She didn't think so. They'd had a fire drill that morning, maybe then... She returned to the classroom and retraced her steps to the outside safety zone, but it wasn't there. By now, she was too frantic to remember anything. It was all she could do not to start crying.

I didn't want it, Crawdaddy. Why wouldn't you take it back?

He was the closest thing to a father she'd ever had, and she liked him. He acted like she was doing him a favor by staying with his family and told her to call him Crawdaddy, like his own kids did. But he'd be mad at her if she'd lost his phone, and if anyone saw a cell phone lying on the ground, they'd take it for sure. Cell phones cost lots of money, and everyone wanted one.

The bell rang, signaling the end of lunch. The kids who'd been hanging around outside drifted toward the doors. Tishanna pushed her way through them, head down, searching the sidewalk and the bushes for the phone, praying that she'd find it.

"Hey Tishanna." It was Grace Crawford. "You're going in the wrong direction. Hey, wait up."

Cornered, Tishanna let Grace catch up with her. "I'm not feeling too good," she said. "I'm going to walk home."

"Won't be anyone home now. You ought to talk to the school nurse. She'll let you lie down in her office and call Momma to come pick you up."

Tishanna dug her toe into the dirt. She didn't want to tell more lies, but she couldn't admit the truth.

Grace looked at her funny. "Were you going to cut class?"

"No."

"Hey, look who's here." One of the Players, the tall one who'd kicked her, was walking toward them. "It's Lady Pee-In-Her-Pants. I knew I'd seen you around."

Tishanna jerked her head up. Two more Players stood across the street, watching. She knew they were looking for her, but she'd been so worried about losing Crawdaddy's phone that she'd forgotten to stay out of sight. She felt Grace's hand on her arm.

"Don't you call my cousin dumb names," Grace said. "And you don't know her from anywhere. She's visiting from Chicago, just got here last weekend." Grace's fingers dug in. "Come on. We're going to be late for class."

If Grace hadn't hold of her, Tishanna would have fallen over right there. She put one foot after another until they got inside then collapsed against the wall. "That was fast thinking."

"I heard Crawdaddy tell Mr. Winslow next door that you were our cousin from Chicago. I borrowed his lie." Grace said. "You better call him right now."

"You better get to class. More than five minutes late and you'll have to stay after school."

"You going to call? Joy and I are supposed to look out for people bothering you."

"I'll call from the nurse's office. Soon as I catch my breath. Go to your class."

Grace walked away, but she kept looking back, hesitating. Tishanna waved at her to keep going. Grace meant well, but she'd made it worse.

Everyone knew who Grace and Joy's father was. Now the Players knew she was staying with a police detective. They'd be waiting after school, so she'd better leave now and not by any door they'd be watching.

She hurried down the hall, ready to tell any teacher who asked that she was looking for the school nurse. No one challenged her, and no one saw her slip into the teacher's lounge, empty now that lunch just ended. A door off it led to the parking lot.

Staying low between the cars, Tishanna sprinted across the lot and out to the street where she took refuge in a bus shelter. The first bus that came, she climbed on. When she showed the driver her student pass, he asked why she wasn't in school.

"I left early 'cause I have a doctor's appointment. I've been sick." It was the first thing that came into her head, and he acted like he believed her. When she got off downtown, he said he hoped she felt better soon. She thanked him and caught the next bus that went to Desire.

Tishanna left her grandmother's apartment wearing old jeans and a black tee shirt, not the school uniform she'd always had on when the Players saw her. With her hair pulled back tight and tucked under a baseball cap, she could be a boy. There was nothing about her to cause anyone to look twice, and no one at the bus stop looked once, all of them thinking about their own problems. When the bus came, she took a seat in the back, slouched down, and looked out the window.

Downtown, she got on the Saint Charles streetcar. She rode it all the way to the end and walked around a park in a neighborhood the Players had never heard of, debating whether or not she should tell Dorcas good-bye. On the other side of the park, she found a stop for the 91 bus, and made up her mind.

By now it was rush hour. The bus moved slowly in heavy traffic, then stopped and just sat there. People stuck their heads out the window, looking to see what was the problem. The man sitting next to Tishanna griped he was going to be late.

"Me too," she said, although she was really just killing time by going in a big circle.

A fire truck passed, siren wailing. Next came an ambulance and two police cars. When the bus started up again, it was stop and go until they reached the accident.

An SUV had t-boned a delivery van in the middle of an intersection. That must have been what happened to Claire's boyfriend. She'd seen the wreck on the news, and Crawdaddy told her the guy who got hurt was a good friend of Claire's. The way he said it, worried looking, she knew what kind of a friend. Claire and him must be back together.

A person in the SUV slumped over the steering wheel, not moving. Another person lay on a stretcher behind the ambulance. Tishanna crossed her fingers for them. A policeman waved the bus through the intersection, and the driver sped up on the other side.

She got off at Prytania, along with six or seven other people, and walked down the block to the grocery store where she bought a soda to go with the sandwich she'd brought from Grandma's. She wanted a bag of chips, too, but Grandma had only had $63 hidden in her drawer, and it was going to have to last. The sun had gone down and the streetlights had come on.

She rubbed her arms. The day's warmth had gone with the sun, and both her sweaters were at Crawdaddy's house. She should have taken one of Grandma's, even if the sleeves were too short.

Tishanna had expected the locked kitchen door, but not the board that covered the glass. All across the back, boards covered the first floor windows. Staying between the house and the bushes, she crept around to the side. These windows weren't boarded up, but they were way too high for her to reach. She didn't want to go in the front. She'd have to walk up the steps, and someone might see her.

Uncertain what to do, Tishanna squatted behind a shrub at the front corner of the house. The hedge blocked her view of the street, which meant no one could see her either. Unless they were at the end of the walk and looking, and no one was. Leaves rustled in the wind, and a car to far away to see honked its horn. Footsteps approached and moved on past. A door slammed at one of the neighbor's houses, then silence. All she needed was one clear minute to make it to the front door.

Tishanna abandoned her hiding place. She leapt the front steps two at a time, raced across the gallery, and grabbed the doorknob. It didn't turn. On either side, boards covered the big windows. It wasn't like this when she and Claire got the books. Claire hadn't even locked the door when they left. She pounded on the door.

"Dorcas, help me. Open the door, please."

Nothing happened. She kicked the door and rattled the knob. It still wouldn't turn. Dorcas wasn't going to let her in. Was she mad at her for moving out? For letting Claire read Mary's books?

"I'm sorry, Dorcas. Whatever it was, I'm sorry. I've come to say good-bye, or maybe you want to come with me. I'm taking a Greyhound to Atlanta tonight. A friend of my mother's lives there." She rested her forehead against the locked door. "Don't be mad, Dorcas, please."

"Hey, Lady Pee-In-Her-Pants."

Tishanna slid to the floor.

"We been looking for you."

CHAPTER 21

Claire tapped her foot, while the machine whirred and groaned, scanning copies of the old survey. Scanners and computers made it possible for her to create polished client presentations, but all these miraculous technologies always took longer than you thought they were going to. A final grunt and a box popped up on the screen. The document had been saved in the computer. She removed the survey from the scanner and put in her diagram of the first floor.

Maybe she should call it quits and come in early tomorrow to finish up. She wasn't happy being at the office alone after dark—not with that gang still at large. At some point, she was going to have to tell Tony what was going on. He'd called that morning, sounding stronger, but they'd not talked long. He didn't want to discuss either the accident or his injuries. She didn't want to add her troubles to his. Her mobile phone rang.

"Have you seen Tishanna?" Bea's voice was tight with tension.

"Not since I dropped her at Crawdad's house Monday night. We have plans for tomorrow, and I've been meaning to call, but..." But all she'd thought about all week was Tony. "She's missing?"

"Since lunch time."

"And you've just started looking for her?"

"It's a long story, and no-one's fault. Crawdad's on his way to Chestnut Street."

"If she got there before the workers left, she could have gotten inside. Otherwise she's locked out. We secured the property. She might have gone to my house. I'm not sure she could find her way, but it's worth checking."

"Where are you?"

"At the office and about to leave. I'll stop by Chestnut on my way home."

"I'll tell Crawdad you're coming. Bring your keys."

Claire shut down the computer and hurried out the door.

The first light on Saint Charles turned yellow as she approached, and the car in front of her stopped. She slammed on her brakes and squealed to a stop inches from its bumper, earning a startled look from a man on the sidewalk and a raised middle finger from the driver she'd almost rear-ended.

"Sorry," she mouthed.

The light turned green, and the one on the next block turned red. Claire pounded the steering wheel with her fist. Other cities coordinated their traffic lights. Why not New Orleans? The light turned green, and she made it through the next one on yellow. Then her luck changed, and she hit a run of green lights, all the way to Jackson, where she turned left and left again onto Chestnut.

Three police cars, doors open and blue lights flashing, sat at the curb in front of the house. A clump of people stood halfway up the walk. She pulled in behind a squad car and hit the ground running. All these policemen—if Tishanna was inside, she'd be terrified.

A uniformed officer grabbed her arm. "Sorry, ma'am. You have to stay back. This is a crime scene."

"This is my house. I'm bringing Detective Crawford the keys." She tried to pull her arm out of his grasp. Then she saw the tangle of skinny legs and crumpled clothing at the base of the gallery stairs.

"Tishanna." She wrenched herself free.

A man broke away from the group and blocked her path. Crawdad wrapped his arms around her. "You don't want to go any farther, Claire. There's nothing you can do." He frog-stepped her backward and gently pushed her into a police car. "Bea's on her way. I'll sit with you until she comes."

"Tishanna?"

"Tishanna is dead. One of your neighbors called it in half an hour ago."

"No." Claire slumped back against the seat. "No, no, no." Unshed tears burned her throat.

"I'm sorry. I know you cared about her. I did too."

"You were supposed to keep her safe."

He didn't answer.

"I locked her out," Claire said. "I told the carpenters to make sure no one could get in."

"It's not your fault," he said. "It's not my fault. Everything went wrong."

"I want to see her."

"No, you don't."

"Did they hurt her?" That night in the house, Tishanna had been terrified. She'd said that if the gang caught them they would rape and torture and kill them.

He turned his head away. "Yes, they did."

"They wanted their gun back, and she couldn't give it to them because I took it and gave it to Bea."

"Tishanna witnessed a homicide, Claire. Gun or no gun, they intended to kill her. It's not your fault, and it's not mine, but I promise you that I will not rest until we have the criminals who did this."

There was a knock on the window. Bea stood beside the car. "Come on Claire. I'll take you home."

"My car's here."

"You're in no shape to drive."

Claire didn't have the energy to argue. She let Crawdad help her out of the police car and obediently followed Bea to an unmarked sedan.

"Drop me at the gate," she said. "I don't want to take you away any longer than is necessary."

"You're not taking me away from anything. I want to talk to you." Bea looked over. "How are you doing?"

"Coping. How about you?"

"Coping is a good word."

They reached the driveway, and Bea punched in the code to open the gate. Watching her, Claire thought, Tishanna would have been safe here. She could have walked in the side gate and sat on my porch until I got home. Why didn't she come here? Why didn't I make sure she knew how to get here?

"I know you're beating yourself up," Bea said. "There's a lot of that going around. But there are also some hard truths I want to share with you."

"Like what?"

"Later, when we get inside."

Claire unlocked the front door and led the way into the kitchen. "I have an open bottle of Pinot Grigio." She pulled it out of the refrigerator and took two wine glasses from the cupboard.

"Pour yourself one," Bea said. "I'll have water. I'm on duty."

"You can't break the rules to have a glass of wine with me? Not after what happened?"

"Claire, I treasure your friendship. But, at this moment, I'm a police detective about to conduct an interrogation as part of a homicide investigation."

Bea's statement took away the last hint of unreality and the last vestige of hope. Tishanna was dead. It wasn't a bad dream or a horrible misunderstanding. Claire's head bowed.

"When are you going to tell her grandmother?"

"Crawdad is probably there already. It would have fallen to me, but we thought it would be better if I talked to you." Her half smile was rueful. "Because we're friends. Don't be mad at me, Claire."

They carried their glasses out onto the porch where she and Tishanna had sat and rocked and talked and ate ice cream, where Tishanna had laughed and said they were acting "like two old ladies." Claire wiped away a tear.

"Tishanna and I sat out here. We saw Venus rising and talked about astronomy."

"It was always a race," Bea said. "Everyone was looking for the witness. Would we find her first or would they? Could we build a case for arresting them before they eliminated her? You found her for us, but she wouldn't cooperate. Vernon wanted to put her in a juvenile home. We convinced him that she'd be safer with Crawdad, certainly more likely to become cooperative."

"She gave you a statement on Monday. Today is Friday."

"We pulled in a group of possible suspects, including the two punks we'd picked up outside your house. We put them in a line-up—this was Tuesday afternoon. Tishanna wouldn't identify anyone. She told us that she hadn't gotten a good look at the men in the alley and had no idea who they were. She'd never seen them before that night and the only other time she saw them was when they trapped the two of you in the house. Today they saw her at school. Instead of asking for help, she lied to Crawdad's daughter and ran away."

Claire sipped her wine, buying time while she thought about what Bea had said. "She did know who they were, maybe not their names, but she recognized them."

"Tishanna confided in you." Bea set a tape recorder on the table. "I'm sorry. I know it's a tough time, but the sooner the better. You know the drill."

"I understand." She waited while Bea recorded the time and date. "My name is Claire Marshall," she said. "I'm participating in this interview of my own free will because I want to help the police. I do not want legal representation."

Bea led Claire through her encounters with Tishanna, and then said, "What did Tishanna tell you about the men she saw beating another man in the alley?"

"They call themselves The Players. Some hang around in the park across the street from Tishanna's school. Some attended that school last year—at least part of the year." Claire relayed every single thing she could remember Tishanna saying about this gang.

Bea interrupted with an occasional question or request for

clarification. When she finished, she said turned off the tape recorder. "That was helpful. You've confirmed some things we suspected and filled in the blanks on others."

"It didn't seem like much," Claire said. "Too many somes, too many maybes."

"We're building a case, and every piece of information helps. Now, if you're up for it, I want to go back over all your encounters with this gang." She stood up. "First let's get something to eat. We need to keep our strength up, and you deserve a break."

"I keep thinking there must have been something I could have done differently."

"You did all you could, Claire, and so did I, and so did Crawdad. Tishanna witnessed a homicide. The moment she ran away rather than running for help... She could have gone into any one of the bars or restaurants and told the people inside what had just happened in the alley, but she didn't. We all tried to help her, but when she was frightened, she ran again."

"She was frightened and running away. Is that your hard truth?"

"There's more. I waltzed around it before." Bea stared at nothing for a moment before continuing. "Tishanna told one of her friends that she found a gun and you stole it from her. That friend told another friend who told another friend. You know how it goes. We think word got back to the gang and that's why they came after you."

"I don't believe it."

"Crawdad's daughters heard the story and told him." Bea reached out a comforting hand. "Tishanna didn't mean you any harm, Claire."

"She warned me that they'd come after me."

"Yes, she did. And now I'm warning you."

"Now, but what about the day those thugs came after me? Did you and Mike and Crawdad know then?" When Bea didn't answer, Claire pulled away. "You didn't think I deserved to know that some thug thought I had his gun?"

"Mike and I both had warned you about the gang. We knew, because you had told me, that Tishanna warned you about the gun. If we'd told you that she had, unwittingly, set the gang on you, what would that have accomplished?"

"It might have shown that you trusted me, that you didn't consider me undependable, inept— Just because I'm not a police detective. The arrogance—"

"Claire, you're tired and upset. We can finish tomorrow."

"Do you really think I'll stop cooperating with your investigation of Tishanna's murder because I'm angry?" She pointed to the tape recorder. "Turn it back on. Finish your interrogation; then you can leave."

CHAPTER 22

Saturday morning, Claire woke early and exhausted, the sight of Tishanna dead at the bottom of the gallery stairs burned into her eyelids. Or was it a vision of Dorcas dead at the base of the front stairs? The two had intermingled in a nightmare collage that haunted her dreams.

Then there was Bea. She'd been furious with Bea last night, had blamed her for everything, which wasn't fair. She rolled over and returned to a troubled sleep. Mid-morning, she woke again. The phone was ringing.

"I heard it on the radio," Jack said. "Are you okay?"

"I'm going to be okay. But the house is a crime scene. Can you pull everyone off?" The police hadn't asked, but they would.

"No problem. We have plenty of other work. Do you want me or Marie to come over?"

"Thanks, but I'm fine."

Claire scoured her little house like a robot programmed to clean. She vacuumed and dusted, scrubbed the sinks, washed and waxed the kitchen and bathroom floors. She cleaned the oven and defrosted the refrigerator. Bea and Crawdad had assured her that she bore no responsibility for Tishanna's death. She wished she believed them.

I took her gun. I locked her out of the house. Was protecting those front windows so important?

She thought back to when she was thirteen, young, unformed, and a

171

million miles away from Desire and gangs that killed. She'd been thirteen when she met Tom, twenty-one when she married him. In between there had been parties and proms, picnics and rides in the country. She remembered Tishanna dancing across the porch, bragging about how hot she was going to be, how many boyfriends she was going to have. Tishanna would never know the thrill of first love, the joy of married love.

Claire didn't call Tony. She couldn't tell him about Tishanna moving in with Detective Crawford without admitting that she'd misled him about their encounter with the gang. His adamant refusal to consider her visiting imbued even a simple "I miss you," with potential controversy. Yesterday morning's conversation had been an awkward search for safe topics, a relief when it ended. She didn't have the strength to stagger through another one.

She was wiping pollen off the porch furniture when the phone rang. Midnight in Italy, this couldn't be Tony.

"How are you doing?" Bea said.

"I'm fine."

"You can't be, but I called to apologize, not argue. I pushed you too hard last night, and I'm sorry. You've helped our investigation, and you deserve our trust."

"I took everything out on you."

"I know that. And I know you wouldn't stop cooperating because you were annoyed with me. Peace, Claire?"

"Peace. I'm sorry I lost my temper."

"That's okay. I've been thrown out of better places."

"I've spent the day doing housework. Come on over and admire the results."

"I can't, not tonight. I'm working, and I'm still asking for your cooperation. We want to go over your Chestnut Street property with a fine-toothed comb—inside as well as out."

"I anticipated, and I've already called off the workers. Crawdad has a key and you all have my permission to go inside. Just let me know when you're finished." She almost added, "No rush." She was in no hurry to return to that house. If it hadn't been haunted before, it was now.

"Through Wednesday ought to do it." Bea said. "Back to your invitation. How about tomorrow night? I'll bring take-out."

"Sounds good. Sixish?"

Sunday morning, Claire went to a service at a church she hadn't visited in months. On her way home, she ran Felicia Miata through a carwash and, that afternoon, waxed her bright blue finish until she shone. The day passed without her calling Tony or him calling her. He still didn't know about Tishanna. Sooner or later, she'd have to tell him. Sooner or later, he'd have to let her come see him.

Bea arrived a little after six, carrying two bags. "Food and drink." She put them on the kitchen counter. "Thai One On has fantastic pad thai."

"Tony used to get take-out from there."

"Have you told him what happened?"

"No. He has enough on his mind." *Why not just admit it?* "Truth is I haven't had the chance. We last talked Friday morning." She busied herself setting out the food.

"A lot has happened since then. You ought to call him."

"It's the middle of the night in Italy. Maybe tomorrow."

Tony called her first. The ringing phone brought her out of a deep sleep and a dream that vanished immediately, leaving only an impression of a world gone very wrong. She picked up and croaked a hello.

"Good morning, sweetheart, this is your wake-up call. I wanted to catch you before you went to work."

Claire sensed the effort behind his cheerful tone and tried to match it. "You can wake me up any time."

"You're hoarse. Do you have a cold?"

"A little sore throat, nothing serious. How are you? Are you still in the hospital?"

"I'm leaving tomorrow for a private clinic outside Zurich, one of Europe's top rehab facilities. Their orthopedic department specializes in sports injuries. I'll be hobnobbing with a bunch of skiers."

"How long will you be there?"

"I've told the doctors that I have a date in New Orleans on June 17th."

"And what did the doctors say?"

"We're still negotiating. What have you been up to? Did you have a good weekend?"

She couldn't tell him, not over the phone. "I want to come see you."

"I'm in a wheelchair, Claire, a wheelchair or my bed. Until my arm heals I can't even use a walker, much less crutches. Ninety-year-olds can totter around in walkers, but I'm not up to it. My most recent achievement is learning how to transfer in and out of the wheelchair so that I can use the toilet without help. I don't want you to see me like this."

Why don't you trust my feelings for you? She wanted to ask, but she couldn't risk his answer. Even now she was lying by omission. Why should he trust her? Her shoulders sagged under the weight of things not said.

"I'll call you when I get to Switzerland," he said. "Now tell me what you've been doing. How's Tishanna?"

She shook her head, unable to speak.

"Claire, are you there?"

"I wasn't going to tell you. You have enough to deal with." She forced the words past the lump in her throat. "Tishanna is dead, murdered by that gang. It happened Friday night."

"You should have called me."

"It was the middle of your night, and even during the day I can't get through. There's a wall around you, Tony, and I'm on the other side." She plunged ahead, "I know it's partly my fault. I hold back, especially on the phone."

"Things are going to be different when I get to Switzerland. I promise. Say something, Claire. Are you all right?"

"I'm hoarse because I spent hours talking to Bea last night—she's the detective on the case. I really want to talk to you. In person." *I need you, Tony.*

This silence came from his end, and she waited.

"I'll call you when I get settled," he said. "It might be a day or two."

That evening Claire contacted an orthopedic specialist, a woman who'd gone to med school with Tom. They'd been friends, but she hadn't seen Suzanne since Tom's funeral. Suzanne had lived in Chicago then, and, it turned out, still did.

"Of course I remember you," Suzanne said. "How have you been? Are you in town? I'd love to get together."

"No, I'm still in New Orleans. I called because I have a question about broken bones, and I'm hoping you can answer it."

"I'll try."

Claire repeated what Dr. Chinetti had told her, a comminuted fracture of the femur at the site of a prior break. Because the old break had not healed properly, they'd had to use an internal plate and screws rather than a pin. "I know it's serious, but I don't know how serious."

"A lot depends upon the age and condition of the patient," Suzanne said. "This isn't your mother is it?"

"No. This is a physically-active man in his mid-thirties."

"I'm glad it's not your mother; osteoporosis is often a complicating factor with older women. But if it doesn't take, mid-thirties is awfully young to lose a leg."

Lose a leg? Claire's heart stopped. Dr. Chinetti's "complete recovery" had sounded far less certain when they spoke after the operation, but she hadn't realized the severity of the situation, certainly not the possible consequences. Tony's driving career would be over, but it was more than that. He was such a physical person. He'd be devastated.

"What are the odds of that happening?"

"I can't begin to predict the outcome without knowing more about the individual case. The challenge with a comminuted fracture is to reposition all segments of the bone and maintain that alignment long enough for the bone to mend. The orthopedist's first choice is an intramedullary nail, a pin surgically inserted through the center of the bone. Second choice is an external bar attached to the bone above and below the fractures to hold the bone in place until the patient can tolerate surgery. An internal bar is the last tool in our bag our tricks. We use it when the fracture extends into the hip or knee joint."

"I don't believe that's the case."

"Or when the bone is so weak or so damaged that a nail isn't an option. From what you say, it was severely damaged."

"And if that doesn't work?"

"We have to consider amputation." Suzanne paused. "This is someone you care about?"

"Yes." She cared deeply. "How long does it usually take for a fracture like this to heal completely?"

"Six months? A year? Some patients will always limp. It's hard to predict—even for the physician on the scene. The prognosis is better for a relatively young person in good shape. Was he in an automobile accident?"

"Yes."

"Good luck, Claire." Suzanne said. "To you and to him. Make sure he obeys doctors' orders. His leg is at stake."

CHAPTER 23

The ambulance rolled to a gentle stop, and an orderly opened the back door. Tony got his first glimpse of Clinique Rothman; it looked like a picture postcard. Beyond a cluster of attractive stone and mortar buildings, a broad lawn sloped down to a brilliant blue lake. A scattering of pines along the far shore thickened into a forest that climbed steep slopes and then thinned out again, giving way to snow and rocks, craggy peaks against a sky as blue as the lake.

"*Un bel posto*," he said to the men maneuvering his stretcher onto a trolley. It was a beautiful place, but any place would have looked beautiful after four hours in the ambulance with a stranger driving. To make things worse, they'd sat him backwards, so he couldn't see where they were going. His jaw ached from four hours of clenched teeth.

He was going to have to get used to being a passenger. The doctors said he couldn't put any weight on his leg for another week, and then only a toe tap. Pain was no longer an issue. His leg itched more than hurt, especially along the line of stitches that ran from hip to knee. His arm didn't bother him unless he moved it, and his ribs only hurt when something jarred them—as was happening right now. The trolley bounced over an uneven bit of ground, and he winced.

An orderly, Max according to his nametag, apologized. "Transferring you from the ambulance is the hard part, and it's over. From here to your room, I promise, a smooth ride."

"Thank you."

"Just like a Ferrari 456."

Tony looked away. The accident that put him here had occurred when he was riding in a 456. "How about turning me around so I can see where I'm going," he said.

A wide paved walk inclined gently to double glass doors that slid open at their approach. Upholstered chairs clustered around patterned area rugs, brass lamps on shiny wood tables, and live plants gave the lobby the appearance of a luxury apartment building. The receptionist wore street clothes as subdued and tasteful as the décor. Only the row of wheelchairs behind the desk hinted at this building's function.

Check-in was a model of efficiency, and ten minutes later, Max wheeled him down a wide hall into his new quarters, a two-bedroom, two-bath suite that was a huge improvement over the hospital room he'd occupied until this morning. He'd asked for two bedrooms although he was still on the fence about Claire coming to visit.

"Room for a lady friend." Max gave him a big grin. "You can't hold a good man down."

"*Keep* a good man down," Tony muttered. Garbled translations of everything American were part of living abroad. The previous hospital had tried to cheer him with piped in music they thought he'd like, including an Italian group covering Lynyrd Skynyrd. Tony, who had grown up with southern rock, wasn't sure which had hurt more, his injuries or listening to the full nine minutes of a tortured *Free Bird*.

"When will she arrive?" Max said.

"No time soon. I'm planning ahead. I'll be here for a while." How long remained up in the air. The gallery opening was less than a month away, cutting it close the doctors said. They wouldn't commit to a departure date.

"Many of our patients invite lady friends to stay overnight, especially the skiers. They are passionate those skiers. Broken legs don't stop them. Even those with a bar from here to here." Max indicated the distance from knee to hip. "One broken leg, it can be done. Two, it's still possible."

Tony raised an eyebrow, and Max responded with an exuberant demonstration of techniques for making love with one leg disabled. He had just assumed his first two-broken-legs position when a nurse marched in, barking orders. Max scrambled to his feet, and Tony bit back the laughter that was killing his cracked ribs.

The nurse, a middle-aged woman built like a fireplug, oversaw his transfer to the bed and showed him how to operate the controls and call buttons. "Would you like a bed pan?"

"Leave the wheelchair by the bed, and I can handle that myself."

"Already? Very good." She nodded approvingly, and he felt a little less like an overgrown baby.

The next thing he knew, a different nurse was turning on the lights in his room. This one was young with light brown hair pulled back from a high forehead. The dusting of freckles across her nose reminded him of Claire.

"I must have dozed off," he said. "What time is it?"

"Dinnertime. Every night you have a choice of meat, fish, or vegetarian entree. Tonight, the meat is veal, and unless you're a vegetarian, I'd recommend it."

"I'm not really hungry."

"All the more reason to get the veal." She had a nice smile. "One bite and you'll be hungry for more."

"Okay, the veal. I'd like to make a long distance phone call. How does that work?"

She pointed to a phone beside his bed. "Just like a hotel. Dial zero zero for the international operator."

Claire was at police headquarters. "I'm looking at mug shots," she said. "Trying to identify the gang that killed Tishanna. Are you at the rehab hospital?"

"Were you there when it happened?" He didn't remember her saying anything about that.

"No, but the police believe it was the same people that came after us the other night. I saw them then." A pause then conversation in the background. "Bea says hello. I told you, she's the lead detective."

Claire's voice had the same careful tone Dr. Chinetti used when discussing the prognosis for his leg. Either she was feeding him the truth little pieces at a time, holding back what she thought he wasn't ready to hear, or she was censoring herself because other people were in the room. Or both.

"Is this a bad time to talk?" he said.

"It's a good time. I've been looking at pictures so long that I'm cross-eyed." More conversation in the background, a man's voice as well as Bea's, then the sound of a door closing. "I've just gone into an empty office. Now we can talk. Are you in the rehab hospital yet? How is it?"

"I arrived this afternoon. It's nice as hospitals go. They make an effort. The scenery is what you'd expect in Switzerland, a lake and mountains. Tell me more about why you're looking at mug shots."

"There's not much more to tell. I saw six of them at night and from a distance; one of them another time or two and closer. I must have looked at a hundred pictures."

That same careful tone—why do I have to pry information from you, Claire? "Did anyone else see them?"

"Only Tishanna."

"Did she know them?"

"Yes. I think so. Tony, you're interrogating me. Bea has already done that." There was an edge to her voice.

What could have erupted into a full-blown argument was interrupted by the arrival of an aide bearing a tray. "You ordered the veal?"

"Thank you. Just put it down. I'll be off the phone in a minute." He waited until he was alone again. "I miss you Claire, and I'm worried about whatever you've gotten yourself mixed up in."

"I miss you too, and there's nothing to worry about."

"I'll call tomorrow or Thursday. Meanwhile, here's my number. It rings directly into my room. No switchboard this time."

"Call me anytime. Two a.m., I don't care. I'm keeping my phone with me and on."

"You can call me, too. I miss you."

Tony had been prepared to tell Claire that, in not too long, she could come visit. But unlike every other conversation, she hadn't mentioned wanting to be with him. She'd made a big point of being with Bea, although she knew that he and Bea didn't like each other, and he'd heard a man's voice as well.

Is Captain Mike Robinson back in the picture?

Robinson was head of homicide, he could be involved in this case if he wanted, and he'd want to if he saw it as an opportunity to get Claire back. She was upset about Tishanna's murder; she'd be vulnerable. Tony stabbed a piece of veal. It was delicious and his appetite better than expected. This place also was better than he'd expected, a rehab clinic masquerading as a resort, but he didn't like the direction his thoughts were taking. He'd never said word one about Claire's social life when he wasn't around—that sword cut in two directions—but he'd assumed she'd be faithful. Now he wasn't so sure.

Wednesday, Tony's first full day at Clinic Rothman, began early. He went from breakfast to X-rays to physical therapy. The fully equipped gym was a surprise. He surveyed the rows of weight machines. What was he doing here?

A tall blonde, who might be carrying two ounces of body fat but was unquestionably female, strode in. "Mr. Burke? I'm Bette Anders, your physical therapist. Are you ready to begin?"

"Begin what? I'm not supposed to put any weight on my leg or any stress on my ribs, and my arm is in a sling."

"Your broken bones are all on the right side, Mr. Burke, and so we will start with the left. Do you need help transferring from your chair to this machine?"

By the time Bette finished running him through a workout of his left side, Tony thought of her as a slave driver, not a woman. He wiped sweat from his face with his good arm. "Are we through?"

"With the left side. The doctors say you can start limited isometric exercises with your right arm. You are familiar with isometrics, yes?" Tony groaned and she laughed. "I thought so. You're well-muscled, stronger than most of the amateur skiers I work with."

"But not better than the pros?" Tony prided himself on staying in top physical condition, and until the accident, he had been.

"Keep that competitive spirit and perhaps by the time you leave here." Bette gestured toward a long pad. "Now, place your right arm on this."

Thirty agonizing minutes later, she said, "That's it for today. We start small. Tomorrow we'll do more."

"Small?" He feigned a collapse against the back of his wheelchair. "Have you ever heard of Simon Legree?"

"You are my third American patient to mention this name. After the second, I purchased a copy of *Uncle Tom's Cabin.*" She lowered her lashes then looked up and smiled into his eyes. "No whips or chains will come into play, unless you request them."

Surprised by the come-on, Tony chuckled.

"See. It wasn't that bad." She walked past him, and her thigh brushed his left shoulder. "You're feeling better already."

Tony accepted the invitation. "Another day or two, and I'll be ready for an evening session. You could stop by my apartment."

"We'll see."

He watched her walk away, hips swaying just for him. Clinique Rothschild was looking better by the minute. A physical therapist would know all the tricks. The black mood that had hovered at the edge of his consciousness since he came out of surgery retreated.

When the phone rang, Claire knew it was Tony. "How are you?" she said. "How is the clinic?"

"Therapeutic. I have physical therapy in the morning, occupational therapy and hydrotherapy in the afternoon. There's a TV in my room and a stack of movies, but I've not had time. It's nine o'clock here, and when we hang up, I'm going to sleep."

"They may be running you ragged, but you sound happy."

"Working up a sweat did me good."

"That's wonderful news. I'm so glad."

"Another week and I'll be ready for a visitor. You can stay in my suite. There are plenty of things to keep you amused while I'm going through therapy. Hiking, boat rides on the lake, and Geneva's only an hour away."

"Next week? That's sooner than I expected." She had promised Bea that she'd be available to answer questions, look at pictures, or view a line-up.

"I know you have a job, but you can make short trips. Don't worry about airplane tickets. I have thousands of frequent flier miles."

"I want to come see you. There's nothing I want more, but I can't, not yet."

"This is a switch."

"I'm the only person who can identify the gang that killed Tishanna. The police asked me to be on call. As soon as this is over, I'd love to come. And stay as long as you want me. I'm not worried about the business. Jack can handle it." *Please understand.*

"Keep me posted."

His tone was distant. He could have been talking to a stranger. They didn't talk much longer, and after they hung up, Claire stared out the window for a long time.

CHAPTER 24

A patrol car sat, motor running, in front of 368 Chestnut. Claire pulled in behind it. She could see someone in the driver's seat, but he didn't appear to have noticed her, so she climbed out of her Miata, walked up, and tapped on his window.

"I'm Claire Marshall. Have you got my keys?"

He looked her over. "I'll give you the keys as soon as you show me some identification."

She fished out her driver's license and handed it to him. He studied it, looked at her, checked the license again, and finally, after another examination of her face, handed it back along with the house keys.

"You look like your picture," he said.

Claire nodded. *Most people do.*

He jutted his chin toward the house. "A girl was murdered here."

"Friday night."

"There's been a lot of trouble in this neighborhood."

"I was at headquarters yesterday, looking at mug shots, but..." She shrugged. "I'm going to try again later this afternoon."

"A person can only do what a person can do." Without waiting for her response, he accelerated away from the curb.

Bea had said that an officer would meet her at the house and make sure it was properly secured before handing over the keys. This policeman hadn't even gotten out of his car. Bea was a smart person working long hard hours, but if Office Obvious was typical of the support she was getting... No wonder the investigation wasn't making any progress.

Claire twirled the keys she didn't want to use. Inside this house was the last place she wanted to go. Just checking the front door would require passing that dark stain at the base of the steps.

Tishanna.

Slowly, Claire stepped around the bloodstain and climbed the gallery steps. The front door opened easily. She took a deep breath and stepped into the foyer, dark and shadowy now that the windows were boarded over. The mermaid sconces no longer brought a smile. They and all the lovely old details that once delighted her had been tainted by sorrow. Her reflection in the mirror stared back with somber eyes. Pale light flowed down the stairwell and onto the marble tiles. Claire stepped into the puddle of light, and cold raised goose bumps on her arms.

You're still here aren't you, Dorcas? Why didn't you help Tishanna? You could have let her in, slammed the door and scared that gang away? Claire shook her head. Blaming Dorcas was tempting but bogus. She hadn't locked Tishanna out. *I did that—to protect the windows.*

Dorcas and Tishanna, both dead at thirteen, neither had a chance at life. Anger washed over Claire, a fury so intense she trembled. Her hands formed fists. She wanted to smash those damned windows, rip the sconces from the walls.

"Claire? Yoo-hoo Claire."

Startled, she spun around.

Ellen Ledet was tottering up the sidewalk. She stopped and leaned on her cane. "I saw your car. Do you have a minute?"

"Of course. Don't rush. Let me come to you." She hurried to intercept Ellen before she reached the bloodstain.

"Lindsey Tice is the one who found the body," Ellen said. "As if that poor woman hasn't already been through too much. She screamed loud enough to break glass, and I came out to see what had happened. I swear, for a minute I thought it was Dorcas lying there. It looked just like her, and at the base of the stairs. I almost had a heart attack." She put a fluttering hand to her chest. "You would have had two dead bodies on your sidewalk."

"Her name was Tishanna Tenier. She'd been staying in the house, camping out, before I bought it."

"And she came back. I wonder why. Have the police arrested anyone? Do they have any leads?" Without waiting for answers, Ellen said, "I was about to fix myself some lunch. Will you join me?"

"That's kind of you, but I have to get back to the office. May I have a rain check?"

"At least have a glass of iced tea. It's already made."

"Thank you, that would be nice. I could use a sit down." Claire's intense anger had receded, leaving her shaken. What had come over her?

Once again Ellen suggested they have their iced tea on the gallery. She went inside to fix it, insisting she needed no help, and Claire sat in the same rocking chair she'd sat in twice before. The front yard looked as well kept as it had last week and the week before. The impatiens bloomed as profusely, but the world had become a harsher, uglier place.

"People don't know what to think." Ellen put a tray holding two glasses of iced tea and a plate of sesame sticks on the table between them. "Those who believe in ghosts will tell you that Dorcas was involved. No one knows anything, and I was hoping that you could tell me more about what really happened."

"I've gotten the impression that everyone believes in Dorcas."

"Well, some more than others," Ellen said. "I really don't, but you have to admit it's a strange coincidence. What have the police told you?"

Claire considered her response. Tony had told her that you couldn't fight gossip. The harder you tried to keep something secret, the more interested people became. Your best option was to manage the flow of information. Tell people what you want them to know, act as if you're taking them into your confidence, and you'll control the story. She had accused him of being manipulative, but now she was going to take his advice. Ellen, self-described as the neighborhood gossip, could be a valuable ally. Plus, she kept an eye on the street.

"The police think the murder is related to recent gang activity, possibly the same gang that mugged Lindsay's husband," Claire said. "I know the detective in charge of the investigation. We're friends." She fiddled with her napkin, giving Ellen time to digest the information. "Remember the young man we saw the other day? If you see him again, call the police."

"I'll tell the other neighbors to be watchful."

"And careful. Whatever you do, don't attract his attention."

"What about your house?" Ellen said. "I noticed that the police removed the crime scene tape this morning. Will you resume work soon?"

"Eventually. I don't know how soon." She wouldn't leave the house to blight the neighborhood, but she could use some time away, and so could her workers.

"The neighbors are concerned. We were so pleased when you began work."

"We have several other ongoing projects. It's a matter of re-scheduling." Claire raised her hands in supplication and embroidered the excuse. "Carpenters, plumbers, electricians—restoring an old house is like a play where you have actors moving on and off the stage. We've been thrown off-balance, but we'll recover."

Ellen nodded, but her expression remained concerned.

"Timing is everything," Claire added.

"That's what my children say." Ellen's face brightened. "Which reminds me, dear. Mary's birthday is tomorrow. We had discussed your going with me. I hope you won't be too busy. To be perfectly honest, I need a ride. My son usually drives me, but he's going to be out of town. Of course if you can't, I can make other arrangements."

"I'd be happy to drive." Claire had forgotten all about it. "What time should I pick you up?"

Claire left Ellen's house certain that everything she had said would be all over the neighborhood by dinnertime. She picked up a sandwich on the way back to the office, planning to eat a late lunch at her desk while she caught up on the paperwork she should have done yesterday. When she walked in, Jack was talking on the phone. He looked up and waved.

"Hey, here she is. Don't hang up." He handed her the phone. "Tony."

"Hi sweetheart," Tony said. "I'm glad I caught you."

"Me, too. But why did you call the office and not my cell phone?"

"This is a business call. I'm looking for a contractor, preferably a beautiful redhead, who can modify the downstairs of my house in New Orleans to make it wheelchair accessible."

"Why?" Her question came quickly and unbidden. Had the doctors failed to save his leg? Was he going to be in a wheelchair for the rest of his life? "What's happened?"

"I don't see any reason to wait until the opening to come back. There are doctors and nurses and physical therapists in New Orleans. And there is a certain *bella testarossa*."

"Tony." She choked out his name, unable to say anything else. She felt Jack's alarmed look and turned to show him the smile behind her tears.

"When can you start?" Tony said.

"Right away. As soon as we figure out what we have to do."

"I've been gathering information." Tony described measuring his rooms, the halls, and the gym. "The physical therapist became suspicious when I wrote down model numbers for the exercise machines. One of the doctors asked if I was planning to build my own clinic. This evening, the administrator dropped by and asked more pointed questions. You should have seen the reaction when I showed him my drawings and asked if I could use his fax machine tomorrow morning." Tony's chuckle ended in a curse.

"What?"

"Laughing hurts my ribs, but every time I remember the expression on his face, I can't help it."

"Ouch." She sympathized.

"The clinic office opens at eight tomorrow morning, 1:00 a.m. your time, which is a little late for you to be in the office. Leave your fax machine on overnight, and my drawings will be waiting when you come in."

"You've given this some thought."

"I have. The double front parlor will make a fine gym, and the den can become my bedroom. I think all the doorways are wide enough. The tricky part is the downstairs bath. If you combine the half bath and laundry, there should be room for a roll-in shower. I don't know about the whirlpool."

"We could put a tub in the middle of the kitchen, like they did in the old West." Claire laughed. "Whatever it takes, we'll do it." The excuse she'd given Ellen Ledet had just become truth. She'd take everyone off the house and put them to work converting Tony's downstairs.

They talked a bit longer, about details and the timing of his return. "Tell anyone who asks that you're preparing the house for my visit in mid-June," he said. "What the clinic offers that New Orleans doesn't is a guarantee of privacy."

"I'll have to tell Jack why it's a rush job."

"Can you trust him not to mention it to anyone else?"

"Of course."

After they hung up, Claire explained the situation to Jack, who was doubtful, as usual. But when she pulled her old drawings from the file, even he had to admit all Tony's suggestions were right on target.

She set up a new file for the project then sat at her desk studying the laundry half-bath combination. If they stacked the washer and dryer, there might be room for a whirlpool. It depended upon the size of the tub, and she didn't know what was required. She wanted to dive in, but she couldn't do anything without Tony's drawings and, possibly, other information. She'd need permits. What's more, she'd promised Ellen Ledet to take her to see Mary Beaudry tomorrow afternoon, and she wanted to read the last of Mary's diaries before they went. Nineteen sixty-three was still at the house.

"My last meeting is at three," she told Jack. "I'm not coming back afterwards, but I'll be here early tomorrow."

"Early as in before ten?"

"I'll be here before you are."

Her meeting was in Uptown, and when it ended, Claire drove from there to the house. Rather than park out front where Ellen and any other neighbors could see her car, she pulled into the driveway and parked behind the house.

Entering through the back door was easier, no blood-stained sidewalk and no cold spot to traverse on her way up the stairs, but being inside still brought a bleak despair edged with anger. She climbed the back stairs to the small bedroom and went directly to the mantle and the toggle Tishanna had shown her.

The mirror slid aside, and Claire picked out Mary's 1963 diary. She flipped through and saw that clumps of pages remained blank. Others had been scribbled over or ripped out. Reading this wouldn't take as long as she'd feared.

That night, Claire discovered that the torn and blank pages described the onset of Mary's increasingly severe illness. Her entries would become shorter and less rational, her handwriting more illegible, more and more sections would be scribbled over, pages would be ripped, and then there would be weeks with no entries.

When Mary resumed writing, she would be coherent, but it never lasted. Nor did the source of her distress ever change. Mary believed herself to be possessed, literally. Her tantrums were expressions of Dorcas's anger, not hers.

Any passage that might have revealed the reason for Dorcas's anger had been scribbled over or ripped out. Claire turned out the light and tried to find sleep. She remembered the anger that gripped her when she was in the house. Before then, she'd been sad, not angry. Had she been feeling Dorcas's rage?

Tishanna had said that Mary's diaries gave her nightmares. "Me, too, Tishanna," Claire murmured. Mary had not been in her last nightmare, but she would be in her next.

CHAPTER 25

Claire was up before the sun and in her office by seven. Tony's fax lay in the tray, six pages of detailed drawings to scale. He was indeed an engineer. She worked straight through until it was time to pick up Ellen. The plans were finished, but she didn't have time to go downtown and pull the permits. She asked Jack to do it.

"You're better at that than I am," he said.

Claire heard the unspoken words. They divided work in their partnership, he who can does, and this was her job. "I have an obligation I can't wiggle out of. I'll have my phone with me and on. Call if you have any questions." Jack's frowned didn't lessen, so she played a trump card. "I supervised demo on Chestnut Street. Remember?"

"It can't wait until tomorrow morning?"

"Tomorrow morning, I'm meeting the plumber at Tony's house. I'd like to have the permits in hand."

"Okay, but stay by your phone."

"Thank you." She ran out the door, already late, which meant no time to grab a sandwich.

Driving past the house, she slowed. Her mind's eye saw the yellow crime-scene tape that was no longer there, the bloodstain on the sidewalk that would fade long before its memory did. She kept going and pulled up in front of Ellen's house.

Ellen stood, waiting at the top of her gallery steps, cane in one hand

and a bouquet of bright blossoms in the other. Claire hopped out, apologizing for being late, and helped her down the steps. "I hope you haven't been standing there long."

"I thought you'd drive your pick-up." Ellen looked askance at the bright blue Miata. "How do you expect me to get into that little thing? I'm seventy-eight years old. And where can I put these flowers?"

"A spry seventy-eight," Claire said, "and it's easier than it looks." She took the flowers and the cane. "Turn sideways and back up to the car. Now take my hand and sit down. Good. Swing your legs around, fasten your seat belt, and you'll be all set." She handed back the flowers and cane.

"There's a plate of cupcakes on the table by the front door. I couldn't carry everything."

"I'll get them." The cupcakes were frosted with buttercream and dotted with chocolate shavings. Resisting the temptation to pop one in her mouth, Claire carried the plate to the car and handed it over.

"I'd rather make a birthday cake," Ellen said, "but the staff prefers you bring cupcakes. They're easier to serve." She settled back with the cupcake plate in her lap, the flowers on the floor, and the cane beside her. "This car is quite comfortable once you're in. I haven't ridden in a convertible in decades, but I had my hair done yesterday and do appreciate your keeping the top up."

"Up it will stay." Claire put the car in gear. "Now, where are we going?"

"The other side of the lake, a few miles past Slidell. It shouldn't take more than thirty or forty minutes."

Thirty minutes there and thirty minutes back, plus they'd have to stay at least an hour. They wouldn't get back to New Orleans until after the permit office closed, which meant no time to fix things if Jack had a problem. Claire pulled away from the curb, trying hard not to resent this time taken away from working on Tony's house.

"The trip will give us time to talk," Ellen said. "I saw those young men by your house last night. I called 911, but they were gone by the time anyone came."

"If you see them again, call me."

"I almost did, but it was late, and I didn't want to disturb you. Next time I will."

Claire waited until they were on I-10 before bringing up Mary Beaudry. "I finished reading Mary's diaries last night. She was a disturbed young woman."

"Mary's at peace now." A quaver in Ellen's voice suggested otherwise.

"Her diary ends in October of 1963. There were other breaks but none longer than six or eight weeks. Do you know what happened?"

"I believe that's when Mary had her lobotomy."

"A lobotomy? In 1963? But doctors stopped doing those back in the fifties."

"Louisiana gave violent criminals lobotomies well into the sixties. It calmed them down."

"I can't imagine... Their own child..." *Oh, Mary, what did they do to you?*

"It was a last resort." Ellen's already sad expression became more sorrowful. "They'd tried everything, a special hospital, electroshock. Mary would become her old self, and they'd send her home, but after a short while, it would start all over again. The lobotomy was supposed to be a permanent solution."

They were on the causeway now, crossing the vast waters of Lake Pontchartrain. The lively tomboy who'd written in the first diary had loved to go boating on this lake—before she became obsessed with Dorcas and didn't want to do anything. Before she believed that Dorcas lived inside her head. Claire had a sudden crazy image, a doctor sticking an ice pick in Mary's brain and stabbing Dorcas.

"You could say it worked," Ellen said. "Mary's peaceful now, but she's not whole."

"What do you mean by 'not whole'?"

"The medical term is affectless. She doesn't care deeply about anything. You'll see what I mean."

"Has she forgotten Dorcas?" Ellen fidgeted in her seat, obviously uncomfortable with the questions. Claire persisted anyway. "She seemed to be obsessed with Dorcas' death. Is she still?"

"Mary still remembers Dorcas, but she realizes that what she thought were memories were really fantasies and bad dreams. She was a highly imaginative child."

"I can be highly imaginative, too," Claire said. But the slamming windows and doors were no fantasy, nor was the cold spot at the base of the stairs.

Ellen leaned forward. "Turn here, dear. We're almost there. Let's talk about something pleasant. I'd like to compose myself before we go inside. And I don't think we should tell Mary what happened the other night."

The group home was a rambling one-story brick ranch in a well-maintained residential neighborhood. Only an outsized mailbox and a ramp leading up to the front door set it apart from its neighbors. The young woman who opened the door recognized Ellen and ushered them inside.

"Mary knows you're coming. Everyone does. They'll all be very glad to see you. They're in the TV room. We can eat in there. I'll get napkins."

"Let me carry the cupcakes." Ellen handed the flowers to Carolyn. "Can you put these in water?" she said and led the way down the hall.

"Hello Mrs. Ledet." A heavyset woman came over to hug Ellen. Her pasty pale skin and gray hair made her look far older than fifty. Mary Beaudry moved ponderously, head drooping and shoulders sagging, as if she could hardly bear the burden of her large body, but when she pointed at the cupcakes, her face lit up with delight.

"Is the one with the candle for me?"

"You know it is." Ellen put the cupcakes down. "Mary Beaudry meet Claire Marshall. Claire drove me here so I could celebrate someone special's birthday."

"I'm pleased to meet you, Claire." Mary spoke slowly. The hand she held out was soft, flaccid as if there were no bones beneath the flesh. Everything about Mary was subdued—her appearance, her manner, her voice. Her only enthusiasm was for the cupcakes.

Claire struggled to connect this defeated old woman with either the mischievous tomboy or the raging adolescent who had written in those diaries. She wished Mary a happy birthday.

"I forgot my birthday, but Mrs. Ledet remembered."

Carolyn joined them. She set the flowers on the table and said, "Lissie remembered, too. She called you this morning."

"That's right. I forgot." Mary returned her attention to the cupcakes. "They're red velvet cake aren't they?"

"Of course," Ellen said. "I know they're your favorite."

Everyone sang "Happy Birthday," and the cupcakes were consumed in a reverent silence that demonstrated what a treat they were. Because it was her birthday, Mary got two. Once the food was gone, Carolyn cleared the table, and the other residents turned their attention back to the television.

"Claire is fixing up your family's old house," Ellen told Mary. "It's been empty for a long time, but now Claire's going to live there."

No, I'm not. Claire wished that she'd never seen 368 Chestnut, that it would vanish from the face of the earth so that she never had to look at it again, much less go inside. "Do you remember living there," she asked Mary. "Back when you were a little girl?"

"Uh huh," Mary nodded. "There was a big tree I used to climb. I'd bring food up with me, books to read. It was my secret hideaway." She looked sideways. "I had other secret hideaways but that was my favorite."

I know you did, I read your diary. "I used to have secret hideaways, too," Claire said. "Trees were the best. No one could see you but you could see them."

Mary laughed, a loud hoot. She stopped abruptly, as if surprised by the noise she'd made, and put her hand over her mouth.

"I used to read Nancy Drew books up in my tree."

"Me, too."

"And *To Kill A Mockingbird.*"

Mary's attention shifted, and her eyes grew hazy.

"I think she's tired," Ellen whispered. "It's time for us to go."

After dropping Ellen at her house, Claire called Bea's office. "I'm glad I caught you. One of the Chestnut Street neighbors has seen young men hanging around the house. She called 911 but got a slow response. I told her to call me if she saw them again. If she does, I'll call you. Is that okay?"

"The person to call is Detective Lawrence Burnette. It's his case now, and I'm not at all sure Larry will want you to be that involved."

"What?"

"Mike took me off the case, Crawdad too."

"Why did he do that? Why didn't you tell me? Why—?" Claire bit her lip to stop the stream of questions.

"I just got out of the meeting, Claire. Informing you was on my list but not at the top." Bea paused. "I'm sorry. That was unfair. I haven't told you because I just found out myself. There's a lot going on that you don't know about. Look, I can't talk right now. Are you going to be home tonight?"

"All night. Come on over."

"I'll try." Bea sounded exhausted.

CHAPTER 26

Claire opened the door. "It's after nine. I'd given up on you."

"I told you that I'd try." Bea was impeccably dressed as usual. Today's pantsuit was a soft gold that set off her brown skin. But fatigue had drawn dark circles under her eyes and etched lines beside her mouth. "It's been a long day," she said, "and I'm starved. Do you have anything I could eat?"

"You're in luck. I bought one of those roasted chickens from the grocery and only ate half."

"You ate half a chicken? You're not pregnant are you?"

"The only thing I'd eaten all day was a cupcake. I was starved. And that's not funny."

"I wasn't joking. The other morning you picked at your breakfast, two bites of toast and you were done. I wondered then." Bea chuckled. "Don't look so shocked, Claire. You and Tony? That *is* where babies come from."

"Well, there's not one coming." She led the way into the kitchen and rummaged through the refrigerator. "I have the chicken, some pasta salad to go with it, and I can slice up a tomato. What do you want?"

"All of the above. I haven't eaten since lunch."

"It's not like you to miss a meal."

"I met Tishanna's grandmother after she got off work, and I just left her."

"I thought you were off the case?"

"I am, but I'd made the appointment before that happened."

"Why didn't Crawdad talk to her, like before?"

"Crawdad's not around. A lot has happened. Let me get some food in my stomach, and then we can talk."

Claire waited until Bea pushed her empty plate to the side then said, "I want to talk to Tishanna's grandmother, tell her how much I thought of Tishanna and how much I enjoyed spending time with her." After Tom died, people's reminiscences about him had comforted her, and she wanted to offer that small solace to this woman.

"In my experience, Grandma is more interested in talking about Dorcas than in talking about Tishanna. She warned me that Dorcas was still angry."

"Tishanna told me Dorcas was angry. I'd like to know why."

Bea leaned back in her chair. "Maybe you *should* go talk to Grandma. Her name is Margaret Tenier. You can trade ghost stories."

"When I bought that house, Jack told me it was haunted, and I laughed at him. I imagined him trading ghost stories with the workers—what you just said about me and Mrs. Tenier—but I'm not laughing anymore."

"Do you really believe your house is haunted?"

"I can't deny my own senses." Claire shrugged. "I've seen windows move up and down on their own, heard doors slam when no one touched them, and felt a cold hand on my arm. It's not just me. My workers are, to a man, unhappy inside that house. I've had to shame, bribe, and cajole them into staying on the job."

Bea folded her arms across her chest. "Grandma blames Dorcas for Tishanna's death. In her eyes, the gang members were mere instruments of Dorcas's revenge. She has little interest in helping us apprehend them and no memory of Tishanna ever mentioning any gang or anyone who threatened her. No memory of Tishanna's concerns, period."

"Did she say why Dorcas was seeking revenge?"

"No and I didn't ask. I just spent more than two hours trying to convince her to cooperate with our investigation, and all she wanted to discuss was Dorcas. I'm tired of the topic. Can we talk about more terrestrial matters?"

"Okay," Claire said. "Mike took you off the case. What happened and why?"

"He did, and he was right. I'd gotten too close."

When Claire started to protest, Bea held up her hand. "I have an analogy for you. Your husband was a doctor wasn't he?"

"He was and so was my father."

"Would either of them operate on you?"

"Neither was a surgeon, but I get your point. If you're emotionally involved..."

Bea finished the sentence. "...it can be hard to do what you need to do."

"I never got the impression that you were letting emotions interfere with your job."

"No one says I did. The risk was that I would."

"Mike took you off the case as a preventive measure?"

"There's nothing wrong with that, and he didn't demote me off the case, he promoted me off. I was Homicide's liaison to the gang task force, but he chaired it. Now I'm the chair. We're not just trying to apprehend kids who have committed crimes. We're trying to intervene before they step over the line. That cause is dear to me."

"I know."

"Mike did me a favor, two favors really. I'm lucky to be working for him."

"What happens to the investigation into Tishanna's murder while this new detective gets up to speed?"

"That's not an issue. Burnette has been working with us since the beginning, and we're moving toward closure. Regardless of what Mrs. Tenier believes, we know that gang is responsible. We found physical evidence at the scene, fingerprints that match evidence gathered at other scenes and DNA we've sent off to be analyzed. It's just a matter of time before we identify the specific individuals involved. Once we do, we should have sufficient evidence to charge and, if there is any justice, convict them."

"I guess congratulations are in order, and I'm sure you deserve to be promoted. Mike wouldn't put you in a job unless he thought you'd do it well." Claire could testify, from personal experience, that Mike never let emotion interfere with his work, but she let it slide. Bea wouldn't welcome the implied criticism of her boss.

"We're still counting on your help, Claire. Detective Burnette will be contacting you."

"I'll look at all his pictures, attend all his line-ups, anything I can do."

"He can be prickly," Bea said, "but he's a good investigator."

"What does that mean?"

"You shouldn't call him every time one of the neighbors sees a black kid walk up the street, nor should they. He'll contact you when he wants your help, which will be soon. We're widening the net, and he's assembling more mug shots for your viewing pleasure."

"I cooperate with him, but he won't cooperate with me? And I don't think you're being fair to Ellen Ledet. "

"Apprehending Tishanna's killers is our job, not yours."

"I'm not a policeman."

"No, and if you were, you'd be taken off the case." Bea's smile was wry. "Thank you for dinner. I'm ready to go home and get some much-needed sleep." On the way out, she hugged Claire. "We appreciate your cooperation. Burnette will be in touch."

After Bea left, Claire realized that she hadn't asked about Crawdad, but maybe she didn't need to. If Bea was too close to Tishanna, so was he. She understood the need for objectivity and distance. What she didn't understand was how or why Tishanna's grandmother could refuse to cooperate with the police.

Dorian rubbed against her legs, and she picked him up. "I bet you miss Tishanna. She really liked you." She scratched behind his ears as she'd taught Tishanna to do.

"That girl never had a chance. Her mother was a criminal, and her grandmother beat her; I locked her out of her refuge, and Dorcas didn't protect her. There's blame enough for all of us, but it was the gang that took her life."

I'm sorry, Tishanna. I'll do everything I can to see that they pay.

CHAPTER 27

Claire sat in her car, wondering why she'd felt impelled to come by here again. Nothing had changed. The house stood silent, its doors locked and windows boarded over. Bits of yellow crime-scene tape were still caught in the front hedge. If she were close enough, she'd see the stain on the front walk. She'd thought this house was a bargain, never imagining a cost measured in human life. *If I'd known then...*

Jack would have a motto to cover the situation, perhaps something about twenty-twenty hindsight, certainly nothing she wanted to hear. She put the car in gear. She was meeting him at Tony's house in ten minutes.

Yesterday had been spent getting her ducks in a row: electrician, plumber, and the permit office. Things had not gone smoothly for Jack, but he'd gotten the process started, and she'd been able to finish it. Barring a new disaster, work should be underway. She crossed her fingers and kept them crossed until she turned the corner and saw the line of pick-ups at the curb.

The plumber and his helper were under the house, laying pipe. Inside, Zach and Banjo were taking out a section of the new wall that had separated half bath and laundry. The electrician was adding a circuit for the whirlpool tub, and Jack was directing traffic.

"Thank you," she greeted him. He'd griped when she asked him to work on a Saturday morning but quickly agreed when she explained that she couldn't cover it because the police wanted her to look at more mug shots. "I see everyone but the carpenters."

"I told them to come this afternoon. No point in paying them to stand around waiting for demo to finish. Does Tony know what the speed-up is costing?"

"I talked to him before coming over," she said. "He's more than happy to pay time and a half for weekend work." He'd already okayed it once, but Jack, suddenly Mr. Financial Responsibility, had asked her to double check.

"You promised Zach and Banjo double time."

"I did. And that's okay, too. Tony remembers them from the first time they worked here. Matter of fact, he told me to tell them hello. And you, too."

Jack harrumphed. The concern and sympathy he'd shown right after Tony's accident had been short-lived. He was, once again, disapproving. Claire wished he could see beyond the trappings of wealth and celebrity to the individual behind them, but she'd learned that arguing with Jack about Tony's character was a waste of time. And there had been days when she'd thought he was right.

"I shouldn't be more than a couple hours," she said. "You can only look at mug shots for so long."

"I'll be here all day," he said.

A uniformed officer met Claire at the front desk. "Detective Burnette was called into a meeting. He asked me to get you set up. I'm Officer Norville."

"Nice to meet you." She followed him to a viewing room.

Looking at picture after picture numbed her brain even more than it strained her eyes. After forty-five minutes, she needed a break and some caffeine. On the way to the cafeteria, she spotted Mike, Bea, and a man she didn't know talking in the hall. They appeared intent on their conversation, so she decided not to interrupt.

When she returned with her coffee, Officer Norville handed her two new photos. "Do you recognize either of these individuals?"

These pictures were eight by ten glossies, not mug shots, and the subjects' eyes were closed. They could be sleeping children, except... "I think these are two of the kids who came into the house the night

Tishanna and I were there. I'm not absolutely positive. It was dark, and I was looking out a second-story window as they were coming up the front walk, but it looks like them."

She studied the pictures again. One had dark fuzz shading his upper lip, but the other had no trace of a beard. "They're dead aren't they?" She'd never before seen a picture of a corpse, but somehow, she knew.

"Captain Robinson would like to talk to you in his office. I'll escort you."

"Thank you, but I know where it is."

"He told me to escort you."

"Really?" *Does he think I'm going to run away?*

Claire entered Mike's office prepared to ask why the escort was necessary. Her annoyance evaporated when she saw the grim expression on his face. Bea and the man they'd been with in the hall were there, too. Bea gestured to the chair next to hers.

"I thought you were off the case." Claire kept her voice low.

"I'm involved through the gang task force." Bea leaned back in her seat and gestured from Claire to the man sitting on her other side. "Claire Marshall, Larry Burnette."

Claire extended her hand. "How do you do."

"Nice to meet you." Detective Burnette was medium height and stocky, with light brown skin, black hair and striking, almost opaque, blue-green eyes.

"Thank you for coming in, Claire," Mike said.

"Is this because I recognized the kids in the pictures? I told Officer Norville I couldn't be absolutely, testify-in-court certain."

"We know who they are. We picked them up running down the street after they'd entered your property. As I'm sure you remember, we had to let them go." Mike ran his fingers through his hair. "We picked them up again and put them in a lineup, but Miss Tenier didn't identify them."

Miss Tenier—it sounded so strange. Dead, Tishanna was getting the respect the world never accorded her in life. Claire leapt to her defense. "Tishanna was terrified, and with good cause."

Bea put a hand on her arm. Restraining or comforting, Claire wasn't sure, but she shut up and waited to hear what else Mike had to say.

"After she was killed, we looked for them, but they'd dropped out of sight until this morning when Houston sent these over." Mike pointed to pictures, identical to the ones Officer Norville had shown her. "They were looking for help identifying two John Does with bus tickets from New Orleans to Houston in their pockets. Detective Burnette recognized them. " He turned the pictures face down.

Claire wanted to ask when and how they died, but Bea's hand, still on her arm, was definitely restraining. Mike would tell her what he thought she needed to know.

"They were killed the day before yesterday," he said. "We've matched the fingerprints Houston sent to some found on Miss Tenier's belongings."

Claire had a thought that would not be suppressed. "You're not going to assume these two were the only ones responsible for her death and just close the case are you?"

"Claire," Bea interrupted.

"I'm sorry. Of course you're not. You're all working on the weekend, doing everything you can. I really do know that."

"No, we are not," Mike said. "The two dead juveniles were executed. We consider it possible, if not likely, that our interest in them led to their deaths." He leaned forward, his expression intent. "If the gang sees any member as a weak link, that person's life is in danger. If the gang sees any individual as a threat to them, that person's life is in danger."

"I'll be careful," Claire said. She remembered the young man at the bus stop. She'd be very careful. "I always have a mobile phone with me."

"You've mentioned a trip to Switzerland," Bea said. "Now would be a good time to take it."

"I thought you wanted me to stick around in case you arrested a suspect."

"That was yesterday," Detective Burnette said.

Claire felt her temper rising. "Actually, it was this morning."

"Houston has witnesses." Mike interrupted what could have become an argument. "A store video cam and physical evidence. Add that to what we already have, and this case is solid. We've identified several gang members, but until we're sure it's all of them, we won't be bringing anyone in."

"Because if you do and have to release them, the rest of the gang might kill them?" Claire looked from Mike to Bea and back to Mike, waiting for a denial, but none came.

"We haven't been able to infiltrate this gang," Bea said. "Unlike most, they don't advertise their affiliation. If the other kids know, they aren't talking."

"What about Crawdad's daughters? They went to the same school."

"After Tishanna was killed, Detective Crawford moved his family to a safe location. Today, he's joining them." Mike said. "Which should demonstrate how seriously we view the immediate threat."

"What about Tishanna's friend, CeeCee?"

"What about not telling us how to do our jobs?" Detective Burnette said.

Claire glared at him and felt Bea's hand tightening on her arm.

"Stay away from CeeCee," Bea said. "Don't try to track her down or even ask anyone about her—for your protection and for hers."

"Enough." Mike held up his hands. "We can't order you to leave town, Claire, but we can strongly advise it. You can identify at least one gang member, and they know it."

"I won't go into the office, and I'll stay away from Chestnut Street. Those are the two places they know to look for me. But I'm not leaving town."

CHAPTER 28

Margaret Tenier splayed tense hands on the tabletop. Claire glanced at them then looked away. Those hands had wielded the cane that left welts on Tishanna's legs. Those stubby fingers, now digging into the linen tablecloth, had left the bruises on Tishanna's arms. Mrs. Tenier cleared her throat.

"They said you'd contact me and I ought to talk to you."

Claire didn't have to ask who "they" were. Bea had told her that Tishanna's grandmother relied upon voodoo for guidance.

"Weren't for that," she continued. "I wouldn't be here."

Here was the Pontchartrain Hotel's dining room, a popular lunch spot for New Orleans socialites. The room was lovely with high ceilings, tall windows, and sparkling chandeliers. A mural featuring magnolia trees decorated the back wall and gave the room its name.

The Magnolia Room had been Mrs. Tenier's choice for a meeting place, an unexpected and expensive choice, but Claire had gone along. "Please accept my condolences," she said. "I'm very sorry about Tishanna."

"We buried her Saturday afternoon, and the State of Louisiana wouldn't let her mother out long enough to attend the funeral. Her only child, but she wasn't allowed." Mrs. Tenier retracted her hands.

"I didn't know or I would have come." The funeral had been delayed, no date set, until the police released Tishanna's body. Bea must have known. They'd seen each other Saturday morning. Why didn't she say anything?

"Just as well. You would have stuck out like a sore thumb. The police was bad enough." Margaret Tenier cackled. "Detective Washington in her fancy clothes stuck out bad as I do in this here restaurant."

She was right. Sideways glances had followed them to their table, but that wasn't what Claire wanted to discuss. "Detective Washington told me that she'd talked to you."

"Talked is right. She talked, but she didn't listen."

A waiter glided over to their table and introduced himself. "Can I bring you ladies a glass of wine before lunch?"

"Not for me," Claire said. "I'm working this afternoon, but please don't let me stop you, Mrs. Tenier."

"I'm working too." She adjusted her dress, a maid's uniform from a one of the downtown hotels. "I'll have the chicken salad plate and sweet tea."

"Of course, madam."

"I'd like the same thing, please, but unsweetened tea." Claire handed back her menu and turned to Mrs. Tenier. "Did Tishanna tell you about the astronomy book she was reading? She was learning to identify the stars and planets."

"She showed it to me."

"We were going back to the mall to look for a model of the solar system. I'm sorry that never happened."

"That's three times you've told me you're sorry. You needn't be sorry about Tishanna. Nothing that happened was your fault."

"I'm still sorry."

"Those boys who killed her are going to pay. That's not what happened with Dorcas. If you want to be sorry about something, be sorry about that."

"I didn't know Dorcas. I knew Tishanna, and I liked her."

"Dorcas knows you. You think you own that house, but Dorcas ain't going to leave until she gets justice. That's all she cares about. Not you, not me, not Tishanna. I warned Tishanna to stay away, but she didn't listen. I tried to explain the situation to Detective Washington, but she wouldn't listen neither. Now I'm telling you. The trouble ain't going to stop 'til Dorcas gets her justice."

"Tishanna said Dorcas was angry."

"Wouldn't you be angry if someone killed you and got away with it?"

Claire nodded. The conversation had gotten away from her, as Bea said it would. The women at the next table were practically falling out of their seats trying to catch every word, but if Mrs. Tenier had noticed, she didn't care. The arrival of the waiter with their lunch brought a merciful distraction.

Throughout the meal, Claire struggled to make small talk, the weather, traffic, the food. Only the latter engaged Tishanna's grandmother, who kept her eyes on her plate and her fork in motion. Mary Beaudry had eaten her cupcake with the same devout attention.

"Did Tishanna tell you about Mary Beaudry?" Claire said.

"She didn't tell me much about anything. Thirteen years old and she thought she knew it all." She forked up the last morsel and pushed her plate aside. "The chicken could have used a bit more seasoning, but it was pretty good."

"Would you like dessert?" Claire looked around for their waiter.

"Don't have time." She laid her napkin beside her plate. "Thank you for lunch. I got to go. If I'm late they dock my pay."

"I enjoyed meeting you."

"If you did or if you didn't makes no difference to me, but don't think for one minute that I didn't care about my granddaughter." She averted her face. "I loved that little girl. Her momma used to work here, washing dishes." Margaret Tenier departed, plowing through the room of ladies-who-lunch like a tugboat chugging through a flotilla of sailboats.

Claire watched her depart and signaled the waiter for her check. She felt as if she should to do something. But what? As far as she could tell there wasn't a thing she could do about anything. That was certainly how Bea saw things. Bea who hadn't listened. Who hadn't even told her about the funeral.

On the way home, Claire stopped by Tony's house. Work had stopped yesterday, Memorial Day, but today, things hummed. She went to see how the downstairs bathroom, the only difficult part of the conversion, was coming along. Workers were installing water resistant drywall where the new sink would go. The whirlpool bath had been framed in, wired and plumbed. The bath itself sat, boxed, in the middle of the kitchen.

"This is temporary, and he wants marble on the walls?" Jack had walked up behind her.

"I'm not at all sure he plans to change the bathroom back after he recovers."

"Installing the backer board, setting tiles, grouting, it takes time. You have to let one thing dry before you move on to the next."

Claire nodded. She knew this. She also knew that ordinary ceramic tile required the same process. Jack, once again, disapproved of just about everything to do with Tony. If it weren't the marble, he'd find something else.

"Did you bring me those files?" she said.

"They're in my truck."

"Walk out with me. I want to talk to you."

"You're not going to tell me Tony's changed his mind about something, are you? We're on a tight schedule. Plus we've got a lot in this job and no money from him yet. You know I pulled everyone off our other projects to fast-track this one, so no one else is paying us."

"We're fine, Jack. Tony is scheduled to fly back Tuesday—which is still a secret, so don't say anything—and I promise you, he's good for it." She waited until they were out of any worker's hearing. "I wanted to ask you about the house on Chestnut."

Jack scowled, and she knew what he was thinking: another project that wasn't providing any income.

"You told me that everyone knew it was haunted. What's the story? Why is it haunted?"

"Didn't the police tell you to stay away from that house?"

"I haven't been near it." Claire crossed her heart. "I'm just asking a question.'"

"I don't remember. It's been a while. You want me to ask around."

"No, don't do that. It will stir everyone up, and sometime soon, we have to go back there and finish."

"Good luck with that, Claire. The girl getting killed—wait a minute, it's coming back. Another girl was killed there, the maid or something. The people who lived there said she fell down the stairs, but the story is she was pushed."

"Then what?"

"Then nothing. That's why she haunts the house."

"I had lunch with Tishanna's grandmother today. That's pretty much what she said. I wondered if this was a story everyone knew—everyone but me."

"If you want more details, you ought try the old lady who lives down the street. Didn't you say she moved in right after World War II?" He wagged a warning finger. "Call her up. Don't go there."

"Not until the police say I can." She picked up the files. "Thanks for getting these. I'll be working at home for the rest of the afternoon. There are some invoices I can send out, including Tony's. You're right, we need to get the cash flowing."

After Claire prepared the invoices, she walked them over to the post office. On the way home, she stopped by a coffee shop and treated herself to a latte and a pecan sticky. Her promise to stay away from Chestnut Street left the option of talking to Ellen Ledet on the phone, but she decided not to. It would be a waste of time. Ellen might not have liked Charles Beaudry, but Lucinda had been her friend, and she was loyal to her memory. Mary's diaries might offer an insight.

That night, Claire went back through the diaries, this time focusing on Dorcas and looking for the anger that Tishanna's grandmother had described. She finished 1961 without finding any, although there was a consistent undercurrent of resentment, an us-against-them perspective that set Dorcas and Mary against Mary's parents and her big sister.

Dorcas may have been attempting to enlist Mary in her crusade, but there was no indication that she saw Mary as responsible for her death.

Anger first surfaced in January 1962 when Mary threw a glass of water at her father and blamed Dorcas. Once unleashed it quickly gathered momentum. By May, Mary believed herself to be literally possessed. She had become the instrument through which Dorcas expressed her anger. Her 1963 diary documented the cycles of breakdown and recovery that ended with her lobotomy.

Deciphering the entries that described Mary's descents into madness was slow going, tedious and uncertain both. The handwriting sprawled into near illegibility, words were written over others and on top of themselves, and whole sentences were scribbled through. Claire held the pages up to a light, trying to tell what words had been written first and what lay beneath scribbles so violent that some tore the paper.

What she found reinforced what Ellen Ledet had said about Mary's troubled relationship with her father. On one page, Mary had traced the word Daddy over and over. On several other pages, what looked like Daddy emerged from beneath scribbles. By the time Claire reached the end, her eyes hurt from squinting into light, and her shoulders ached from hunching over. And she'd read enough to know that Mary blamed her father for Dorcas's death.

Ellen's reticence now made sense, and so did her remarks that had seemed off-topic. If Charles Beaudry had been accused of killing Dorcas, the tense atmosphere created by the civil rights movement and the Birmingham bombing was not irrelevant.

Too edgy to consider bed, Claire fixed herself a cup of chamomile tea and carried it out onto the porch. Dorian jumped into her lap and nudged her, demanding attention. "Fine," she said, "you can be my rubber ducky."

A programmer she'd hired to digitize Authentic Restorations' records had introduced her to rubber duckies. When the code won't run, he'd said, talking things through with an inanimate object helped pinpoint the fallacy in the logic. She'd assured him that she often talked to her computer, sometimes harshly.

He'd laughed and said that didn't count. "Your rubber ducky has to be something you—at least the child you once were—can imagine talking to. A bath toy, a stuffed animal, a doll, whatever."

The next time a design problem was giving her fits, Claire had discussed it with Dorian and found a solution. Cats don't make ideal rubber duckies because they tend to wander off in mid-conversation, but if she kept scratching behind his ears, he'd hang in.

"Where does the truth lie, Dorian?"

No one had told her a complete story, but there was an internal consistency to the fragments. Did that prove Charles Beaudry had been responsible for Dorcas's death? Or did it mean only that Mary Beaudry had, while suffering multiple breakdowns, accused her father of killing Dorcas? Mary could have been over-reacting to the fact that her parents lied to her when Dorcas died. There had been nothing in the diary to substantiate anything bad about Charles Beaudry, except that he wasn't much fun to be around, an opinion Ellen Ledet also expressed.

Claire circled around what was known and what was supposed, and she came back to Dorcas. If you believed in Dorcas, the ghost, you believed that Charles Beaudry had been responsible for the death of Dorcas, the girl. Nothing else made sense. But what on earth was anyone supposed to do about it now? She was back to "What does Dorcas want?"

CHAPTER 29

Mr. Z's was a classic dive, a dimly lit room in the back of an old warehouse. Small wooden tables jockeyed for space on a cement floor bounded by an elevated stage on one end and a bar on the other. The location, four blocks off Esplanade in an iffy neighborhood where tourists didn't venture, added to the ambiance.

Claire would never have known this place existed if Mike who loved jazz hadn't brought her here. It was his favorite club, a hangout for local musicians and a destination for jazz greats looking to kick back after a gig at a bigger venue. On any given night, a famous musician might walk onstage with his instrument and turn the advertised trio into a surprise quartet.

Coming here alone could be considered foolhardy, but Claire was desperate. She hadn't left town, as Bea had suggested, but she'd barely left her house. Other than brief visits to project sites, her only excursions had been lunch with Tishanna's grandmother, a post office run, two client meetings, and a trip to the grocery store. She had worked from home, watched old movies at home, ate and slept at home, and become sick and tired of her own company at home.

"Welcome to Mr. Z's," The scruffy man at the door held out his hand. "There's a ten dollar cover tonight."

Ten dollars? Someone special must be playing.

She sat at an empty two-top near the back and looked around the

214

rapidly filling room. She needn't have worried about being conspicuous. Other people were here by themselves, and no one paid her any attention. Mr. Z's was not a place where singles went to meet singles and definitely not a hangout for teenaged thugs. The only person who talked to her was the waiter who took her order and asked if she wanted to run a tab.

The room was packed by the time the MC introduced the night's performers, a five-man combo made up of cousins from one of New Orleans' celebrated musical families. Each one was famous in his own right, and they rarely shared a stage, but tonight was a benefit for a local musician who had serious medical problems and no health insurance. The room erupted in cheers when the musicians filed on stage. It fell into reverent silence when they picked up their instruments. Coming here had been a brilliant idea.

Thank you, Mike.

Someone tapped her shoulder. She jumped, but it was only a man from another table asking her if she was using that extra chair. She shook her head, and he carried the chair off. Claire watched him and, through the opening he created, caught a glimpse of Mike Robinson at a table up by the stage. It looked as if Mike was also here alone. She couldn't tell for sure before the crowd closed back in, blocking her view.

When the musicians took a break, Claire asked the people at a neighboring table to save her place while she visited the ladies' room. There was the usual long line, and by the time she returned to her table, the lights were dimming. Before sitting down, she looked over the heads of the crowd. Mike was still there, and no one sat across from him. She cut through the tables.

"Hi. Isn't the music fantastic?"

"Claire, how are you?" The smile that lit his face when he recognized her faded. "I thought Tony wasn't coming back for another two weeks."

"I'm here by myself."

"As am I. Please join me."

"I left my drink."

"I'll buy you a fresh one. Sit down, the show's about to resume."

"Thank you." Claire waved good-bye to the people holding her table.

"What are you drinking?"

"Strawberry Abita."

"Strawberry beer? Really, Claire?" He signaled a waiter.

"The taste of springtime." She smiled. "Don't knock it if you haven't tried it."

The musicians returned, and they both turned their attention to the stage. For this set, the combo played a long improvisation, sliding in and out and around the melody, one instrument after another taking the lead. When they finished, the audience clapped and stomped their feet. Someone in the back yelled, "Amen, brother, amen."

The saxophone player wiped the sweat from his face "This is supposed to be the end, but we're having too much fun to quit. Give us a ten-minute break, and we'll be back for one more short set."

Mike glanced at his watch. "It's after midnight. Are you good for more?"

"Absolutely. I was suffering acute cabin fever, and this is the perfect cure."

An elderly man returned with the five original musicians, two of whom helped him to the piano. He looked to be a hundred years old, but he hit the keyboard with the vigor of a young man. Until now, they'd played a Dixieland-tinged modern jazz. This final set was gospel. It ended with a transcendent rendition of "Amazing Grace," a vocal solo accompanied only by the piano played with the delicacy of a butterfly's kiss.

"That was beautiful." Claire said. "I feel so lucky. Coming here tonight was just a whim, and to witness this."

"You mean you weren't following me?" Mike said, and they both laughed.

The waiter brought Mike's check, and Claire reached for her wallet. "I started out in the back and changed tables," she said. "I owe you for an oyster poor boy and two beers."

"No problem, baby. The gentleman paid."

"You shouldn't have, Mike, but thank you."

"You're more than welcome. You didn't drive here by yourself did you?"

"No, I took a cab."

"In that case, allow me to drive you home. My car's around the corner."

The crowd dispersed quickly, the street was dark, and rain threatened. Claire was happy to be in Mike's car and not standing alone on the sidewalk, waiting for a cab.

"I never expected to hear gospel in a jazz club," she said.

"Gospel is the common denominator. Have you ever heard of the Million Dollar Quartet?" When she shook her head, he said, "Back in 1956, when they were just beginning their careers, Elvis Presley, Jerry Lee Lewis, Johnny Cash, and Carl Perkins bumped into each other at Sun Studios in Memphis. It was pure happenstance, and they decided to make a recording, right then and there. They sang bits of this and that, some country and some rock, but the songs they all knew—beginning to end and every verse—were gospel."

"That's a neat story."

"I'm afraid the story is better than the music. I have a copy, but..."

"I knew you were a jazz fan. It seems your musical tastes are broader."

"Gospel might be my favorite. When it's good, there's nothing better—as you just heard. This Jazz Fest, I spent more time in the Gospel Tent than at any other venue."

"You went to Jazz Fest?" Surprise made her laugh. "Bea told me the police dread Jazz Fest."

"Traffic cops, yes, but not this policeman. Have you ever been? No? Next year, I'll take you. It's the last weekend in April and the first in May."

Next year? By then Tony would have recovered, he'd be back to racing, the season would have begun, and she'd be alone again. "Be careful what you promise," she said. "I might hold you to it."

They were almost to her house. Claire took a deep breath and raised the topic both had avoided. "I've been taking your advice, but I have to go back to the office sooner or later. We've stopped work on the Chestnut Street house, but that's got to change."

"Another week or two, Claire. This gang is not going to get away with murder."

"Tishanna's grandmother said the same thing. She's sure you'll catch them."

"When did you talk to her?"

Claire glanced over. Mike's eyes were on the road, and his expression gave nothing away. It had been a nice evening, but he was back to being a homicide detective. "Tuesday," she said. "I invited her to lunch because I wanted a chance to express my condolences."

He stopped for a yellow light most people would have run. "I hope you're not playing detective."

"I'm not." She thought a moment. "Take that back. I am, but it's a decades old crime. The killer got away with it, and he's long dead. Did Bea tell you about Dorcas?"

"Is this your ghost?"

"Mrs. Tenier says the trouble won't stop until Dorcas is mollified."

"She told Bea the same thing."

"I know—to Bea's frustration. Unlike Bea, I'm paying attention. I own the house that Dorcas haunts, and I'd like her to leave so that I can sell it."

"You're taking this ghost seriously?" He chuckled. "Claire, I'm surprised at you."

"I bought that house at auction for next to nothing because no one else wanted it. The rest of the world knew about Dorcas. I didn't. Over the years, she's caused a lot of grief. Mary Beaudry, the daughter of the man probably responsible for Dorcas's death, had a series of breakdowns. She believed that Dorcas possessed her. Tishanna believed that Dorcas protected her, and she did. Twice that I witnessed and, according to Tishanna, three times. But then she didn't." A stab of pain made her pause.

"Claire, you are in no way responsible for Tishanna's death."

"Tishanna talked about Dorcas and Mary as if they were her friends, but she was horrified by what Dorcas did to Mary. She told Bea that she'd seen the gang kill a man because she didn't want his spirit doing the same thing to her." The pain grew, squeezing out the joy the music had brought. She looked at Mike and saw genuine concern.

"I didn't realize how hard this has been on you," he said.

"And now you think I'm falling apart? Like after Tom died?" She put her hand on his arm. "Don't worry about me. I'm sad about Tishanna but otherwise fine."

"I wish you'd take advice from people who care about you. You need to get away. Visit your mother. Take a cruise. Go to Switzerland."

"Can I tell you something in absolute confidence?" He nodded and she said, "Tony's flying back Tuesday."

"Why is that a secret?"

"The press said he sustained a broken leg, which is true and what they were told, but it was a very bad break. He's in a wheelchair, and he doesn't want people to see him as an invalid. He needs to recuperate in privacy, but if the media finds out he's here..." She shrugged. "You know."

Mike's surprise had morphed into concern. "I suggest you bring him up to date on the situation. Pass on my suggestion that he arrange protection for both of you until we have that gang in custody. Celebrities often employ bodyguards. I'd be amazed if he hasn't."

"I'll talk to him," Claire promised. Mike was right, of course, but she'd have to approach the topic carefully. Tony was prickly about the limitations his injury imposed.

"You could call him when you get home. It's morning in Italy."

Claire shook her head. If she called Tony now, he'd ask what she was doing up in the wee small hours, and she'd have to tell him she'd been with Mike. Even if she explained that they'd just bumped into each other, it wouldn't go over well.

"A little lead time wouldn't hurt," Mike said.

"I'll call him tomorrow. And please don't say anything about him coming back early. I haven't even told Bea."

CHAPTER 30

D-day. Claire wandered from room to room. Everything was quiet now, quiet and clean. You'd never know that the last three days had seen a flurry of activity so intense it approached chaos. Jack, the crews, and the subs—bless them all—had stepped up and done whatever needed to be done.

The den had been converted into a downstairs bedroom and outfitted with a hospital bed. A custom-made rubber mat created a safe path across the kitchen's potentially treacherous tile floor to the expanded bathroom with its sunken whirlpool tub and accessible shower. The dining table had been shoved to the side, making room for a sofa and TV set moved in from the den, and the rest of the downstairs furniture had been put in storage. The double front parlors, dotted with exercise machines, looked like an exceptionally elegant gym.

Tony's house was ready for a man in a wheelchair, and he was on his way, flying non-stop from Geneva to New Orleans via private jet. His plane should be on the ground by now. Claire sat on an exercise machine with a view out the front windows and waited.

Somewhere outside, Stephanie was watching. Tony's response when she passed on Mike's suggestion about arranging protection had surprised her. She'd been braced for uncomfortable questions like, "Why did it take you so long to tell me what was really going on?" But all he'd asked was if she'd prefer a man or a woman. Either could be arranged. The only hint of reproach came in his insistence that her protection begin immediately.

If he'd known what was going on, it would have begun long ago.

She wished she'd gone to the airport to meet him, but the security agency had argued strenuously against it. The fewer people involved, the less chance anyone would notice Tony's arrival. More to the point, wasn't she the source of danger? Anything that linked him to her put him at risk. Is that what she wanted? Cowed, she'd agreed to wait at his house.

The whole bodyguard situation made Claire uncomfortable. She tried to imagine living in a world where hiring protection was commonplace, a deductible business expense, according to Tony.

Light flashed on the street. Three sets of headlights approached. The first car continued past and parked in front of the house next door, the middle one turned into the driveway, and the third stopped short of it. A man got out of the car in the driveway and pulled a wheelchair out of the trunk. Another man climbed out of the back seat and helped Tony from the passenger seat to the wheelchair.

Claire ran to the front door but stopped short. If she could touch the doorknob, she would turn it, and they'd told her to stay out of sight until everyone was inside. Holding her breath, she watched the man push the wheelchair up the ramp her carpenters had installed over the front steps.

Finally, the front door opened. Tony's tan had faded, and beneath the pallor he was gray. His face was thinner; he'd lost weight. Still, the sight of him filled her with joy.

"Tony."

"Hello sweetheart."

An IV stent protruded from his right hand. She looked at it, inquiring.

"It's just for the trip. It comes out tomorrow." He reached for her with his other hand, and when she leaned down to hug him, turned his face for a kiss.

"I've missed you." They spoke in unison.

"How was the trip?" She wanted to tell him that he looked tired and needed rest, that she would take care of him, that she loved him. "I'm glad you didn't have to change planes in Atlanta."

"They've taken good care of me all the way." He held her close with his good arm.

"No hanky-panky." It was the man behind the wheelchair. "My patient has had a long day, it's past midnight where he came from, and he's tired. Where is his bed?"

Claire led them to the ex-den. "In here," she said. "The bathroom is on the other side of the kitchen."

"He'd be better off if you put the bed closer to the bathroom. By the way, my name is Alexander. I'm his nurse. And you are?"

"Claire." She started to put her hand out but stopped when Alexander kept both of his on the wheelchair. "This is what I thought you wanted, but I can have people in tomorrow to change things around."

"I'm the one who wanted it this way. More privacy." Tony sent her a quick smile. "How about leaving us alone, Alexander."

"No hanky panky," Alexander repeated before walking out without closing the door.

Claire pulled it shut and danced a little hokey pokey over to Tony. "No no hanky panky," she sang. She kissed him again. "I'm so glad to see you, but you have to be exhausted. Don't you want to go to bed?"

"Is that an invitation?"

"A standing invitation. I'll be here tomorrow and the next day and the next day and as long as you want."

"Push my wheelchair over to the bed, and I'll show you what I've learned in rehab."

Tony stood up then sat on the bed and swung his legs around. "Come lie next to me. I still have one good side." He patted the bed on his left.

She snuggled beside him and soaked up the sensations, his warmth, his heart beating under her cheek, his chest rising and falling with each breath, his scent. His breathing slowed and his arm, which had been tight around her, relaxed. Claire disentangled herself and moved to the chair by the bed. She sat quietly, watching him sleep, until the nurse opened the door and beckoned to her.

"Now you can show me around," he said. "Where are we sleeping?"

"Excuse me?"

"That came out wrong, didn't it? Well, don't worry; you're not my type. Tony, on the other hand." He smacked his lips. "Too bad he likes women. W O M E N as in more than one. But I'm sure you don't need me to tell you that."

"How long will you be here?" *And what is your problem, Alexander?*

"Two of us are doing a 24 hour on, 24 hour off schedule for the rest of the week, at which point the doctor will reassess. Meanwhile, where are we sleeping?"

"There are two bedrooms upstairs. I'm using one; you and your colleague can take turns in the other. It has twin beds. The call button beside Tony's bed is set up to ring in both upstairs rooms."

"Both?" He raised his eyebrows.

"Both." Claire looked him in the eye. "The house was renovated and barely lived in before Tony went back to Europe. We just finished making it accessible. There may be glitches that haven't been discovered yet. If you find any, let me know, and I'll have them fixed."

"Yes, ma'am," he said with exaggerated courtesy.

"Will you be doing any cooking?"

"Me?" Alexander pressed both hands to his chest and assumed a look of horror. "I'm a registered nurse. A home health aide will come in mornings to tidy up, do laundry, and cook the day's meals. Under my supervision."

The question had not been intended as an insult, and Claire saw no reason to apologize. She showed Alexander around the house and when the tour was over said, "I'm going to take a book into Tony's room and read for a while before I go to bed." *And I dare you to tell me I can't.*

"We haven't gotten off on the wrong foot, have we?" Alexander said. "We don't want you getting us fired."

"Good night." If he were working for her, he would have been fired an hour ago.

Some time later Claire woke. The book lay on the floor beside her chair, and the sky outside was lightening. Just as she wondered what had wakened her, Tony groaned. He was either having a nightmare or he was in pain. She touched his shoulder. "Tony, wake up. It's okay."

He opened his eyes then squeezed them shut. His breathing was ragged. "My leg."

She pressed the call button. "The nurse is coming." *Quickly, I hope.* She wiped the sweat from his face.

"We've got it." Alexander brushed her aside and opened a bag he'd brought with him. "We were afraid this would happen." He picked up Tony's wrist and injected the IV stent. "You overdid it yesterday, but we'll fix you right up. Count backwards from twenty. Come on, Tony, twenty, nineteen, eighteen, seventeen... Before you know it, that leg is going to stop bothering you. Fourteen, thirteen..."

Tony's breathing became regular, his face relaxed, his eyes closed and stayed closed.

Claire kissed her fingertips then laid them gently on his forehead. "That was fast."

"Intravenous morphine, nothing better for pain."

"I wasn't talking about the morphine. You must have flown down the stairs. But what if he was having a nightmare?"

"We can tell the difference." Alexander disabled the syringe and disposed of it in a medical waste bag. He looked at her through narrowed eyes. "You were here before me."

"I rang the bell." She explained although it was none of his business. "I'd nodded off in the chair. Tony's moans woke me. Unless he objects, I'm going to move my bed into this room."

"I hope we're not seeing ourselves as Florence Nightingale."

Claire took a deep breath. *Why are you being such a jerk?* "My husband was a doctor. I know enough to know better."

"Married to a doctor, my dear, no wonder you rubbed us the wrong way."

"You know what really annoys me?" she said. "People who refer to themselves in the plural." She assumed an expression of wide-eyed innocence. "Unless they're suffering from multiple personality disorder."

CHAPTER 31

Their odd little household quickly settled into a routine. Lucy, the home health aide, arrived by eight and made breakfast while the nurse helped Tony shower and get dressed. After breakfast, Lucy tidied up. Claire took a shower, and Tony read the paper and talked by phone to his business manager, one of the few people who knew he was in New Orleans. The arrival of his physical therapist, at ten, was the signal for Claire to leave for work.

Ever-present bodyguards kept an eye on the house. When Claire left, one went with her. If the protective services agency had its way, she'd never go anywhere. In a compromise, she stayed away from her home and her office and, of course, the house on Chestnut Street. She met Jack on work sites, clients at restaurants, and city officials in their offices. She brought files back to the house and worked at the dining room table until she heard Lucy rattling around in the kitchen making dinner.

Claire had moved her bed into Tony's room, but there'd been no more nighttime wakening. Nor had there been any exchanges of affection. After a day devoted to exercise and therapy, Tony was too tired for anything but halfhearted dinner table conversation and an early bedtime. The nurse helped him prepare for bed, and Claire retreated to the now empty upstairs bedroom, where she read until she was tired enough to go downstairs and sleep. The routine was okay for weekdays, but Claire dreaded the weekend.

Friday at breakfast, she poked at the omelet Lucy had prepared, and wondered what she would do with herself while Tony was exercising or resting or working with his therapists. There was nowhere she needed to go, nothing she needed to do, and hanging around Tony's house, getting in the way of the people there to help him recover, would drive her crazy. To make it worse, Alexander was on duty all weekend. Gloria, the other nurse, was as pleasant as he was nasty, but she would be attending a family wedding in Texas.

Claire had mentioned Alexander's hostile attitude to Gloria, who said he was going through a rough time in his personal life. "Please be tolerant, he's a good nurse and underneath a good person." Claire wasn't convinced about either, but she said nothing more to Gloria and nothing at all to Tony.

She watched him across the table. He was reading the morning paper and deeply engrossed in an article about the Canadian Grand Prix. Qualifying runs began today.

"Is it hard, missing the race?" she said.

He looked up. "I missed Barcelona two weeks ago, and in three weeks, I'll miss France. After that there's England then Germany, Hungary, Belgium. I can't spend the next six months feeling sorry for myself every time there's a race."

"No, that wouldn't be your style." Their eyes met. His were stormy gray. "What?" she said.

"Wedinger is still in a coma."

"I'm sorry." She rested her hand on his. "I hope there are no serious accidents this race."

"The new rules will be in effect." His eyes drifted back to the article.

"Time for me to hit the shower." She stood, dropped a kiss on his head, and left him to his newspaper. She had two meetings this morning, and a potential client wanted her to look at a house he was considering this afternoon. The busy day was good for business and better for her mental health.

Claire was eating lunch alone at an Uptown restaurant when Detective Burnette called. "Good news," he said. "We arrested several gang members last night and this morning. We think we have them all."

"All right. Congratulations."

"How soon can you come down and look at a line-up?"

"I have two more bites of my sandwich, and it will take me fifteen minutes to drive to headquarters."

"One-thirty would be good. They'll be expecting you at the front desk."

"I'll be there."

Freedom. No more bodyguards. No more worries about bringing danger to Tony's doorstep. She could go to her office, go home, go wherever she wanted. If she left right now, she had time to pick Dorian up from the kennel and bring him home before driving downtown. The poor cat had never been kenneled before, but she hadn't wanted to hire a cat sitter—not when the police thought the gang might be watching her house. She called Tony and got Lucy, who said he was with the occupational therapist. Rather than interrupt, she left a message.

She signaled the waiter for her check and, when he brought it, gave him a twenty. "Keep the change."

"Thank you very much."

"You're very welcome." She floated out the door and waved to Stephanie.

Detective Burnette was waiting at the front desk when she arrived. He explained how the line-ups would work. "We're going to have you look at four groups of individuals," he said. "I want you to tell me if anyone looks familiar, and when and where you've seen them before."

He was in the second group. His expression as he stared straight ahead showed the same threatening insolence he'd displayed when watching her office. She felt his eyes boring into her. Maybe he couldn't see her through the one-way glass, but he knew she was there.

"The second man from the right," she said. "I've seen him on Chestnut Street twice and once across the street from my office. He led the charge the night the gang came after Tishanna."

"Anyone else?" Detective Burnette said.

She shook her head. "Not yet."

"You're halfway there. We have two more groups for you to look at."

Claire wasn't able to identify anyone else. "I'm sorry," she said when the last group walked out. "The only individual I saw well enough to identify positively is that one."

He held up his hand. "You said exactly what we were hoping you'd say. Let's go talk to Detective Washington."

"She did great," He announced as they walked into Bea's office. "One positive ID, the one we needed, no false positives and no maybes."

"Told you." Bea held out a package of cookies. "Hungry? Macadamia nut white chocolate. I'm celebrating."

"Thank you," Claire took one and sat down. "I'm celebrating too."

"What the hay?" Detective Burnette grabbed a cookie. "I've got another witness coming in momentarily. This is lunch."

"In that case," Bea said, "take two."

"Thanks." He grabbed another and backed toward the door. "I'll be in touch." He half saluted and was gone.

"He's in a better mood than last time," Claire said. "He was actually pleasant."

"Deep down, he's not really a jerk."

"What did he mean by 'no false positives'?"

"Cooperative witnesses who are emotionally invested in a case, as you are in this one, can be unreliable. They're so anxious to help us identify the criminals that they talk themselves into recognizing people they've never seen before. I knew you wouldn't do that."

"Falsely accuse someone?"

"Exactly." Bea helped herself to the last cookie. "I told Larry you'd been on the wrong end of that stick. Do you have to get back to work or can you join me for lunch? I'm weak from hunger."

"I have plenty of time, but I've eaten, and you just polished off a bag of cookies." Claire pointed to the now empty package.

"A mere appetizer, and I shared them." Bea pushed back from the desk. "Why don't you come along and keep me company? My current favorite is an Italian restaurant on the ground floor of the Carroll Building. It's five or six blocks. Are you up for a brisk walk?"

"Fresh air, sunshine—I'm up for anything that gets me out." Bea gave her a sharp look, and she said, "I'll tell you about it when we get to the restaurant. You eat and I'll whine."

The restaurant was empty except for a bartender putting up clean glasses and two waiters chatting by the back wall. One of the waiters looked up.

"Can I help you ladies?"

"Can you feed me?" Bea said. "I know lunch is over, but I'll never make it to dinner."

"Sure, baby. Come on in. There's some of the lunch special left. You like andouille chicken lasagna?"

"I'll take it, and my friend wants a glass of wine."

"That's not the whine I meant."

"I know." Bea grinned. "But you're not going to just sit there and watch me eat."

"No, but I have to be awake all afternoon. I'll have a cappuccino."

The waiter disappeared into the kitchen, and Bea said, "The gang's in jail, Tony will be here soon, so why are you whining?"

"Tony's been here all week. Don't tell anyone. His presence is a secret."

Bea raised her eyebrows. "How's he doing?"

"He's recovering, but it's a long road, and he's still in a wheelchair, which is why he's in hiding. Wheelchair says invalid, and he thinks that would undermine his public image."

"What about the showing of Jim Burke's art? Isn't that coming up soon?"

"Tony is determined to walk in on crutches—no wheelchair and no walker. The physical therapist says he has maybe a twenty percent chance of making it. She underestimates him."

"I'm waiting for the whine."

"Ever since Tony got back, I've felt like the princess in the tower. I told him about the gang, and he hired bodyguards."

"You're unhappy because Tony wants to protect you? Am I missing something?"

"Tony wants to protect me. The bodyguards want to protect Tony. He's the client, and the company has worked for him before. From their perspective, I'm someone who has wandered on stage and is making their job more difficult. If they'd had their way, I'd never leave my room.

"I'm exaggerating, but they actually suggested I not leave the house because the people who are after me might follow me back."

"We've arrested the gang," Bea said. "It's over."

"It would be if it were really about me, but it's not. After Larry Burnette called, I told Stephanie, my minder, that I didn't need her anymore. She disagreed. Protecting Tony means they have to keep an eye on me too. She's probably in here, lurking under a table." Claire shaded her eyes and pretended to search the restaurant. "Everything at Tony's house is organized around his recovery, as it should be. He has nurses and therapists in every day. They have jobs to do. I don't.

"I feel like a fifth wheel. One of the nurses gives me a hard time every chance he gets, and if he keeps it up, I'm going to become a squeaky fifth wheel."

"Have you discussed this with Tony?"

Claire shook her head. "I can't. Look at what's happened to him. This racing season has been pure hell, two drivers dead and another still in a coma. They were his friends. He was badly injured in an accident that was totally not his fault, but he's not whining. I know he's unhappy. Tony's a joker, and there haven't been any jokes, but he's not complaining either."

The waiter set a cream-covered mound of pasta, chicken and sausage in front of Bea. "*Buon appetito.*" He returned a minute later with a cup of cappuccino, its saucer heaped with biscotti. "I gave you extra." He put the coffee down. "Now wipe that frown off your pretty face."

"Thank you." Claire forced a smile, and he left satisfied.

"Back to Tony," Bea said. "He would have learned early not to complain. You met his mother. Imagine how she responded when little Tony came crying to her."

Claire didn't have to imagine. Tony had told her that when a horse he was riding too fast stumbled and fell on him, Geneviève had been furious with him for endangering the horse, which wasn't injured. She'd waited hours to be sure the horse was okay before taking Tony to the hospital, where the doctors discovered that he'd broken his leg. That was the break that hadn't healed properly.

"This isn't the first time you've mentioned Geneviève's influence. Last time it was a warning. This time it's an excuse?" Claire stood two biscotti on end and laid a third across the top. "Stonehenge," she said.

"An explanation, not an excuse." Bea watched Stonehenge totter and fall. "You're too old to be playing with your food."

"And too old to be whining, but thank you for listening. How are things on the gang task force?"

Between bites, Bea said that arresting this particular gang was a big step in the right direction. "Most muggers are thieves. Give them your wallet, and they run away. These kids wanted to make sure no victim would ever testify against them. 'Dead men tell no tales' was their motto. They're responsible for at least five homicides in addition to Tishanna. If their strategy had worked, other gangs would have started emulating them, and we would have been up to our necks in homicides. Worse than it is now. Larry Burnette isn't big on saying thank you, but you better believe that he and I are both grateful for your help, as is Mike."

"I didn't do much."

"Don't sell yourself short. You showed courage and compassion. You almost saved Tishanna." Bea reached a hand across the table. "I know that still hurts."

"I talked to her grandmother—you know that. She says the trouble will continue until Dorcas gets justice."

"Please." Bea rolled her eyes.

"No, listen. She says Dorcas was murdered and her killer got away with it. I told you about Mary Beaudry's diaries. They say the same thing and blame her father."

"Mike told me you were poking around in an old mystery." A grin spread across Bea's face. "I believe he called you incorrigible."

"Tishanna read Mary's diaries, too. She told you about the mugging because she didn't want the man in the alley doing her like Dorcas did Mary. That's a direct quote."

"Okay." Bea sighed. "For the sake of argument, I'll go along with your ghost story. Now tell me, how do you propose to provide Dorcas with justice?"

"I don't know."

CHAPTER 32

Claire put the bags on the kitchen counter. "I brought take-out Italian, enough for everybody. You haven't started dinner yet have you?"

Lucy shook her head, no. "I've been upstairs, changing the linens. Gloria left early."

"Alexander's here?" Claire's heart sank. There went her pleasant evening. "I thought he was off until tomorrow morning."

"He's in with Tony."

"Can you put the food in the refrigerator, please? I have to run. Please tell Tony I'll be back by six."

She was meeting a potential client at a house he was thinking about buying. She'd recognized the address, a neighborhood developed during the 1920s, but this house was a 1950's ranch built on what had been the side yard of the older house next door. The client had described it as Greek revival. *Because there are white columns on the front porch? What is he thinking?*

Ten minutes later, she had her answer. He wanted to demo the ranch and build a new house. "Six thousand square feet," he said, "five bedrooms, six and a half baths, a laundry upstairs and one downstairs. I've sketched out rough plans; you can finalize them."

Claire looked askance at his sketch of a neoclassical mansion that would be horribly out of scale in this neighborhood. "Authentic Restorations is a small company," she said. "We do renovations, not new construction."

"I know. I was thinking this would be an opportunity for you to move up. If you give me a good price, we could do business."

"Thank you but no. This project is not for us," she said.

He departed in a huff, and Claire sat in her car, staring at the house. If you got rid of those pseudo Greek columns and replaced the elaborate front door, you'd have a nice example of mid-century modern architecture. Ranch houses were out of fashion, but no one could deny that they were comfortable and well designed for modern living. On a whim, she called the broker listed on the for sale sign.

"You're at the house?" he said. "I'm two minutes away and can be there in five."

"I'm really just curious." Claire explained why she was there. "I hope I haven't killed your sale."

"I can guess who you talked to, and don't worry about it. He put in a lowball offer that the seller is refusing to counter. See you in five minutes."

Inside, the house was exactly what she'd expected—a master bed and bath plus two smaller bedrooms and another full bath to the right, a large living room straight ahead, dining room and kitchen to the left. If there were a basement, it would have been transformed into a rec room with knotty pine paneling, but houses in New Orleans didn't have basements.

"This is a nice house," she said.

"At a very good price."

"There's another house I have to sell first."

"The seller might entertain an offer with a contingency clause."

She shook her head. "It wouldn't be fair. The other house has problems." *Starting with a ghost named Dorcas.* "But if this house is still on the market when I get rid of that one, I'll be in touch." She gave him her card and thanked him for his time.

What, she wondered, had inspired her to contact the realtor. Was she that bored? Was she halfway serious about this house? Or was she looking for something, anything, to get her out of Tony's house? And what was she going to do with herself now?

After a moment's thought, she pulled out her phone and called Dr. Felix Rubio, Mary Beaudry's psychiatrist. They'd been playing phone tag for several days. This time he answered.

"Ms. Marshall, I'm sorry I've been difficult to reach. One of our staff is on maternity leave, and I've been seeing her clients as well as mine."

"I've been difficult to reach too," Claire said. "Did you get my message about Mary Beaudry's diaries?"

"Yes. You say they document her decline."

"Document and demonstrate." She described the contents. "Do you think I should give them back to Mary? They are hers, but reading them could upset her."

"I've talked to Mary once a week for the last two years, but we've never identified the source of her illness. Nor has she ever mentioned anyone named Dorcas. If, as you say, she documented the onset of her psychosis in these diaries, reading them may help her, and me, unravel the mystery. Of course, I'd like to see them first."

"What if Mary was telling the truth?" Claire said. "What if her father really was responsible for Dorcas's death?"

"I think it's more likely that she believed herself to be responsible." Dr. Rubio paused and Claire heard papers rustling. "The extreme reactions described in her records were triggered by an emotion beyond Mary's capacity to control. Guilt has enormous destructive power."

"Dorcas accused Mary of not wanting to remember what happened, not of being responsible for it. Her anger was directed toward Mary's father."

"Ms. Marshall, you're speaking as if you believe Dorcas's ghost spoke to Mary. I assure you that the voice came from Mary's subconscious. What this voice said was intolerable, and so Mary ascribed it to someone else."

"I could drop the diaries off this afternoon if you'd like." Claire said. Bringing up poltergeists and saying that she had firsthand experience of Dorcas would do nothing but undermine her credibility. Let Dr. Rubio read the diaries for himself.

"My office is in Slidell," he said. "Where are you?"

"New Orleans, but it's no problem. I'd enjoy the drive, and I have the time."

"It's Friday. Rush hour can jam up the causeway."

"I wouldn't mind a drive, and I can leave as soon as we hang up." She was already sitting in her car. She jotted down his office address and said she'd be there within the hour.

Traffic had thickened in town but thinned as she approached Lake Pontchartrain. Just short of the causeway, she pulled over and put Felicia's top down. She stayed in the right lane, close to the sun-sparkled water. Her tires hummed on the pavement, the wind whipped her hair, and she could almost smell the fish that were attracting a cluster of boats off to her right. All too soon, she reached the other side.

Dr. Rubio stacked the diaries on his desk. "Nineteen sixty-one through sixty-three. More than thirty years ago, but only yesterday for Mary, if those are the memories causing her such pain. Thank you for bringing them to me."

"Dorcas died in 1953," Claire said.

"Ah, the ghost." Dr. Rubio shook his head. "Blaming mental illness on external forces has a long history and, unfortunately, a persistence in popular culture. Modern psychiatry has to acknowledge a debt to shamans and witch doctors. We still use hypnosis and psychotropic drugs, but we've left the old superstitions behind. We no longer attribute disease to malevolent possession, mutter incantations over the mentally ill, or trephine skulls to release evil spirits."

"And you no longer perform lobotomies to calm disturbed individuals," Claire interrupted the lecture. "But it's not been that long, has it?"

"No, it hasn't, and in parts of today's world, mental illness is still diagnosed as demonic possession and women are still executed as witches. In New Orleans, clergy still perform exorcisms, and I'm sure you're aware that voodoo is a living religion."

"Mary Beaudry," Claire said.

"You're right, I digress. I sense your outrage on Mary's behalf, Ms. Marshall, and I share it. The impacts of her lobotomy limit her, but I don't want them to limit our attempts to help her enjoy the life she is still capable of living."

"I have other books that belonged to Mary. *To Kill A Mockingbird*, *Marjorie Morningstar*, and several Nancy Drew mysteries. They were hidden on a secret shelf in the mantel of what was her bedroom. You'll find them mentioned in her diary."

"I'm quite sure Mary lacks the power of concentration required to read a novel. You might consider reading to her on your next visit. First, however, let me see what's in these diaries."

"I didn't realize..." Claire wanted to cry for the girl who had loved to read but no longer could. She stood up. "I'd better be going. I'm supposed to be back in town by six."

"You should be in plenty of time, and you'll be going against the flow of traffic." Dr. Rubio walked with her to the door. "I'll read those diaries over the weekend and be in touch."

Rather than drive straight to Tony's, Claire stopped by the old house to pick up Mary's books. Chestnut Street was quiet. You'd never suspect that just three weeks ago, a girl was brutally murdered here. Today, her killers were in jail, but Claire felt no sense of closure. Tishanna's grandmother wouldn't either. She'd said the trouble would continue until Dorcas got justice.

Tishanna is dead, and Mary is badly damaged. What kind of justice is that?

Behind its tall hedge, the house looked forlorn, the first floor windows boarded over and the upstairs windows staring like empty eyes. Weeds had already retaken the front yard and encroached upon the driveway. Claire stepped over the stain on the walkway where Tishanna died. Recent rains had washed most of the blood away and what remained had faded, but it would always be there, visible or not.

Claire squared her shoulders and climbed the front steps. The wood and plaster smells of construction had replaced the stench of decay that greeted her the first time she opened this door. Spring had moved toward summer, but the house remained cold. As she walked through the icy spot and up the stairs, grief wrapped around her like a cloak. Why was she bothering with the books? Why bother with anything? Nothing she did would help Mary. Nothing could bring Tishanna back.

She trudged down the hall to the back bedroom that would forever smell of fear. That was the scent she hadn't been able to identify. She put her hand on the doorknob and felt a rush of anger. Her jaw clenched, and she drew her foot back, ready to kick the door open.

Stop. What is the matter with you? This had happened last time she was here. She'd felt overwhelmed with sorrow and futility and then cold fury. She turned around and retraced her steps.

At the top of the stairs, she paused to look down. Hers were the only footprints on the dusty floor, but every sense told her she wasn't alone. Her breath caught in her chest as if she was going to have a panic attack. She grasped the banister and wobbled down the stairs, stumbled across the foyer and out the front door. Safe outside, she kept going, down the steps and into her car, where she sat until her heart stopped pounding.

She could have broken her neck falling down those stairs. *The heck with those books. Dorcas can keep them.*

CHAPTER 33

Tony watched the blue Miata pull into the driveway. Claire climbed out and walked toward the house, shoulders hunched and head bowed. She didn't want to come inside. He'd returned too soon, too damaged, and too distant.

"I'm going to take a quick shower," she called to Lucy and started up the stairs.

"Claire," he said.

She turned around. "Oh, hi. I didn't see you." She came over and bent to kiss his cheek. "How was your day?"

"Making progress," he said about a day that had been just like yesterday and the day before. "I hear you tried to fire Stephanie."

"I did fire her. Didn't you get my message? No?" She frowned but recovered quickly. "The police called this morning. They've arrested the gang. I don't need a bodyguard anymore, I don't have to worry that they might follow me here, I can go home, to my office..." The smile that blossomed as she described her regained freedom became rueful. "To my haunted house."

"Is that where you've been?" His question came too quickly, and she gave him a sideways look before answering.

"I just came from the house. Before that I was talking to a psychiatrist in Slidell and before that to a potential client I turned away. I'll tell you about it later, but right now, I really want a shower." She paused halfway up the stairs. "I got takeout for dinner. Chicken andouille lasagna. I hope you like it."

Tony watched her disappear upstairs where he couldn't follow— *fucking wheelchair*—and waited until he heard the water running before wheeling into the kitchen. Alexander was leaning against the counter watching Lucy putter around. They both looked up.

"Claire left me a message today," he said. "I never got it. What happened?"

The quick glance Lucy cut at Alexander confirmed his suspicions. "Next time, Lucy, don't ask Alexander to deliver a message. Do it yourself." He looked from one to the other. "My leg is broken, but my eyes and my brain continue to function. I can replace both of you, but I can't replace Claire, nor do I want to. Do you understand me?"

Lucy nodded, her brown eyes brimming with tears. Alexander remained stone-faced.

"Claire is taking a shower. When she comes down, I don't want her to know there's been any unpleasantness. Tonight, we're going to have dinner together—just the two of us—the take-out she brought home. After dinner, she and I will adjourn to my room. Lucy will do the dishes and then go home. Alexander, you will leave right now and not return until eight tomorrow morning."

"Who will help you prepare for bed?" Alexander said. "You can't manage by yourself, and Lucy isn't properly trained."

"Claire and I will manage." Tony wheeled himself back into the slapdash family room that used to be the dining room and turned on the television.

The local news was full of stories about the gang that had been apprehended. The mayor praised the police force and described the gang as particularly vicious, a priest bemoaned their youth and called for mercy, victims' relatives expressed satisfaction that the gang had been apprehended and hopes that they would be executed. Multiple victims. He heard Claire coming down the stairs and pressed the mute button.

"That's Tishanna's grandmother." She pointed to the screen.

"Do you want to watch?"

She shook her head. "No, but I should. Is she talking about Dorcas?"

Whatever she'd been talking about, she'd finished. The station went to a commercial, and he turned the TV off. "Tishanna was one of several victims. Did you know that?"

"I knew they'd killed other people before they killed her."

"You never mentioned it." He stopped himself. There was a long list of things Claire had never mentioned, but he didn't want to squabble, not tonight.

"Maybe I should have, but you couldn't do anything from Europe, and I didn't want to worry you. The good news is they're all in jail. Bea says they won't get bail." She smiled. "That rhymed. I'm a poet."

"And your feet show it," he said. "They're long fellows."

"Third grade." She smiled.

"Fourth for us. Children in Louisiana weren't as advanced as children in Michigan."

"Do you want to get out and go somewhere tomorrow? It's supposed to be a nice day. We could rent a van and drive down to the beach." She stood behind him and massaged his shoulders. "Wear sun glasses and a floppy hat, and you'll blend in with the crowd."

"You go. I imagine you're ready for a change of scenery."

"Aren't you?"

"I can't afford a day off. The opening is a week from tonight. I've got seven days to get out of this wheelchair and up on crutches."

"There's no shame in being in a wheelchair, and you don't want to risk hurting that leg again."

He gritted his teeth. This argument was familiar territory. "Crutches say you broke your leg; a wheelchair says you're an invalid. It's all about image."

"I know. That's why you have to be seen with beautiful women." She released his shoulders and walked over to the window.

"There are other drivers as good as I am, but no one makes as much money. Advertisers hire me to endorse their products because their customers want to be like me, not the real me but the playboy who dates movie stars." He wheeled around to face her. "No one wants to be an invalid. Look at me, Claire. No one wants this."

"Hugh Hefner might as well be an invalid, lounging around in his housecoat, but he maintains his playboy image by surrounding himself with half-naked women."

"Smoking jacket, sweetheart, not housecoat."

"What if I get myself a push-up bra and fishnet stockings, a little something cut down to here and up to there?" She ran one hand between her breasts while the other climbed her thigh. "I'll get all dolled up and push your wheelchair around the gallery."

He grinned. "You're not kidding are you?"

"Nope."

"You'd really do it?"

"I would."

"We'll continue this discussion later." He wanted to pull her close and hold her body tight against his. The best he could manage was his good arm around her hips in a quick half hug. He watched her walk away.

Over dinner, Claire told him about her conversation with Dr. Rubio, whom she described as pleasant but pompous and in love with his own voice.

"You seemed on edge when you came home. Was he that annoying?" *Or were you so reluctant to come back here?*

"It wasn't him. It's that house. I walk inside and a black cloud descends. I'm saddened and angry about Tishanna's death, but that's not it. The house really is haunted, and it gets to me." Claire pushed a piece of sauce covered chicken around her plate. She shared her suspicions about Dorcas's death then told him what Tishanna's grandmother had said and what Ellen Ledet had said and not said.

He took a drink of water—no wine for a man taking painkillers. "If I wanted to get rid of a ghost, I'd hire an exorcist."

"Really?" Claire looked surprised.

"What church do you go to?"

"When I go, which isn't often enough, St. Michaels."

"Talk to a priest. I know Catholics do exorcisms. I think Episcopalians do too."

"Dr. Rubio mentioned exorcism—negatively. He was setting up a straw man." She pushed her plate aside. "If I hired an exorcist who drove Dorcas away, where would she go?"

"Straight to Hell." He hoped.

Claire opened her mouth as if to speak but closed it without saying anything. He changed the subject by praising the lasagna. It was delicious but heavy. A heart attack on a plate, Alexander had said. That crack may or may not have sealed his fate. Tony hadn't decided.

After dinner, he suggested they retire to his room. He transferred himself to the bed and invited Claire to sit beside him. "I'm vetoing the fishnet stockings," he told her. "I want people to admire Dad's art, not your legs, but I do think you ought to get a new dress."

"How do you know I don't have the perfect dress?" Her smile teased. "I have lots of dresses."

"That you wore to work at the insurance company. No."

"No?"

"Are you free Wednesday morning? My shopper is bringing clothes over for me to consider. I can tell her to select some dresses for you. I see you in an elegant little black dress, cut halfway down to here." He ran his thumb down her cleavage and caressed her breast.

"Tony." She removed his hand. "What if Alexander or Lucy comes in?"

"They won't." He lifted her hair off her neck. "Most women look more elegant with their hair up and sexier with it down, but not everyone. The French consider a lovely neck, which you have, to be highly erotic." He released her hair. "We can decide, once we have your clothes."

"You're planning to dress me as if I were your Barbie Doll?"

"Why the outrage? You volunteered to dress like a Playboy Bunny." And he was grateful. If she hadn't, he would have had to bring up the clothing issue himself.

"That would have been a joke. You're serious."

"Image is serious business."

"For you," she said.

"For you, too. You don't meet clients dressed in jeans and work boots. Appearance matters. This gallery opening is your debut, and it's true about first impressions. You're a beautiful woman, and you want to look your best."

To his relief, Claire gave in gracefully. "I'm free Wednesday morning. Between now and then, I'll think about what image I'd like to project."

"Which you do every time you get dressed. It's not so different." He kissed her the way he used to when he had two good legs and could take care of himself. He felt her start to surrender then pull back.

"Lucy and Alexander have left and will not return until tomorrow morning—my orders. I told Alexander you'd get me ready for bed. I said you've had lots of practice and were quite good at it." Claire blushed and he winked. "That's a slight exaggeration, but they are gone, and I've been waiting too long to make love to you." He lay back and pulled her close.

"Are you sure this is okay?"

"I'm positive." That night with Bette, he'd done everything but take notes.

CHAPTER 34

Monday morning, Dr. Rubio called to say that he had read Mary's diaries and wanted to confer with his colleagues before venturing an opinion on what to do with them. "I found their contents to be extremely disconcerting."

"I did too," Claire said.

"It may be impossible to know the truth after all these years, but I believe it is worth pursuing for Mary's sake. It is possible that she witnessed a disturbing scene."

"I'm going to explore other avenues which might provide some insight into what happened—talk to the neighbors and the police. I'll let you know if I learn anything."

"Please do. I'll be back to you by the end of the week."

Claire hung up and dialed Bea's work number. "I'm calling to ask for your help. Whether or not you believe in Dorcas the ghost, you have to believe that Dorcas the girl existed. She died in 1953 when she fell down the Beaudrys' front staircase and broke her neck. There must be records—police records, hospital records, an obituary. She's buried somewhere."

"As are any records," Bea said. "Do you really think digging them up will accomplish anything?"

"You don't have to believe in ghosts to consider her death worth investigating. "

"I believe in the statute of limitations."

"Not if she was murdered, but this isn't about punishing a killer. Mary Beaudry's psychiatrist thinks that her mental illness goes back to whatever happened to Dorcas. I want to help Mary. If you could see what's become of her, you'd understand."

"Wait a minute. Mary's still around, and you've met her?"

"I thought I'd told you. No?"

"You never mentioned it."

"When Mary accused her father of causing Dorcas's death, her parents took her to psychiatrists, who prescribed medication and, when that didn't work, electro-shock. She continued to accuse him, and they had her lobotomized, which has left her half a person. She lives in a group home outside Slidell. I've gone to see her, and I'm going back, but I wanted to talk to you first."

"What was Dorcas's last name?"

"I don't know. I don't remember seeing it in Mary's diaries."

"No last name means no hope of finding anything. Ask, and while you're asking, an approximate date of death wouldn't hurt."

"I should have thought of that. Thank you, Bea."

"I'm not promising anything. Having her last name doesn't guarantee that we can locate any record of her death, but it would raise the chances somewhere above needle in a haystack."

"I'm reluctant to mention Dorcas to Mary, but I'll ask around the neighborhood. At least one woman has lived there forever and knew the Beaudry family."

Ellen Ledet was pleased to hear from her. "Does this mean you're ready to resume work on the house?"

"I'd like to talk to you about that and some other things. Are you free later this afternoon?"

"Why don't you come by about three? I'll make sugar cookies."

"Thank you, but could we make it four?" Even that would crowd her day.

She should have spent the weekend returning files to her office and putting things in order, but she'd spent most of Saturday at her house, tidying things that did not need to be tidied and discussing her life with Dorian. Sunday, she'd driven down to the Gulf. The sea breeze had cleared the cobwebs from her brain, but hours spent walking the beach and watching waves hadn't produced any solid answers. The more things changed, the more they stayed the same. She'd decided to do nothing until after the opening. She owed Tony that much.

"I'll see you at four, then," Ellen said.

Claire grabbed her purse and headed for the door. Tony was in the living room gym, sweating on a weight machine. She waved good-bye and he grunted a response.

Jack looked up when she walked into her office. "Ten fifteen. Back to your old habits?"

"I certainly hope so."

"I saw that the cops got that gang, and hoped that meant you'd be back in the office."

"Where I belong." Claire dumped an armload of files on the desk. "I want you to know that I've been up since seven and on the phone since nine."

"Any new clients?"

She shook her head. "I'm afraid not. I've been trying to get things on track with Chestnut Street."

"Claire, that's not going to happen."

"I know. The house is haunted. Tony says we should get an exorcist." She massaged her neck. "I have a crick from talking on the phone."

"An exorcist isn't a bad idea."

"If Dorcas won't leave under her own accord." She started stacking the files. "It's going to take me all morning and half the afternoon to get everything back in its proper place. What's your schedule?"

"Hagan Avenue, all day. You know, Marie's sister is looking for work. She used to run the office for a big construction company. She quit to have a baby, but now she's ready to go back. If you need a hand, she'd be perfect."

"Not yet, but I'll keep her in mind."

Jack stopped halfway out the door. "Hagan Avenue is over by Bayou Saint John. Saint John's Eve is coming up. Have you ever been?"

Claire shook her head. "I've heard of it though."

"You ought to go. Someone there will know where you can find an exorcist."

He left and Claire settled down to filing and answering messages and returning her office to order. At lunchtime, she walked over to Ralph and Marie's grocery.

"Hey baby, where've you been?" Ralph greeted her with a wide gold-toothed smile. "Marie and I were just talking about how we hadn't seen you in a while."

"How's Marie doing?"

"She's all better now, I'll tell her you asked, but my lumbago is acting up." He massaged his lower back.

Several minutes of medical detail later, Claire asked if she could have a muffaletta and a ginger ale. Ralph insisted that she get a lemon tart to go with it. A meal wasn't a meal without a taste of the sweet.

"Can't argue with that." She carried lunch back to her office and ate at her desk, happy to be back in her own life.

They sat on the now familiar porch. Ellen set out a plate of cupcakes, pecans dotting the butter frosting. "Red velvet," she said. "I remembered how much you enjoyed the ones I made for Mary."

"Thank you." Claire took a cupcake. "How is Bill Tice doing?"

"He's home and in a wheelchair, which he hates, but he realizes that he is lucky to be alive."

"I know a man who's in a wheelchair after an automobile accident. He hates it, too."

"Of course he does. Wouldn't you? And it's harder for men. They think they're supposed to be the strong ones." Ellen poured their iced tea. "I saw that the police finally arrested those hoodlums. We'll all breathe easier knowing they're in jail."

"What do the doctors say about Bill's prognosis?"

"It's still uncertain, but he already has more control over his legs than they expected. Lindsay has been his rock. I have the greatest respect for that young woman."

"Please let me know if there's anything I can do to help her—or Bill."

"You could help everyone on this street by finishing work on the Beaudry house."

"That's what I wanted to discuss with you." Claire cut to the chase. "As you know, Mary blamed her father for Dorcas's death."

"I don't believe that's still true."

"I gave Mary's diaries to her psychiatrist. He thinks she holds herself responsible."

"What does this have to do with the house?" Ellen unpleated her cupcake wrapper.

"It all comes back to Dorcas. What was her last name?"

"I don't believe I ever knew it. She was just a child."

"Didn't her mother work for the family?"

"Dorcas's mother was named Martha. She was a pleasant woman, we always said hello, but I never knew her family name."

"Do you think Lissie would know?"

"I'd be amazed if she did." Ellen smoothed the wrapper. "Back then people called household help by their given names. Most still do. It wasn't disrespectful. Lissie and Mary might have called Martha, Miss Martha." She looked up, a puzzled frown creasing her forehead. "Why do you want to know?"

"Records of Dorcas's death would be filed by her last name. Dr. Rubio thinks knowing the circumstances of her death might help Mary— or help him treat her."

"Wanting to help Mary is admirable."

"It could also help me. You asked about the house. It's haunted. I can't get workers in there to rehab it. I don't like being inside myself. The air is full of anger and sorrow."

"Don't you think you're being melodramatic, dear?"

"I'm not the melodramatic type." Claire smiled. "That said, I'm convinced that I'll never be able to finish that house, much less sell it, as long as Dorcas is on the scene."

"What are you going to do?"

"I'm going to get rid of Dorcas, and that begins by figuring out why she's there." She looked Ellen in the eye. "Do you know who was responsible for her death?"

"It was an accident, Claire. No one." Ellen sounded weary. "I hope you don't decide to abandon the house."

"I won't." Claire stood up. "Thank you for the tea and cupcakes."

"Thank you for stopping by. Would you like to take some cupcakes home with you? I'll never eat them all."

That evening, Claire called Bea. "I'm not getting anywhere on Dorcas's last name."

"Don't spend any more time on it. I talked to Mike. He says we can't do anything no matter what you find."

"Not even add a memo to the file?" She had thought that might appease Dorcas.

"A person accused of a crime is entitled to face his accusers," Bea said. "Beaudry died years ago. And the sad truth is we have barely enough resources to address recent homicides."

"I'm not giving up on this."

CHAPTER 35

Laughter and snatches of conversation drifted in from the art gallery. People were discussing Jim Burke's art, but they were also asking about Tony. Wasn't he supposed to be here? Al, an ex-boxer turned bodyguard, wanted to check the premises one more time, but Tony shook his head.

"Not necessary. You've got back-up outside and in the main room." He reached for his crutches. "Showtime."

A short hallway separated the private office where they sat from the public rooms where art was displayed. Claire led the way, followed by Tony, then Al, who would protect Tony's back and catch him if he fell. The roped-off seating area that was their destination was on the far side of the main room.

"Excuse me." She cleared a path through the crowd, glancing back every step, terrified that someone would jostle Tony or, worse, that she would stumble in her spike heels and throw him off balance. He stopped to speak to someone he knew, and she wanted to scream. Didn't he know how at risk he was?

Al stepped in with a suggestion that they chat later. He nodded to her. "Keep going."

"You bet." She could have kissed him.

She reached the corner and undid the clasp on the velvet rope. Tony walked past and handed her his crutches. He sat on the far side of the sofa, next to the wall, a few feet behind the podium where he would speak. She sat beside him, and Al stood against the wall behind the sofa, keeping an eye on the crowd. They'd made it. Everything had gone as rehearsed.

"How are you doing?" she said.

"Happy to be sitting. Although it was a pleasure to walk behind you." He winked, the old Tony. "I plan to do that more often."

The gallery owner brought them glasses of sparkling white grape juice that looked like the champagne being served to everyone else. "The podium mike is on stand-by," he said. "We're ready whenever you are."

"Give us fifteen minutes," Tony said. He rested his arm on the back of the couch, his fingers grazing her shoulder. A man came over, wanting to discuss the racing season. A woman asked Tony if he remembered her. "I was in your fifth-grade class."

A reporter from Times Picayune approached, a photographer in tow. "Hey Tony, how about a picture of you and your lovely lady?"

Tony introduced her as Claire, his *bella testarossa*, and then had to spell it.

Claire smoothed the skirt of her outrageously expensive little black dress and arranged her face in a pleasant expression. Things were going well, and in two hours it would be all over.

Claire's face ached from smiling, and her feet ached from being imprisoned in shoes that were never meant for walking. She leaned back in the leather seat—she and Tony were in the backseat of a Ferrari sedan imported for the occasion—kicked her shoes off and massaged her poor toes.

"Congratulations, Tony," she said. "You did it, and you did it in style."

"So did you. Every man there envied me." He put his hand on her thigh, and she covered it with hers. Moments later, he was asleep. The playboy of the Formula One Circuit looked like a little boy. Claire stared out the window. She'd tell him tomorrow.

Her mother called the next morning, before she'd had a chance to talk to Tony. "You were on The Sunrise Show, Claire Marshall. I hardly recognized you, you looked so glamorous, but it was definitely you. And with Tony Burke. You told me that you worked on his house, but you didn't tell me you were playing house, which is what the reporter implied." She paused. "My daughter and Tony Burke. Should I be worried about you?" Mom the matchmaker, who had been desperate for her to become romantically involved with a man, wasn't too sure about this one.

"It was a public occasion," Claire said. "Tony needed a date. It was all about image."

"The reporter described you as a stunning redhead who didn't take her eyes off Tony all night."

"I was watching him because I was afraid he was going to fall. His leg is far from healed. Tony and I are friends, nothing more." She felt Tony's eyes on her—please, no—and looked up. He sat in his wheelchair not six feet away. She hadn't heard his approach—damned rubber wheels. How long had he been there? "I've got to go, Mom. I'll call you back tonight."

"Friends, nothing more?" he said.

"We need to talk. Let's go back to your room where no one will interrupt."

"Or overhear. That can be inconvenient." His eyes had darkened to the stormy ocean color that signaled trouble, but he followed her and shut the door behind them.

He sat in his wheelchair, while she paced, too on edge to be still. "I'm moving back to my house," she said. "I was waiting until after the opening to tell you."

"Why?"

"Waiting because I didn't want to do anything that might undermine your rehab. Leaving because I can't stay." She lifted her chin. "The Friday night before you came home, I went to a jazz club by myself. I was going stir crazy. I ran into Mike Robinson who was there alone, too. When the show ended, he offered me a ride home, and I took him up on it."

"I knew Robinson was back in the picture. Did this just happen to be a club where he had taken you before?"

253

"This isn't easy, Tony. Let me finish, please."

He nodded. A neutral expression replaced the anger that flashed when he asked about Mike, but his hands were fists. Claire stared at them, remembering. Tony had been a boxer. He'd almost killed a man, and he'd sworn that he'd never hit anyone again. She knew, because he'd told her his secrets. She had held hers close. She took a deep breath and continued.

"It was after midnight when we left and in a dicey neighborhood, but I felt safe with Mike, and not only because he's a policeman. Mike is solid and dependable, a man you can trust." She took another deep breath and plowed ahead. "I like and respect Mike. I know that he cares for me, and I believe that, with encouragement, his affection could become something deeper. That night, after he dropped me off, I wished that I cared for him."

She had rocked on the porch swing, dissecting her relationships with Tom and Mike and Tony. She had talked to Dorian, her rubber ducky, until a thunderstorm drove them inside. In bed, she lay awake wondering if she had become a woman destined to live alone.

"But you don't?" Tony said.

She shook her head. "Only as a friend."

"That's what you just said about me."

"I didn't know you were listening." She sat down on the bed, deflated by her admission, and made another. "I was lying."

"You're not a woman who would be satisfied with friendship." Tony's eyes met hers and held them. "You'd be wasted on Robinson."

"Mike would be wasted on me. He reminds me of Tom, my husband, whom I loved, and if he hadn't died would still love. But he did die, and I am no longer the woman who married him.

"Tom and I sacrificed our present for the future. He specialized in pediatric oncology and was going to save the world one child at a time." She half-smiled. "We actually used those words. We were so young."

"That was his future. What about yours?"

"I was content being a soldier in his army. But then he died, and I was left with nothing but the boring job that was paying for his education. I was so angry that I repressed all my memories of Tom and so guilty about my anger that I buried it. I had panic attacks, took too many pills, I was a mess." She hurried through her confession. Did Tony really want to hear this?

"I saw the pills," he said.

"But you never saw me take one, because I had stopped. I made peace with my memories. I can remember the good times, look back and value what we had, while knowing it's history. My only regret is that Tom never got to live his dream."

"You've never discussed your marriage before." Tony put his hand on her cheek and turned her face toward him. "This new openness should be a good sign, but I'm waiting for the other shoe to drop. You don't want Robinson, but..."

"Passion isn't enough, either. Last Friday wasn't the first time you'd made love since your accident. You knew exactly how to protect your broken leg."

"I never promised monogamy."

"That doesn't matter anymore." She had tortured herself with the question of whether or not it was cheating when he never pretended to be faithful. After a while, she realized that was irrelevant. He might not be lying, but he was cheating. "I don't want to share you."

"Because you love me, Claire?" He studied her face. "You don't have to answer. Let me tell you about Clinique Rothschild.

"The other rehab patients were mostly skiers, some tennis players, a few runners and bikers. Male and female, they were young, attractive and bored. It wasn't a nightly orgy, but there was plenty of action, and the younger staff joined in. The day I arrived, the orderly who brought me to my room demonstrated techniques for making love with a broken leg. My physical therapist ended our first session with a come-on."

"Life is full of temptations."

"I chose to leave them behind. I flew to New Orleans against my doctor's advice and turned this house into a rehab clinic because I love you. And I was worried about Robinson trying to win you back while I was away."

A tear slid down her cheek. She wanted to believe that love was enough, but she had learned that wasn't true.

"Friday night was the second time," he said. "I asked my physical therapist for a private lesson, because I wanted to know my limits before being with you. Believe me, I paid a price."

"You paid her for sex?"

"I paid blood, sweat, and tears for no sex. Bette was still my physical therapist, and I had insulted her by saying no thank you to any more private lessons. She got even. Every morning, she put me through a workout that brought me to my knees. Or would have if I weren't in a wheelchair."

Claire felt the corners of her mouth turn up.

"Go ahead, smile. Laugh out loud if you want. You're going to need your sense of humor if we're to make it." He gestured toward his broken leg. "The accident has changed a lot, temporarily I hope. Knowing you has made a bigger difference, one I want to last."

"Life has changed me," Claire said. "Being with you has changed me, and not just the transformation into your *bella testarossa* in that little black dress. Although it's a spectacular dress, and I enjoyed the admiration."

"The opening wasn't the ordeal you anticipated?"

"No, but I was worried about you the whole time. What if you'd reinjured your leg?"

"I could have lost it."

"You knew that, and you did it anyway?"

"I took precautions. Look back, Claire. We arranged the furniture, choreographed and rehearsed every movement. There is no such thing as absolute safety, but you can manage risk."

"I don't want to love a man I can't trust."

"If you want to move back to your house, go ahead. If you need some time to yourself, I'll understand. But don't give up on us."

"I'm moving out today, but I'll still visit."

"We're going to make this work."

CHAPTER 36

Saint John's Eve fell on a Thursday. By late afternoon, people dressed in white filled the bridge over Bayou Saint John and spilled out the ends. Mostly women, but with a good sprinkling of men, they chanted and swayed. Their clothing glowed in the late afternoon sun, and their voices soared in sweet counterpoint to the drum rhythms. Many of the women wore small hats or veils. Some carried colorful banners, which they unfurled and waved.

Claire associated voodoo with African Americans, but this crowd was racially mixed, young and old, well dressed and raggedy. "What are they singing? I don't recognize the language."

"It's Creole," Tony said. "Don't look so worried. This is white magic. Saint John is John the Baptist. This ceremony is about transformation and renewal, the clean slate baptism brings, plus guidance from those who have gone before."

No one took notice as they threaded their way across the bridge, past people kneeling at mini-altars decorated with candles, bowls of dried leaves and powders, vases of fresh flowers. On the other side, a woman gestured toward Tony's crutches then slid over and made room for him on her bench, one of several set in the shade. He thanked her and sat down.

"Have a seat." He pulled Claire onto his good leg.

"Why are we here?" she whispered in his ear. "I feel uncomfortable, gawking at these people as if they're some kind of sideshow."

"We're looking for someone who can help you get rid of Dorcas." He put his arms around her. "Relax. Close your eyes and listen to the music. You're not gawking; you're part of the show."

"Why didn't you tell me to wear white?"

"Typical woman, worrying about clothes."

"How do you know so much about this? Have you been here before?"

"Not since I was in college." His crutches slid to the ground, bumping the woman who'd given them the seat. He apologized, but the woman was so immersed in what appeared to be silent prayer that she didn't notice. A few minutes later, she stood and indicated that Claire could take her place on the bench.

"You're welcome here," she said. "The ancestor spirits say that if you keep an open heart, you'll find the answers you seek."

"Thank you." Claire couldn't think of anything else to say. That bit of wisdom could be profound or it could be from a fortune cookie.

"The veil around you is very thin. A blessing can feel like a burden." The woman half bowed and drifted away, stepping to the beat of the drums.

"You've already made your first contact," Tony said. "Good work."

"You're putting me on."

"Says the woman shopping for an exorcist," he teased. "The rituals may seem strange, but substitute angels for ancestor spirits, and the basic beliefs aren't very different from those you learned in Sunday school." His lips brushed her temple. "I'm feeling renewed already."

Claire rested her head on his chest and listened to his heart beating like one more drum. The crowd on the bridge grew and more people set up altars. Eyes closed as if in a trance, groups of people shuffled their feet in rhythm with the ever present drumbeats. At the edge of the crowd, a kneeling woman sang and swayed, moving her right arm with the grace of a ballet dancer. A stream of white powder fell from her hand and formed an intricate geometric design on the ground.

"Look over there." Claire pointed with her chin. "It's the woman who gave up her seat. What's she doing?"

"I think it's some kind of divination."

"How much longer are we going to sit here? I'm getting hungry."

"Good smells are coming from the direction of that tent. Pass me my crutches and we can check it out."

"Do you want to eat and leave?" The sun was approaching the horizon and the thought of lingering after it set made Claire uneasy.

"If we do that, we'll miss the best part. After dark, there'll be bonfires, more dancing, and music. A blazing boat will appear on the bayou. In Marie Laveau's time, she'd arrive on that boat with Zombi, her enormous snake." His eyes met hers. "You don't like it here do you?"

"That woman told me the veil around me was very thin." She rubbed her arms. "Maybe I'm just cold."

Her mobile phone rang while they were eating.

"Your house is on fire," Ellen Ledet said. "The fire trucks are here, but I'm afraid no one noticed until the fire was well underway. Flames are coming through the roof."

"I'll be there as fast as I can."

Driving back to the Lower Garden District, Claire said, "Remember that woman who was supposed to be delivering a message? What kind of a seer can't see a fire a couple hours before it happens? If the house burns down, where is Dorcas going to go? Or did she start the fire? Can poltergeists do that?" She knew she was babbling, but her brain was reeling.

Tony put a calming hand on her shoulder. "It's just an empty house."

"The house was secured; no one could get in. Maybe there was a problem with the new wiring or the rats came back. Painters use heat guns no matter how many times you ask them not to, and old wood can smolder for hours—but not days. No one has worked on that house in weeks. I have to call Jack."

"Give me your phone, I'll call him for you."

She saw the smoke first, dark billows rose into the evening sky. Then she smelled it. She turned the corner onto Chestnut and had to stop.

Police had the street blocked off.

"Park here and go ahead. I'll catch up with you," Tony said.

It looked like a scene from a movie. Police cars on the periphery flashed blue lights. Fire trucks filled the road in front of the house. Their red and white lights shot beams into the evening sky and reflected off puddles of water in the street. Uniformed firemen, their coats and boots black and shiny wet, lined up on a heavy hose and directed water onto the fire. Clusters of neighbors stood on the other side of the street, watching. Some of them had cameras and were taking pictures.

Claire ran up to the closest fire truck.

"Stand back, ma'am. Across the street," a fireman said.

"It's my house."

"I'm sorry, ma'am, you still have to get out of our way. Please stand clear. The captain will want to talk to you later, but not until we get this under control."

Claire walked away, and someone called her name. Lindsey Tice hugged her hard, rocking back and forth.

"Thank God you weren't inside. One of the neighbors thought he saw a woman at one of the upstairs windows." She pointed toward the back corner. "The firemen said no one inside was still alive, and they wouldn't risk more lives to retrieve a body."

"I'm fine." Claire patted Lindsey's back. "It's just a house. Nobody is inside." *No one alive.*

Flames flickered behind every window and poked through holes in the roof. By now, the mermaid sconces would be puddles of molten metal. The bump out crashed to the ground in a shower of sparks. A window exploded, blown out by the heat. The firemen pulled back to the sidewalk but continued to send streams of water onto the walls and roof.

Claire felt Tony behind her. "Is there somewhere we can sit down?" she asked Lindsey.

A neighbor brought rocking chairs, another neighbor made coffee, and Ellen Ledet appeared with a bottle of Irish whiskey, which she added to their cups.

She sat down with them. "I hope you have insurance, my dear."

"The company does." Claire started to introduce Tony.

"I know who you are," Ellen said. "I saw you on TV with Claire."

"And Claire has told me about you."

Leaves on the big magnolia popped and crackled and burst into flame. Claire winced. "Mary's tree is burning. The only thing she asked me about was that tree."

Ellen stared at the tree, her expression impassive. "I'll tell Mary about the fire the next time I visit. Maybe you'd like to come with me."

"I'll call you over the weekend."

"They have the fire under control, but it won't be out for hours. I'm going home." Ellen handed Tony the whiskey. "Dispense as needed."

Neighbors Claire had never met stopped by to say how sorry they were. Most lingered until she introduced them to Tony. Word had gotten out.

"Next thing you know," she said, "someone's going to ask you for an autograph."

"You're as famous as Tony in this neighborhood," Lindsey said. "The police told me that you helped them catch the gang that mugged Bill. We're all grateful. I've been meaning to tell you thank you, but you were never around when I walked past the house. And now this... I'm so sorry, Claire."

"How is Bill?"

"It's been a slow go, but he's doing better than expected. Thank heaven. He's home, but he's in a wheelchair, and it's hard. Speaking of Bill, I'd better get back." She gave Claire a quick hug and Tony a pat on his good arm. "You get better, too."

The flames subsided, and all but one fire truck departed. A fireman came over and asked for her contact information. Several men wearing black jackets with arson written in big yellow letters on the back began going in and out of what was left of the house. Claire watched them for a while, wondering what they would find.

"My husband died in a house fire," she said. "A little over three years ago."

"I know," Tony said. "Is this stirring up old memories?"

"I didn't see the fire. I went by afterwards." She took a deep breath and told him what she'd never told anyone else. "I used to stand on the sidewalk in front of that burned house and try to feel his presence, but he wasn't there. It was as if he'd never existed. After a while, I stopped."

His arm tightened around her shoulders.

"It's been a long day," she said, "like two or three separate days. Remember the people in white, dancing on the bridge, and that strange woman? Do you think they burned any boats on Saint John's Bayou tonight?"

"Nothing as spectacular as this," he said.

She asked the question that was bothering her most. "What if the person in the upstairs window was Dorcas? What happens to a ghost when the house they're haunting burns down?"

"I'd like to sleep on that one."

Claire realized how much walking Tony had been doing and how tired he must be. "Let's go. I'll drop you at your house."

"You don't want to stay?"

"I want to go home."

He studied her face, and for a moment she thought he was going to say something, but whatever it was, he changed his mind.

CHAPTER 37

"Once again, I appreciate the ride. My son is still working out of town." Ellen adjusted the plastic wrap covering the plate of cookies she held on her lap. "I always bring a treat. Mary has such a sweet tooth."

"I brought her books," Claire said. "Copies of two that burned with the house, *To Kill A Mockingbird* and *Marjorie Morningstar.* There were several Nancy Drew mysteries, too, but I don't remember the titles."

"Did you talk to her doctor?"

"He doubts Mary would find either novel upsetting. As you know, the lobotomy has left her unable to feel emotion. He also doubts she has the power of concentration required to read a novel, but thinks she might enjoy having one of her old favorites read to her." Claire kept the anger out of her voice. Ellen had known Mary's parents and been friends with her mother. She sympathized with their decision to have the poor child lobotomized. And, as she'd said more than once, hindsight was easy. "I wonder how she'll react to news of the house fire."

"They dropped a big dumpster in front of your house right before you picked me up."

"Crews will start clearing the lot tomorrow morning and, I hope, be done by the weekend. The rubble is dangerous, unstable and full of glass shards—those beautiful windows."

"Did they figure out what caused the fire?"

"They traced it back to a short circuit in the wall of Mary's old bedroom. The circuit breaker should have flipped, but it didn't."

"Are you going to sue the electrician?"

"It wasn't his fault. Sometimes things just happen." They were on the causeway, crossing the lake she had crossed more in the last two weeks than in the six previous months. "It's beautiful out here isn't it?"

"It's a long way across, but we'll be there soon."

Their visit with Mary got off to a good start thanks to Ellen's cookies, but Mary frowned when Claire showed her the books. She pushed *Marjorie Morningstar* aside. "I didn't like the ending."

"I didn't either," Claire said.

"Marjorie could have been an actress or a writer or somebody special, and she ended up an ordinary housewife." Mary picked up *To Kill A Mockingbird*. "This is a bad book about a bad little girl."

"Scout wasn't bad." Claire defended a character who had been one of her heroines.

"Bad girls cause trouble." Mary glanced at Ellen from the corner of her eye. "I know a story about a bad girl who didn't want to go to church."

"Do you remember the name of the story?" Ellen said.

"The little girl's name was Mary."

Claire and Ellen exchanged glances. Ellen shook her head, but Claire said, "I'd like to hear the story."

Mary pulled on the collar of her blouse. "She had a dress she hated because the collar felt scratchy on her neck."

"Let's go," Momma said. "Your sister is already in the car."

"I want to stay home with Daddy." Mary plopped down on the stairs.

"Your father's not staying home. And let go of your pretty lace collar. You'll get it all wrinkled." Momma sighed. "You'll be the death of me, Mary Amelia Beaudry. Why can't you behave? When Lissie was five years old, she was a good little girl."

Mary stuck out her lower lip. She knew the only reason Lissie wanted to go to church was to see creepy Phillip Rollins, and there was nothing good about that. "Can I wait and come with Daddy?"

"Oh all right. Where's Dorcas?"

"Back in the kitchen. She won't play with me." Dorcas was usually Mary's friend, but this morning she was cranky because her momma was home sick and she was having to do all the work.

"Dorcas," Momma called, "you make sure Mary stays clean. That's a brand new dress she's wearing." Momma held Mary by both shoulders and made her look into her eyes. "Promise me you'll stay out of trouble. That means trees and mud puddles and the garage. You can play with your paper dolls until your father's ready."

Momma and Lissie left, and Dorcas came out of the kitchen. "You better be good 'cause I ain't got time to mess with you."

"You do too." Mary pulled on Dorcas's skirt. "Come on and play paper dolls."

"I gots to wash the dishes before the egg yolk dries. That stuff dries fast and sticks worse than glue."

"Egg yolk is stickier than glue?" Mary thought this was good information. She'd been trying to make a fort for her paper dolls, and the glue that she and Momma bought at the dime store took too long to dry.

"Stickier and it dries hard as a rock. Now you heard what your momma said. Stay out of trouble, while I get you all's dishes in to soak."

Mary waited until Dorcas carried a load of dirty plates into the kitchen. Then she snuck up to the sideboard and grabbed one of the soft-boiled eggs left over from breakfast.

The pieces of her paper-doll fort were in the living room, where she'd left them last night. She peeled the egg and bit off the top chunk of white, thinking that rest of the white would make a cup for the yolk.

She should have left the shell on. The white wobbled and a bit of yolk spilled on her dress. Momma wasn't going to be happy, but it was just one little smudge. She could always say it happened at breakfast.

Mary smeared egg yolk on the front of the fort, pressed it against the side, and held it tight. It didn't dry as fast as Dorcas said, but it worked better than the glue. She had three sides together when Dorcas walked in, took one look, and started yelling.

"What are you doing? Look at your dress! Your momma's gonna kill us both."

Mary looked down and saw yellow splotches of egg yolk all over the front of her new dress. It must have spilled while she was gluing. She was going to be in big trouble with Mama.

Dorcas grabbed Mary's arm so hard it hurt and dragged her up the stairs, all the time saying what a bad little girl, couldn't stay out of trouble for a minute, not even on a Sunday morning.

Daddy came out of his bedroom in his undershirt, fastening his pants as he walked. "What's going on here?"

"Look at her dress," Dorcas said.

Mary was glad Daddy didn't have his belt on yet. He would have taken it off and let her have a whap right then and there. "Dorcas is hurting me." She started crying, hoping that he'd decide she didn't need any more punishment.

Daddy gave Dorcas a hard look. "Weren't you supposed to be watching her?"

Mary stopped crying, happy because someone else was getting the blame. She pulled away from Dorcas and waited to see what was going to happen next.

Dorcas put her hands on her hips. "I was cleaning up after breakfast. I can't do two things at one time, and she knows better than to roll around in her food."

Mary couldn't believe Dorcas sassed Daddy like that. From the look on his face, neither could he. He hauled off and slapped Dorcas so hard her head whipped around and she stumbled backwards. She grabbed at the banister but missed and fell, thumping and banging all the way to the bottom.

Mary peered over the railing. Dorcas lay all crumpled on the floor. "Dorcas!" She started down the stairs, but Daddy pulled her back.

"You go to your room young lady. And stay there 'til I tell you to come out." He swatted her bottom as she ran down the hall, but she was moving away, and it didn't hurt.

Mary stayed in her room, quiet as a mouse except for a bit of sniffling. She changed into a different dress so that she'd be ready for church, but Daddy didn't come to get her. After a while, she heard people talking and moving around, but no one came upstairs. She was afraid to leave her room before Daddy said she could, so she picked up a picture book.

The next thing Mary knew, Momma was shaking her shoulder. "Wake up."

Mary remembered what had happened. "Where's Dorcas?"

"Dorcas hurt herself falling down the stairs. She's gone to live with her family out in the country." Momma's eyes were red like she'd been crying.

"I want Dorcas to come back and play with me."

"Dorcas isn't coming back, and it's your fault for being a bad girl. I don't ever want to hear another word about Dorcas. Do you understand me?"

Mary's smile was sly. "Momma said never mention her name again, but I just did."

"It's okay," Claire said. "That happened a long time ago."

Mary shook her head. "It didn't really happen. It's only a story."

Claire and Ellen stayed a few more minutes, long enough to be sure Mary was not upset. They left without telling her that her old house had burned.

CHAPTER 38

Tony was watching a baseball game when Claire walked in, carrying Dorian. Someone nearby set off a string of firecrackers. The cat leapt from her arms and ran under the sofa.

Tony muted the TV. "Was that orange streak the big fellow?"

"The poor cat is terrified of fireworks. I couldn't leave him home alone."

Tony reached down before she could warn him. "Ouch!" He sucked the blood from his thumb.

"Let me put some antibiotic ointment on that," Claire said. "You can get a nasty infection from cat scratches."

"Does he do this every Fourth of July?"

"And New Year's Eve and Mardi Gras and in between—whenever someone sets off firecrackers. Will I find Band-Aids and ointment in the downstairs bathroom?"

"There's a first aid kit in the medicine cabinet, right where Alexander left it."

"I'm glad he's gone."

"I'm glad they're all gone. Lucy still comes in mornings to tidy up and prepare meals, and the therapist comes three times a week, but other than that I'm alone—unless you're here."

Tony watched her bandage his thumb. When she finished, he patted the cushion next to him. "I think Dorian will feel more secure if you sit above him. After all, he's your cat." She leaned against him and he put his arm around her. "Are you still brooding about Mary Beaudry?"

"Not brooding, but listening to that poor woman talk about a fictional character being robbed of her future broke my heart."

"Have you talked to her psychiatrist?"

"Dr. Rubio sees her story about Dorcas as an enormous breakthrough. He still doesn't believe in ghosts."

"And you?"

"I hope he's right about Mary." She also hoped that Mary's confession, such as it was, had satisfied Dorcas's desire for justice. "Dorcas went out in a blaze of glory didn't she?"

"Do you hold her responsible for the fire?"

"Yes." She looked into the middle distance. "I don't think Ellen Ledet knew. She appeared stunned by Mary's story and was very quiet on our ride home." She pointed to a thick book lying on the coffee table. "What are you reading?"

"Aerodynamics." He held the book up, showing her a page of mathematical symbols. "One of my dark secrets is that I'm a good engineer, but it's been a while, and I'm brushing up."

"Because?"

"Ferrari has asked me to consult with the engineering and design team until I can drive again and, perhaps, after that. We'll see how it goes."

"What does the consulting involve?" Claire held her breath. Tony's leg was mending, and he was getting restless.

"They'd like me to return to Italy as soon as possible. I told them I had business here that needed wrapping up first."

"The dealership?"

"Tony Burke BMW Ferrari is on track. The new manager is doing a terrific job, and the sales team likes working for him. If he keeps it up, I may have to sell the dealership to him." He paused. "I'm selling this house."

Her stomach dropped. Tony was leaving, and he wasn't coming

back. "You're selling it?" she echoed.

"Claire, your company did a fantastic job—twice—but I don't want to live here. I suspected that before going back to Europe, but thought if you lived here, I'd feel differently. When you declined to move in, I decided to wait and see. Now I'm certain. This will always be my mother's house, *Chez Geneviève*." He made a face, as if the words tasted bitter.

"Didn't you live here when you were married?"

"All six months, and it was a poor idea. I wanted to be anywhere but home. This house will always hold bad memories."

"I understand." About the house, but not about him leaving for good. Hadn't he asked her to "give us a chance?" Did that mean hang around until he was ready to leave? She pulled away, damned if she was going to beg him to change his mind. "We can put the first floor back to normal very quickly and without much expense. Except the handicap-accessible bath, and you might as well leave it."

"Bill and Lindsey Tice are buying the house as is—exercise machines and all." His expression, which had darkened when he mentioned his mother, brightened into the smile that could melt stone.

"When did all this happen?"

"After your haunted house burned. Remember I told you I wanted to call Lindsey and thank her for her kindness that night?"

"Uh huh."

"One thing led to another."

"You've been busy." *And you've kept it all to yourself.*

"You've been busy, too, either at work or trying to help Mary Beaudry. You identify with her."

"We both liked to climb trees." Claire tried a joke.

"I think there's more, and I hope it's no longer unfinished business."

She shook her head. "It's not. I've done what I can. Ellen will continue to visit."

"Good. Now let's talk about my unfinished business." He took her hands in his and studied her face. "Claire," he began. Another firecracker went off and Dorian yowled. "Will this go on all night?"

270

"You and I are both thirty-five years old. By this age, we come with baggage. Dorian is part of mine."

"You were right to move out," Tony said.

"It's not as if I haven't visited." *I've come running every time you beckoned.*

"Including sleepovers, but it's not the same as living together. I've missed you, and I hope you'll come to Italy with me, you and the big boy—although he'll have to be quarantined, and good luck to them." He held up his bandaged thumb.

"You want me to come to Italy? For how long? What about my job?"

"I don't have my life all mapped out, I don't think that's possible, but you don't see many drivers over forty. The day I'm not at the top of my game, I'm off the track. That's my job. You have to answer the question about your job. Can you hire a manager to look after things?"

Of course she could. Jack's sister-in-law was looking for work, and she'd be perfect. The business would have to move away from historic restoration—that was her arena—but all Jack needed was a partner who could manage money. "Probably," she said. "Yes."

"We'll need a place to live. My apartment is on the second floor, no elevator. Short-term we can stay at a hotel. Soon as we're settled, I'm hoping you'll take on the house hunt. I looked at a lot of villas last summer. None of them seemed right, but I can't see the potential in a house. You can."

"House shopping for an Italian villa? Tony, you're sweeping me off my feet."

"I love you."

"That's only the second time you've told me you love me. And the first time was during an argument."

"The words don't come easily, but you must know how I feel about you." He held his hand against her stomach.

"What are you doing?"

"Imagining how you'd feel if you were pregnant."

"Pregnant!" Claire gasped.

"I've told you that I think you'd make an excellent mother, and once I dragged out of you that you think I'd be a good father." His hand slid lower. "Making love can also make babies. I'm sure your mother warned you about that."

"You want to have a baby?"

"If I have my biology right, you're the one who has to do that, but I'm willing to help get the process started." He winked.

Claire buried her face in his neck. There was nothing in the world that she wanted more than to have his baby. "I love you, too."

"And people who love each other have babies together. Now let's talk about marriage. My children are going to have a father and mother who are married to each other."

"Children?" She laughed. "If you're talking plural, we'd better get started. My biological clock is ticking. Tomorrow, we'll call my mother and talk about the wedding. Something very small, maybe in Michigan so my old friends can come. Or maybe in New Orleans so Bea can be my maid of honor."

"We could start on the children right now."

EPILOGUE

Translated from the August 19. 1995, Gazzetta de Modena:

Tishanna Beatrice Burke was born on August 17, 1995. She came into the world weighing 8 pounds three ounces and sporting a full head of red hair. Her father, Formula One driver Tony Burke, said he is the luckiest man in the world, living with two *bella testarossas*. Tony and his wife Claire recently purchased Villa Mostaco, one of the oldest structures in Modena. Mrs. Burke, who owned a construction company before her marriage, said they plan to spend the next 20 years restoring it.

The accompanying picture showed a beaming Tony with one arm around his wife and the other holding his infant daughter.

ABOUT THE AUTHOR

As a child, Patricia Dusenbury read under the covers when her parents thought she was asleep. (She still reads into the wee hours but now uses a Kindle.) Despite sleep deprivation, Patricia managed to get through college and a career as an economic analyst/strategic planner. Now retired, she hopes to atone for all those dry reports by writing stories that people read for pleasure. Her first book, A Perfect Victim, won the 2015 EPIC (Electronic Publishing Industry Coalition) award for best mystery. The sequel, Secrets, Lies & Homicide, was a top ten finisher in the Preditors and Editors Readers Poll, and a 2016 EPIC finalist. A House of Her Own, a 2017 EPIC finalist, is the third and final Claire Marshall novel. Learn more about Patricia and her writing at http://PatriciaDusenbury.com

If you enjoyed A House of Her Own, please consider leaving a review on Amazon.